The Eye of the Scarecrow

The
Eye of the Scarecrow

WILSON HARRIS

FABER AND FABER
London

First published in 1965
Published in this Edition 1974
by Faber and Faber Limited
3 Queen Square London WC1
Printed in Great Britain by
Whitstable Litho, Straker Brothers Ltd.

ISBN 0 571 10557 2

For Margaret,
Antony and Elizabeth Tasker
and
Mary Wilson

Sightless, unless
The eyes reappear

ELIOT

Contents

AUTHOR'S NOTE

No introduction to a novel, least of all by the author himself, can smooth over the difficulties the work may present. And indeed the only merit in a short note of this kind lies in highlighting those difficulties as integral to what I would like to call *pace* and *new dimension* in a certain kind of imaginative fiction.

Since *The Eye of the Scarecrow* first appeared I have received a number of questions which relate to conflicting tendencies within the world of British Guiana from the economic depression of the 1920's to the year 1964 when the novel ends and the movement towards political independence in Guyana had virtually come to a head.

That movement, however, as I have tried at times to illustrate in reply to the questions I have received, is not what I mean by pace in an imaginative and profoundly original sense. Nor, in the same token, is the political independence that came in 1966 necessarily a new dimension.

Yet it is clear that over a span of forty years there occurred a series of grave conflicts between capital and labour, between parties and powers, between institutions and masses that set up a convulsion in the psyche of ordinary men and women which it is difficult to describe. (Those who lived through it were often inclined to turn away from it as from a nightmare of history.)

Still that difficulty, in essence, needs to be faced. For it is related to an implicit necessity for change in which the imagination is cornered by the very claims of historical narrative to be identical with universality, to be a general framework of expression bound up with the institutions of the day; to be at the same time a general framework of protest bound up with the institutions of the day.

The pace of revolution therefore as new dimension in the degree that it existed at all within a span of sacrosanct institution, lay concretely in a ceaseless ferment of unwritten lives and hopes that possessed a catalyst of sensibility acting upon the age.

I stress *catalyst* for it was an inner daemon of this nature embodying a paradox of incalculable and unwritten hopes that seemed to hold out a reason deeper than unreason through which the imagination could address itself to the necessary breakdown of historical and economic categories it had long taken for granted; yet reason could not stifle a profound sense of insecurity, blasted dreams, in which history (as universal given tool) was both culprit and nightmare, the ground of nihilism and pessimism. And the cult of the lonely revolutionary making propaganda for change began to mask the self-wounding nihilist armed with self-deception.

Yet paradoxically it is here that the issue of pace becomes bleakly woven into something akin to new dimension.

For nihilism is rooted in a sense of mourning for the death of security extending beyond colonial moorings into the womb of old cultures and institutions across times and seas – a state of mourning intensely related to a private terror of wasted lives and extinguished promises in the past that seem to run into "the ghostly idiot stranger and spectator in one's own breast" (page 20 *The Eye of the Scarecrow*).

Man is both the clown of the nameless sleeping living and the nameless forgotten dead. He seems therefore to possess a passion to caricature history in his own body, to become Idiot Nameless. Thereby he relates himself to a theatre of "the uninitiate" (page 103) and to the enigma of unwritten lives outside given frameworks of pride and consolation.

Yet the strangest irony of the imagination, I believe, resides in this, in that it is from this ground of loss one undermines given categories in order to relate them within a new capacity for self-judgement. And perhaps this constitutes "the striking innermost chemistry of love" (page 23) as an imaginative interior or intuitive grain and dimension within which polarised structure/ animism of fate is imperfectly but subtly and complexly altered and moved within "the dazzling sleeper of spirit".

"The dazzling sleeper of spirit, exposed within the close elements, the refraction and proximity of sun and water, awoke all too suddenly and slid, in a flash, like speechless gunfire, from crown to toe, along the slowly reddening whiteness of the sand, turning darker still like blood as it fell; and ultimately black as the river-bottom descended, vanishing into a ripple, a dying footfall again, darting across the deep roadway of water and rising once more, distinct web or trace of animation upon a flank of stone." (page 49).

Wilson Harris
July 1973

BOOK ONE

The Visionary Company

And so it was I entered the broken world
To trace the visionary company of love, its voice
An instant in the wind. . . .

HART CRANE

There is no man that hath power over the spirit to
retain the spirit.

ECCLESIASTES viii, 8

25th–26th December 1963 This year in the autumn I visited the ancient city of Edinburgh, travelled across the rim of the windswept Pentlands and descended to the steel-grey Firth of Forth. . . .

One pause of sunset, in particular, I recall now, like a station of feathered branches, half-tree, half-bird, lingering a long while in the sky before a train of frozen fire part-extinguished, part-melted itself into the ground. In the fulfilled poise of this moment, like a barrier of absorption between day and night, the reluctant smoke of sky and carriage of earth were drawn into singular consciousness of each other. . . .

Now as I make this—the first entry in this Journal— the winter sky of London travels through the window and falls upon the page before me like the blank fleece of a wayward flock, wayward yet still shepherded by the overcast sun, all shorn to spread in such an absent moment an intimate landscape and illumination.

The entries of an experience related to *1948*, will be written far outside of that year. The fact is I am only now about to embark on making these. Nevertheless—late as it seems—I am hoping it may prove the first reasonable attempt (my Journals in the past were subject to the close tyranny and prejudice of circumstance) at an open dialogue within which a free construction of events will emerge in the medium of phenomenal associations all expanding into a mental distinction and life of their own.

The question arises—who or what indeed is this medium of capacity, this rift uncovering a stranger animation one senses within the cycle of time and the hub of another state of apparent unawareness? . . .

2

1948

WATER STREET

28th December 1963   Nineteen forty-eight, the year of the Guiana Strike, uncertain forerunner of private upheaval and public change in the decades which followed, may now well be symbolically described as another year of local climax for some, universal anti-climax for others. I remember I met L—— early in the year before anything serious had actually happened anywhere as far as I knew. His face wore a normal expression. Still I glanced away abruptly as if involuntarily conscious of something I did not wish to see, then turned back and confronted him again feeling suddenly stricken with foreboding and astonishment. In that instant of my turning away and back again every feature of his appeared shattered, like the smooth but cracked surface of a depression after a naked spell of drought. . . . The incredible image of a scarecrow vanished, as if in passing it had never existed and L——'s face was smiling at some current joke he was telling, his eyes moist as the reflection of rain. He was unaware of anything abnormal in the motionless heat of the day. The silent thunderclap I had heard so loud in my imagination (and which he had in some lightning way invoked) had been an instantaneous explosion, which left not an echo of trespass or crisis upon him though a curious void of conventional everyday feeling began from that moment to take the shape of a moving cloud in my mind.

12th–15th February 1964 Much as I would like to recall —like a ghost returning to the past—the identical map of place which was shattered in a moment I cannot. I cannot remember the colour of the paint on the walls of L——'s room; and only with a great effort am I able to establish that there were others present, a couple of draughtsmen perhaps, in the room which served as L——'s engineering office.

This effort of memory still cannot restore more than an assumption of an essential fabric of person and thing; which hallucinatory furniture appears swept clean—at this distant remove in time and place—of flesh or grit like smooth slabs, neither paper nor stone, in a skeletal grain of bleached wood.

The fact is I find myself conferring the curious baptism of living imagination upon helpless relics, relics which thereby lose a smothering or smothered constitution and character. For if I were to attempt to confine or draw an exact relationship or absolute portrait of what everything was before the stroke fell and created a void in conventional memory, I would have succumbed to the dead tide of self-indulgent realism. On the other hand, to travel with the flood of animated wreckage that followed after, is a different matter, a trusting matter in which I am involved—a confession that nothing immaterial and actual and eternal may have changed in the outlines of the past; and therefore since the nucleus of phenomenal catastrophe one envisages at any particular moment is just as likely as anything else to be an illusion, it is useless to believe one was, or is, ever possessed by articles of spirit without faith.

I am beginning to see now at last, more clearly than ever, why I must never cease to question every vehicle of self-sufficient recollection. . . . The senses of apprehension which endure today within me, to approach a distant place and time, have truly dwindled into correspondences and intuitions. And these are declining still further even now into the purest, frailest instinct of an incalculable faith in a freedom of being.

L——'s room stood at the top of two storeys whose windows glanced in the sunlight across Water Street towards the burning estuary of the Demerara river where the crest of a wave occasionally flickered as if it sought a pencil of relief (or was it extinction?) beneath the shadow of pavement on the sea wall withstanding the Atlantic. . . .

It is this frail visionary organization of memory—one thing against another, and everything apparently laying siege to nothing (while nothing seems to extend into the immaterial capacity and absorption of everything), which highlights the transient figures of the insensible past into ideal erections against chaos, standing within a measureless ground plan of spiritual recognitions, intimacies and identities. . . .

As a child of eight, nineteen years before the great Strike, I climbed the mound—at the northern extremity of Water Street—towards the wall overlooking the river's mouth in the Atlantic. That was long before the Municipal Authority had thought of erecting a bath-hut and converting the desolate foreshore into an open swimming pool. No one was around (or if there was I have now forgotten) but I still remember clearly the spirit which moved in that place; and the dislocated image which re-

16

turns seems strangely to address me within the beckoning associations not only of 1948 but of 1964 when this late entry in time is being made. The air over the foreshore was filled with a tumultuous cloud of palm flies, flying wires of insects with gauze-like wings which seemed, in their cloud-like angelic transparency, like the subtlest dispersal in nature of a nameless fear of demons: the flying wisp of a bandage torn from the blank compulsive heart of sickness and death, the crippled self-deception of beggars—stationed in the shadow of the commercial houses of Water Street as in a depression in a mental landscape (that world-wide depression of the 1920s and 30s)—protesting with the greatest unconscious eloquence, born of a kind of degrading hollow silence, to be rarefied and uplifted from being mere chains upon themselves and rooted stumps and imprisoned castaways.

17th–29th February 1964   And it is along Water Street, a mere trickle of legend in 1948, that a funeral procession returns to my mind's eye like the beginnings of a swollen flood in the world of 1964. The anonymous light but tragic spring of the dead moves secretly and steadfastly across every continent in every falling raindrop. Light as a feather, yet capable of descending like a stone.

I see now through the conscious mask of winter how slowly it seemed then sixteen years ago in the impatient heat of the pitiless struggle, that the unconscious spring of death had come; the longed-for, renascent yet dreadful arrival of incipient maturity: the faces of those who shot up, prematurely, with a conviction of self-righteous organization, and died before they knew it in the battle of the year, strike and lock-out. . . . The signal procession of cars, horse-drawn vehicles, ancient buses, bicycles, men, women, children came half-limping, half-rolling, along the flat coastal road, canvassing the country for the greatest possible witness of support—across the imperceptible relief of the Demerara/Mahaica watershed—descending though unaware of it (the ground looked so uniform) into an erasure of old plantation boundaries forming the Demerara township and capital—pressing into the line of the wall against the sea and advancing to meet the river's estuary. . . . There it turned into Water Street.

One nightmare account accused the native officers of the police of commanding (out of misjudgment ripening into bestiality and fear) their loyal ranks to open fire too quickly—another said cryptically that those who worked to sow the dragon's teeth deserved whatever they got. And it was here—at the crossroads of history (as the placards borne aloft by the revolutionaries in the procession declared)—that the confusing limits of tragedy became apparent in the shattering question of unity: did the stress of comradeship lie in all visualizing and uprooting a guilty motive from amongst themselves and—in exposing each other's mental crime—submitting to the forced spring of movement (however false and untimely) of all? . . . Such a questionable union involved the hideous and logical denigration of every person, high and low, in the horror of a progressive realism which was far more dangerous, because it seemed politic and necessary however aimless and subversive, than the most fertile incestuous fantasy. It was the devil's abyss blocking the way, I dreamt (as if every hopeful intuition I possessed was now all at once overturned in the midst of unexpected perils), the irony and nihilism of spirit I suddenly saw which bore such a close, almost virtuous, resemblance to the un-

18

prejudiced reality of freedom I was seeking to entertain; and one found oneself peering, as a consequence, into the heart of the universal carnival for the grimmest redeeming clue of an open memory, the germ of associating sovereign truth and humility. . . .

There was the sudden awakening clatter of horses' hooves close at hand magnetized into acute consciousness by the mildewed repellent odour of sliced leather or dung which burnt my nostrils: and this harness of sensation was drawn in the same instant into a wilder contorted out-rider of shadow—the common-or-garden vulture flapping its wings grotesquely; it had arisen clumsily after being disturbed from picking at shreds on the foreshore. It appeared at first as if it could not fail to fall like an un-gainly hoof and strike its own rebellious spark on the ground but adjusted its flight and strode, phenomenal poise, equal power, beyond L——'s gaping window into the soaring distance of clouds burning in the sun.

The sharp sound of primary hooves and the torn smell of a sick half-eaten body of leather—combined with the scarecrow of shadow alighting for a flashing moment upon the funeral procession—issued into the starkest bier of grave memory I knew, when as a boy on my way to school I sometimes encountered the "poor man's hearse" rolling towards me, painted black as shining coal.

Rumour circulated the facts—rumour which had long lost its human tongue and facts which existed in the deaf light of some curious unswerving heedless direction—that the nameless paupers of charity who occupied an obscure ward in the Public Hospital were vagrants of the soul and therefore long before each one expired he (or she) was in process of being borne to his (or her) end within an unconscious design, perpetuating the self-sufficient life of doom, the seal upon all eyes, on all the senses of the world, on every visual and palpable certainty that one existed in the corruption of flesh. And I knew no one *knew* for certain that anyone or anything lay in the interior of the blind hearse as it rolled past, which, unlike every prepossessing vehicle of the dead, lacked sides of glass through which the onlooker could spy the shape of a coffin under its growth of flowers. If the two were to confront one another, as sometimes inadvertently happened, the poor man's singular hoax face to face with a number of conventional mourning carriages, the mêlée which ensued cast an engulfing shadow on the blatant capsule of day. No wonder the ghostly idiot stranger and spectator in one's own breast— plunged into awareness of how deprived one was of root and reality—started prompting one to wonder indeed whether the blossoming casket in clear view carried rags of nothing within, or the wheat of something without, resembling a shattered loaf for this or that non-existent stomach.

And as the black solitary hearse grew nearer I was stricken by the devouring faces of the two men, the hearse-riders, sitting high in front, laughing and joking, totally oblivious to my frenzied countenance (as if I were the meagre necessary grain of spirit they had stored out of sight and blissfully forgotten in their own miserly contrivance of a tomb); oblivious, too, of the horses' reins as if these dangled from another's—my own?—life-giving hands. They might have been incapable of truly hearing or speaking or both, while unfeeling and unseeing in the bargain, and the mirth which issued from their lips is still a riddle which taxes all, day in, day out.

That I may still recall them to the consciousness of the

living for the merrymaking bread of sustenance, and they may continue forever to bear my vestigial parts in their dense spirit of self-mockery of death—is a sufficient, indeed alarming, witness of a mutual and living god, the uncommitted nurses of dialogue between agents and persons unknown and things and places unapprehended.

As fearfully and inevitably as the explosive train of memory rolls along (mingling economic and political, metaphysical and dialectical physicians like an ancestral gathering of nurses to help one stomach the banquet of the dead), there follows in its wake the consciousness of a dream: I had my finger upon a trigger—departed lives fired again to ricochet like bullets within the corridors of the mind. *In my Father's house are many mansions.* I dreamt I was standing alone in a large room and the question arose—where did the dying procession of strikers vanish? Were they swallowed in the abyss of Water Street or did they find consolation in some funereal cellar corresponding to the burning of all material ambition? I found myself confronted by a mystery, the mystery involved in a decision to seek those, whom the rage for an ideal may have consumed, down one fiery way or along another which would permit me to retrace my own steps in time.

The room in which I stood was part of a building of two storeys. It may have been my grandfather's lodge in East Street, the meeting place of a small religious group; on the other hand it looked equally like L——'s engineering office in Water Street. . . . I had left my step-grandmother downstairs in the company of other women, cousins and servants of this nebulous establishment. I had been looking out of a window in their company when there rose before me, high in the sky, a purplish balloon, half-carriage, half-bird, floating above the housetops. I suspected who the inmates were—officials and directors of church and state, by whom I was employed to serve in an obscure alchemical capacity, and since I was on sick leave I did not wish to be seen up and about by them. Even as I looked the balloon came down right next door. I turned away from the window and hurriedly began to ascend the stairs, followed by a solicitous attendant, the shadow of the woman who had nursed me in the earliest years I could remember. Her name was Cromwell or Crumbwell or the crumb (of reality)—WHICH—MAKES —WELL. I was grateful for her attention and for the opportunity to explain to her why I had left the company in such haste; and I persuaded her to watch for the arrival of my hypothetical employers. . . . On her reluctant departure I was left alone to explore the large upper room in which I was now aware—as if for the first time—of a number of royally made beds, unwrinkled sheets and blankets. These seemed to me, however, merely the dutiful ward of ruling substitutes in which my heart was now truly sick. I discovered a door in the wall I had never seen before opening into a secret apartment and I stopped dead on the threshold. It seemed an exotic and self-effacing, even subversive retreat to find and yet curiously logical and right in its context, when one bore in mind the paradoxical unity of this commanding house devoted to the religious observance of an absent proprietor and utilitarian conscience. As I stared into it I was overwhelmed for it was—beyond a shadow of doubt—the revolutionary goal I pursued, another bedchamber but this time (unlike the expansive daylight one in which I still stood) devoid of every film or integument of a window. Nevertheless however cloistered it first appeared —it was filled with a rust-coloured light like ammunition

22

fired from distant stars, naked metallic rose, neither iron nor bronze nor gold: the sleep of an immaterial unsupported element: the armour of the poor, and I knew then how dread and necessary it was to dream to enter the striking innermost chemistry of love, transcending every proud chamber in the inexorable balloon of time.

3

1929–32
EAST STREET AND WATERLOO

1st March–7th May   At the age of eleven—in the year 1932—I spent a month in Public Hospital during which I underwent a serious operation. Chloroform. Sickly-sweet smell one never gets rid of, the half-smell of life and of death. The garden of disgust. Bewildering and nauseating fantasy akin to the strangest recollection of riding out of the womb. Finding oneself ushered into and out of a galloping skin. What consciousness of relief to discover one simulates dying in order to live, and pretends remembering when (or how) one was born in order to reassure oneself one lives and must die. . . . For the thought of eternity—unless punctuated by such inflections of relief, hiatus or cessation—would be an unbearable inflation of terror and inhuman timelessness. . . . I lay still under the chloroform—which had been administered by the dutiful hands of my nurse—and stared at corrugations on the slanting roof of a house, white, opaque, and yet inclined to give out such an intensity of suppressed radiant emotion one could almost *feel* an illusion of weight and of weightlessness.

I emerged with a constricting stamen of anxious blood

23

in my throat and was borne away on a stretcher to be fed on liquids. Like a plant in a pot. . . . The garden in front of my grandfather's house was full of voices and flowers at this time of the year, the month of March, the full-blooded hue and cry of tropical spring. A donkey was braying as it appeared to run before its pursuing cart, dogs were barking against the wheels following animal feet. Grasses and blooms, not only loud reds but silent yellows, the sweetpea, the sunflower, kept pace with me on either side of the echoing flagged pathway as one ran from the front steps to the front gate which opened on to East Street. Then there was the abrupt signal of water dividing East Street into northern and southern banks or roadways, and along the striding parapets close to this fluid boundary moved stately pillars of trees. For this waterway was an artery and reserve once within the radius of an anchored plantation encompassing successive owners—French, Dutch, English, African and Indian stock, but now propelled by the stalwart trunks of legacies sharing both obsessions of shadow and circumference. I used to immure myself and stand at the window of the deepset house to glimpse the sliced surface of the canal. The water level sometimes stood fresh and high, shimmering with corrugations in the wind, the tracery of steel, veins of shadow, the enormous outline of frail fingers like elongated petals cast by the high, dark, green and swaying body of a spirit in the trees against the clouds. These would all sound and speak together when the rope of wind sharpened and blew, an extraordinary dense gallows of movement, the hanged trespasser within the sentence of place, the broadcast of an ancient execution and runaway design. It was an unparallelled vision of seed and fruit, the saddle of history and the captive of

24

nature, the recollections of one who shared the severance and the unity of ancestral master and slave. When I spoke of the ghost I saw to my grandfather, half in judgment, half in jest, he burst into a great rage. It was the first time I had seen him so angry. I felt chastened and stricken for confessing to what he declared in my present imagining was no longer the brutal punishment inflicted upon one man by his time but gross self-indulgence followed by pride. Such idolatrous realism he would not tolerate even in an unhappy child. And from that moment my pagan scaffold, my visionary sport in nature, began crumbling secretly beyond the limits of the purity of obsession. . . . And yet little though I knew it this was to prove a life-time's poetry of science and a stubborn terrifying task. It was to prove the re-living of all my life again and again as if I were a ghost returning to the same place (which was always different), shoring up different ruins (which were always the same).

L—— was one of my first childhood friends, soon to be left an orphan by his mother's sudden death. He was then sent to an institution but he visited me from time to time and on each occasion I seemed to recall differently the memory of what occurred between us on the banks of the East Street canal. . . . It was *1929*, three years before my sudden operation that turned its uprooting light on everything like a decisive culminating blend of awareness serving to endorse and create (in a process whose art was one of the purest eradication) the youngest mental and oldest timeless scars. . . .

L—— and I were standing half in the shade of one of the great trees which shepherded the canal along, intent on our own flock of reflections hanging in the water and I was filled with overwhelming curiosity. How could I measure the binding depth of the crowded stream? I instantly pushed L—— in before I realized what I was doing. He fell into the water with a choked outcry and I was filled only then—when it was too late—with remorse and alarm. I leaned over quickly, frightened at what I had done, and gripped his hand, noting, however, at the same time in the insensitive way one gratifies an instinctive curious appetite that the water seemed no higher than his chest against the side of the canal. I pulled and he scrambled to regain the land and I saw from his condition that if he had been double his slight build he might have sunken very deep into the bottom of the canal. As it was his feet were now long-booted and leaden with mud, his clothing foul, dripping and wrinkled into the alien folds of another skin. He was trembling with shock, so much so I was privileged to escape the direct sting of punishment. His memory played an evasive trick on him. When asked by my grandfather to tell what had actually happened he declared he had suddenly slipped and fallen of his own accord. He did not dare to dream anyone (least of all myself) had in reality given him the slightest push.

In this unwitting way he had saved me from the wrath of justice and I had involuntarily and compulsively pushed him into becoming my own gauge of future extremity. This dawning conscience within me of the guilt of freedom was due to his insensibility and instrumentality: while the childish and childlike knowledge which prompted him to assume my enduring innocence was due to my concurrence in his early stumbling of faith in a universal external liability, the commission of error and weakness I found myself unwilling and unable to explain to him he did not entirely and solely possess. . . . Was his privilege greater than mine because of my debt to his unwitting magnanimity or did mine exceed his since it was I who *knew* the instinctive scale and (unpardonable?) reflex of reality which elevated him in all dumb honesty and excuse above myself? . . . This was the suspended root of a question within a question I began dimly to transplant beyond the premises of immediate judgment on myself.

If indeed one were to conceive of each growing point in the judgment of experience—whether the ghost of any year such as 1932 back to the uncertain body of 1929, or the certain body of 1964 melting into the ghost of 1948—as an intimate transplantation of the broken texture and fruit of time in oneself—pointing towards the ultimate uprooting of all preconception in the humility of consciousness—one is bound to marvel at the stubborn renascence and proliferation of the past returning out of every desired goal of nothingness, out of the pitiful seed of vanquished memory, in the midst of evacuation and detritus cast forth from a hollowness of spirit in the service of science or art, law or love. Is it that within the rubble of oneself still lies the key. . . ?

An early childhood companion such as L——, who grows into my closest friend over the years and yet seems totally insensitive to my every mood of crisis so that sometimes it is on the tip of my tongue to accuse him of being deaf and dumb, lives to engineer, I feel, a certain living retrenchment, in those who are aware, of the dead rule of pride: grandfather's puritanical love of justice suffers as a dead consequence in my living time, his stern invariable injunction—to uproot each material god one is forever inclined to uphold—flags and wilts of itself within the poetic logic of the years and survives only by trans-

27

planting the ground of itself into a humbler agnostic reflection of the sovereign loss or gain of a property of place. *He would turn against me now if he knew.* For indeed I cannot tell what evil inspiration prompted me, all of a sudden, to reduce him into my daemon and agnostic. Was it the ghost of himself, posthumous irony? No, how could this be, when such an apparition would stun and appal him? I hear his voice from the grave repudiating everything, accusing me, once again, of fabricating a lie—self-indulgence followed by . . . not pride this time, surely, but the retrenchment of proper pride, the reduction of a proper and sound regard for him. How could I accept this licence to operate upon my own self-appointed guardian of conscience? How could I dream to engage in the subversion of his classic principle? His religious truth of abstention from notions of exaggerated innocence or guilt in regard to the time and place of others is in process of being converted by me into the strangest consistency— the worship of an insensible knife-edge of moving compassion upon all persons and things. And this places me in a peculiar position to exercise peculiar judgment upon him in the realm of his withdrawal into a privileged establishment of trust which may not, after all, be *his* but *my* conceit.

Equally (for one such as myself who confesses himself doomed to live and repair, in a battle with my own will, as it were, the crumbling senses of corruption the other has repudiated in a chimera of ideal existence) the very shock of confronting a quixotic self-righteous inwardness out of the heart of the past—the tragic and sterling rebuff administered by my oldest self—makes me discern, in my surrender (or involuntary loss) of an older and clamouring, indignant, exclusive feeling, the truest subduction of slavery into freedom my older self instinctively desired, dissolving every vain attempt one may be driven to make to maintain another unjust cage (either one proud individual measurement or another) for the perfect dead in the undying hope of the living. . . .

I remember the painting of the Battle of Waterloo which hung in my grandfather's drawing-room towards the end of the year 1929. I became aware of it one afternoon in a questionable even treasonable way I had never drawn from within it nor felt upon it before. I was past eight years old then, my grandfather was close to eighty. It happened when the dying (he was then a very ill man though this was a closely guarded secret) Governor of the Colony rode past along East Street. The ghost of a Commander-in-Chief, thin as a reed wearing the glint of glasses like sun on the canal. He held himself painfully (fleshless and upright) in the saddle less like a living man than a shirt cast over branches of rib and bone. His was a dark rock-coloured, still earthen-looking, horse followed by yet another upon which the jerking leaf of a jacket of an orderly fluttered past. It was the Governor's faceless expression in the tree of the sun which stirred in me the picture of a stricken soldier lying on the painted battlefield in my grandfather's sitting-room. And as I stood in the thin throng on the grass-edge of the street to see the grave stick of a personage ride along, there stirred within my mind's eye the painted forest of battle, fallen sculptures carved out of trunks of trees, wearing scarlet flowers of protest on their uniform. I saw the blood of a ruling image (otherwise assumed to be unfeeling and unapproachable as stone) shed on my own familiar homeground. And I began grieving with a singular passion for

29

the unconscious nutriment of freedom however spectral and forbidding it seemed in the long march and funeral procession of figures of conquest.

My grandfather's tenants occupied a tenement range in Waterloo Street—a couple of blocks away from East Street—which I was taken to visit for the first time the day after the Governor rode past. We arrived at the entrance to the property and turned into the brooding alleyway running between two faces of long squat buildings (one reflecting the iron logic of philanthropy, the other meekly bent to the slow unrepentant dream of recovering the coin of profit). I became aware of a living frieze of subjective figures occupying the frame of each doorway in which a group stood or sat with the hollow darkness of their room at their back. It was Saturday afternoon and everyone seemed possessed of the dreadful ease of an unkempt batallion whose economic gratitude and morale were alternatively aroused and shaken as their old landlord paused to address them. The fact was— this fortnightly visit of his (though I did not immediately realize it) was a pure ritual since no one, with the exception of one family of symbolic tenants, the Anthrops, was able to pay a penny of his rent. A slump existed everywhere (a severe retrenchment of investment in the raw materials of business) and the minimum portion of work which could be scraped together within the granite circumstance of the poor went to keep the link of harsh body and charitable soul together.

Nearly all the tenants were six months at least in debt, some had not paid for over a year, and all they could do was continue to plead to be allowed to occupy the rooms at their back into which I now peered, drawn in spite of myself, with the necessity of contemplating a love of horror as if I glimpsed the subterranean anatomy of revolution. *In my Father's house are many mansions*, an underworld, as well, within which might still be bred progenies of change out of the seeming absurdity and perversity of a corner of affection. The old man had no intention of putting them out when he saw they could not pay anything at the moment (unless one knew how to draw blood from stone) but equally he did not intend to relinquish his professional vocation, like a doctor confronting his patient, a commander his troop, to remind them sooner or later their debt of living duty and community must be paid. And there was Anthrop, after all, the head of one family, who miraculously, it seemed, overcame circumstance and settled with him on each occasion he visited. In truth my grandfather was beginning almost to enjoy (though he would never have confessed this) the paradox of it all in the way an artist may grow in awe of the train of his unpredictable material when it becomes capable of the unique momentum of acquiring its own godlike stamp and redeeming character of life.

The family of Anthrop occupied the last couple of rooms in the range: the remainder of the land, extending to a line of paling stakes, stood vacant save for a row of closets and baths in an open net of shadow drawn by the spreading brushwork of leaves from a wide tamarind tree. The occasional dry sweeping fall of leaf and shell caught the outhouses which were crumbling themselves ripe and fast; a bill ruling the latter unfit was soon to be presented to the Legislative Assembly by the Member representing the Municipality. For who would deny that the time had come for every eye-sore to be abolished?

What profit remained in upholding an art of decay, a canvas of fertile humour, ugly faith, inane, impolitic, thick-skinned, primitive manifesto? Why preserve each brutal wall, judicious hinge, unscientific doorway scored all over by the knife of weather to gape as well as laugh at every patched fruit of initiation into the soil? And yet (wretched economics of nature) here was enthroned the golden centre of inspiration, the most subjective scarecrow earth of all like the religious currency of wood motivated equally by rooted instinct as by growing callouses upon a body of dense spirit leading to an immaterial element of indifference as the quicksilver rain is indifferent to the brightness of the sun. And this treasure of immateriality was the strangest almost undreamt-of experimental thing, a consistency of unrestricted elements within a harsh melting pot of resistances, the crude nature of the sublime long-suffering geography of history.

It was something, however, which in bridging the depth of the mind still leaves one (even after the crossing of many disparate years) vacant and bewildered within a burdensome engagement of prospects. The truth was— in spite of, or because of a natural immunity, fluid raindrop, creative spark—I hated my grandfather's property which seemed capable of turning around in my mind into an unreal triumph over passing time, the relative strength of stable illusion.

I closed my eyes feeling all of a sudden close to sickness: a spinning and sleeping top. The dreaming fit passed. I looked around once again. No one seemed aware that anything had happened. I was subject to these attacks which were accompanied sometimes by spells of vomiting. This time fortunately not. But I experienced once more the resulting chaos I knew, loss of orientation, the unruly pivot around which revolves the abstract globe in one's head. No wonder the mouth of the yard on Waterloo Street seemed to have changed places with its own backside and each legitimate position lay in a contrary direction. This sensation of helpless upheaval, the stigmata of the void, I had first experienced on a Sunday School excursion upriver on which I was forced to go. Sea-sick, fell asleep, awoke when the boat had turned around and was heading back. We were in sight of the station from which we had originally set out save that the pier under heaven had transplanted itself to the other bank as if to advertise a superior disobedience to the laws of hell: I was in fact obsessed with the idea that I was still travelling *up*, chained to an escort, rather than *down* the river back to where and what I wished. . . .

Anthrop's room had naturally swung with alleyway and corridor. And Anthrop himself appeared at the door wreathed in smiles, full of that unwitting gaiety one associates with the unnatural spirit of the poor. He closed the door quickly behind him to conceal the inmates I had seen: half-naked woman, his wife, with twins at her breast. And my reluctant gaze swung to him with the click of his lock, conferring upon him not the wages of consumption by the new-born but the wages of consumption instead of the new dead. For his face was clearly one of self-reversal of the twins of birth into the hearse riders whose frightening image of devouring innocence I had obliquely glimpsed.

I came out of hospital at the end of April 1932, scarcely able to credit my own living senses. A moment of brilliant happiness—sun, sheer spirit of illumination, brightest air of freedom. It began with the gloomy notification that I was to stay in for at least another "couple of days" but this injunction was set aside by my step-grandmother whose whirlwind visit overcame the authorities: I was at liberty to go that very morning. After all (they may have given the matter some helpless thought) what difference would it make? There was nothing more they could do. All so quick and abrupt I scarcely credited my good fortune. Liquids still the nurse warned, and it did not seem to matter. What would have been tasteless in hospital became all at once, with the doctor's sentence of release, a capacity of endless enjoyment. I would soon be well and sound again. It was natural I should be led to tell myself so whether anyone else believed it or not. And yet this turned out to be the case. For within a few days the needle within throat and stomach vanished. And left a peculiar stitched taste to grow slowly in the mouth. Not the torn fabric of weakness any longer. The flavour of a curious unexpected patch of despair: tincture (no longer puncture) following just as swift as the incalculable measure of healing and relief. . . . But why then *despair*?

Why now despair (in the self-evident light of thirty-two years of survival) of the successful march and design of life which begins again and again and which began then for *me*? The absolute emphasis, I know, is absurd and yet I still cannot help it after all this time. The stale accumulative fact is I grew miraculously stubborn and strong with each passing hour, passing day, passing season and year, sixteen "explosive" years (only now can I see their inward helpless explosion), twice sixteen of "ebb and flow". . . . And only now can I begin to penetrate the substance I appeared to gain—the strength of all colourlessness, all hackneyed flavours, the strength to remain within the gratifying spirit of anomaly; not the

34

ghost of freedom I had dreamed I would be, time and time again, in the surrender of everything and every illusion of strength I possessed, but a slave to the futility of hardness, one's everyday conduct, one's everyday meat of existence, one's settlement of helplessness, the fact that one has still not died to it all after all the melted scaffolding of the years (and is only *now* capable perhaps—what self-deception!—of entering into the self-reversing game of reality of the banquet of life on death in one's immortal undiscovered realm, a land of creatures living freely everywhere and nowhere).

The truth is—such apparent delay or procrastination is the tantalizing food of every poor devil's state of eternal convalescence, cruel grace wherein the newly-minted appetite of youth acquires the mould of age, a debased currency within which flickers continuously still like a pot on a fire—the thought of being stricken anew by the lightning debt one owes to the weakest inspired beginnings within each vessel of consciousness.

Then indeed, long ago, in the tragic misconceived beginning (one now dreams to return to with a different paradoxical vision of hope) one chose to purchase the manufacture of despair, unwittingly it may be true, and tasted in this bargain a growing hoard of sensibility one conceived as self-sufficient and original, the newfound coin and cement of freedom, instantaneous harvest which seemed truly ambitious, truly right, anything but a miserly or incongruous investment in one's own human prolongation of misery. It had in fact been sown, strange enough, in its own paradoxical expenditure of fire and energy, my sudden all-consuming delight in abandoning a sick bed at a moment's notice which I had not anticipated since I had, in fact, overheard something and was half-prepared to resign myself to the prospect of not only remaining there but never moving out. . . . And then the last thing one had reckoned on happened; I was out in the street of the open world—all thought of dying suddenly forgotten—as if for the first childish profligate time, devouring the burning sweetness of being cooked alive. Home. Relief. Fear soon forgotten, the fear of cruel (only now it seems gentle) death. . . . Thus it was I opened my first proud store of lifeless and lifelike priorities and absurdities and secrets. Yes, I confessed, I was safe and established in my own private being at last. And therefore because of such a conquest of my own space, such a miracle, I dreamed all too rashly (I see it all now) I could never be deprived of my own selfish purchase of reality with each breakthrough into the hidden world at large I knew and desired with a transparent greediness I had never been able to muster before.

L—— came to see me a month after I returned home. We went into the garden which was soft with rain that had fallen overnight and we fashioned figures out of lumps of rich mud.

BOOK TWO

Genesis

There went up a mist from the earth, and watered the whole face of the ground.

And the Lord God formed man of the dust of the ground. . . .

4

L—— decided to leave when he saw the weather looked
uncertain. I accompanied him to the gate with an irra-
tional sensation of a portraiture of disappointment. The
air was heavy as the trunk of a tree and the face of the sun
was growing into blossom of cloud. It was another in-
stance, I declared, of the bewilderment within each
seasonal person and ghostly thing I cherished: the weather
of reaction—which had set in very early after my return
home continued to demolish each anticipation I had felt
springing out of a sense of recovery.

L—— had appeared wooden and unable to enter into
the spirit of the game of beginning to make everything
new. He looked older than when I had last seen him. I
watched him as he broke and moulded the earth and his
reluctant, sceptical fingers appeared less capable of
strange outer life (I thought a little scornfully in order to
depress my own disappointment) than the elongated dead
creatures they measured as if their life—the scientific
deliberation of his hands—was outside of the pheno-
menon of dust. They (L——'s hands) were growing to
take themselves entirely for granted like implements of
unnatural blood.

I loitered by the gate scarcely in the mood to wave to
him as he hastened along East Street to catch his bus. . . .
At last I turned and began to make my way back to the
house; and stopped at the place where he and I had
crouched, now scarcely able to believe the thing I created

with my own eyes out of one of the pieces he had made and discarded on the ground. For an incredible instant all the sap of life rose anew. I wondered what he would say if he were still here and I were to point to the translated figure and occasion on the ground. I shook my head after a while, slowly, experiencing once again the bewildering pendulum of reaction. Nothing. He would have said nothing and seen nothing. Nevertheless (I shook my head clear again) here was the beginning I sought, the old in the new, whether he was capable of seeing it or sensing it or not. L—— and I (I saw it all within the negative dust which flashed upon my eyes) were to enjoy the enigma of being related. . . . He would acquire a reputation for sober and matchless good sense, judgment, responsibility while I would be the striking unpredictable one. He would never come to blame anyone for the evil which happened to him—as I was often religiously inclined to do—and he would always be restrained, indifferent, in the face of good fortune—as if he could never *see* he deserved any reward which came to him. But even as I counted the measure of his virtues I was conscious that in praising him so highly I was approaching a curious and dangerous subject of apparent generosity and self-satisfaction within myself.

It was all there, the problematic creation and bewildering scale of our lives, in the dutiful expression he had drawn and involuntarily fashioned out of mud as if to make me aware of the surprising and surprised breath of self-critical spirit within his staid and aloof, unco-operative flesh.

The figure which he had made had seemed to me— scarcely five minutes ago—lifeless and unreal. But now the very joylessness with which it had been constructed struck me like a curious revelation of mystical sorrow. I felt cold and strange, a religious stranger to all previous knowledge of emotion; and *emotion*—in such a void or context—became *new*, liberating, oblique, powerless to arouse an expenditure of energy to create the harm I saw I had already inflicted. I could not turn away from the piece which expressed the heart of inarticulate protest in the ground of apparent lifelessness and I asked myself— How did I come to *dream* of one thing and inflict another —the beginnings of such a life of woe on anyone or anything? Was it my impetuous greedy will or L——'s submissive response which seemed to kill one inspiration and feed another? Blobs of breasts, the breasts of mother earth. I came close to laughing—the "dead" figure looked so ridiculously remote from my own flesh-and-blood mother, so unlike that the very distance and unlikeness between the dignity and indignity of her life and the slavishness and imitative mockery of this death stirred a terrifying community and curiosity and an impenetrable need to know whether herein lay the beginnings of the infliction of pain or cruelty on one helpless member by another. Only yesterday it was I was stricken, frozen with astonishment, when I caught a glimpse of my mother's face in a mirror looking like the face of an impossible shadow. Yet it was she, I reminded myself. The door of her room was part open. My step-grandmother and grandfather were addressing her in an ominous persuasive tone and she was weeping bitterly and hollowly, the tears streaming helplessly down her cheeks to mingle like beads of glass in the reflection of her hair. Her fleeting distraught appearance was that of someone in process of being devoured by and in process, too, of devouring a strangled sensation of love. It was the quickest incredible

41

chain of reaction I saw for *they* saw me too and quickly closed the door. There was a silence, the silence within a waterfall when one is suddenly estranged to the music of the self-sufficient senses.

And now the first tinge of nutriment—desire and self-disgust—was born as a shower of rain fell and beads of moisture, the colour of milk, sprouted out of the breast of mud. The mirror of earth and the falling chain grew into a blur as if someone was now veiling herself from the compulsive gaze of instinct; my eyes were torn away from misconceived parent, mesmeric grandparent and step-grandparent into another fold and descending shower of memory—Anthrop's room this time and the naked woman inside, his wife: rolling in fluid procession down the surface of my skin into the corners of my mouth until I felt upon the tip of my tongue the robe of salt. How had the bitter hem of selfish nutriment arrived—did it start by falling from nowhere or was it the native flesh of wisdom within the vehicle of earth? And where did the open fault and dress of inspiration lie which drew every intimate conscription of image into another mourning ancestral cavity standing at one's own tenant's skeleton back?

It was a rainy unstable night following the broken afternoon. Slices of moon now and then appeared like a newborn apparition or the old and declining increment of flesh within a heavy procession of cloud shaped by the dream of my own funeral. The rain ceased to gallop or to shout upon the roof, and the panes of glass in the window glistened, reflecting the transparent assault which had been made upon them. The emotional clamour of the wind—as if the voices of hell itself were let loose—now died down, and the ticking of the grandfather clock within the hall beyond my bedroom door quietly arose growing loud in the new buried silence, uniform and measured, rational and clear.

The sound of the clock was at first distant and somnolent but on gaining one's attentive reflection it developed into something as insistent as everything I had called upon to be made which groaned and protested. Save that its mature and quiet seizure of the stillness of earth now prevailing under the light of the moon led one to dwell with breathless relief upon each erosive trickle of water on the window-pane like a falling minute pendulum pointing to a deeper and ultimate grave of stillness—a creation of silence inhabited by the perfect angelic time of creatures whose presence I dared to hope would outwit all evil and still consent to be shaped by my command and tongue. In dumb animal obedience, a spirit of human (or unhuman) otherness, they would worship and uphold my epitaph and calendar of freedom. . . . I turned on my pillow with a sudden startled moan and a cry I could not suppress. It struck them like an unhappy stroke and they vanished, stripping and unburdening themselves of the slightest trace of clock-work guilt in my order of procession and burial, the pilgrimage of the empire of age back into the colony of youth or—in another sense—the toys of youth obliterated by the march of age I had unwittingly imposed on them; retreating even deeper into their dialogue of genesis.

They were my dreaming instinctive models, Angels (sometimes capable of recall, sometimes elusive and sealed and forgotten) of childhood and ageless transformation, the sword over the garden and the tomb— mother earth L—— had pretended to consent to make,

43

and the wages of self-mockery Anthrop had pretended to enjoy.

The Night of self-initiation, self-kinship, grew into celestial furniture, the great hearse rolled on, stitched planks held by the scissors of the universe, divisions of cloud within which glimmered the operations of space; the moon had been pared right down to lie almost like a needle upon a backcloth of stars: I saw the flagged pathway flutter and roll before me backwards and forwards and backwards until the sheet unwound itself into a stream of cotton, the rippling surface of the bedclothes of East Street canal. . . . The rough-hewn figure of Anthrop descended from beside his dwarf of shadow. The seat of his trousers shone like milk in the frailty of the moon, it was so worn, threadbare if not fleshbare. It was his custom to come once a month to trim my grandfather's nightmare toenails. Sometimes it was a solemn function but often it was merely a duty he performed as with the march of each clown or corpse he drove, and that was why he often joked and laughed in a blunt, even rude, fashion with his idol of a landlord. . . . On this occasion an unexpected thing happened when he arrived. Half-way along the framed carpet running to the sleeping picture of the house he encountered someone who was the spit and image of himself, cast from an identical yet deceptive mould. It was Anthrop's twin brother who had risen high even as Anthrop had fallen low. They passed each other with the barest flicker of a nod, a grain of thread on the forehead of my bedpost, Anthrop, the rude unnatural one, and Anthrop the rich civil engineer.

In the needle's eye of light Anthrop's twin resembled not so much his crude brother but a gentler and younger

44

frame as well: *this was L——'s father, I swore, no one else.* I
half-groaned, half-laughed. It was a joke in poor taste.
Why resurrect such a shameful scandal? Poor L—— It
was rumoured that his dead mother (L—— was an
orphan) was still in love with engineer Anthrop, in fact
had always been his secret mistress.

Even as I *dreamed* I was aware of a bewildered protest I
tried to express. I wanted to protest against an incredible
logic where all frontiers refused to collapse into each
other—innocent prejudice into guilt, death and its unbroken assumption into a new life, motion into the flight
of stillness. How could she—the dead mother of the living fatherless child—live and move with such resurrected
constancy and inconstancy in my dreaming mind, remaining nevertheless subject to the same laws of censure
and propriety, self-hatred and self-love? Would Anthrop's
rich successful brother always exist in no other form for
her (and for me) but that of being her illegitimate lover,
my assumption of twin scandal and bankruptcy, the family
of the void, loveless eternity, solipsis, love's own extremity? . . . But even as I struggled to find a way of new
conviction other than the ancient riddle of protest I knew
the changeless ground of it all would yield ultimately, of
its own accord, when it succeeded in marrying the fearful
strength of the past to the infant freedom of choice
which was still weak in the conviction of the present and
the future: my own impulsive rein of eagerness and repulsive light of action grew brutally fitful and restrictive as
the uncertain spring of day—I was *pushing* her (I was
aware of a contrary rebuke and stillness in the heart of
crude action)—*pushing* her, nevertheless, even as I had
involuntarily pushed him, her son, into the canal and to
the brink of his (and her) total self-acceptance, total re-

sponsibility for my bewildered self belonging to both sides of the blanket, illegitimate one of present speculation and legitimate reinforcement to escape from the prison of past knowledge.

I found myself pushing her into the streaming bedclothes and into my own cupboard and skeleton of shadow—the ghost on the gallows I had once shuddered to see in the mirror of the canal but whose spiritual reflection I now assured myself would bring her no living harm. While it would do me a great service by accepting my dead burden of fright, legitimate or illegitimate, by consenting—without caring—to suffer my technical goad and translation which was consistent, after all, with the daily caress and instrument of callous love.

I pushed her and she fell into these uninspired arms, the engineer of depth, and dissolved into the scaffold of one drowned reflective self to my sudden indescribable horror. I heard myself shout (though scarcely able to believe my own ears) that it was all my fault, plunging forward before it was too late to pull her out and draw her up into my own gauge of budding self-deception, self-knowledge and hanging extremity, my illusion of freedom. She rose and I was established in *him*, in his phallic technical right, the dead man's living right, thereby abolishing the necessity for him at one stroke. (*The news arrived yesterday that her engineer had been drowned—the police were investigating. . . .*) I turned away from his subjective memory to fulfil our mutual engagement: *but it was my own mother—and no scapegoat of woman—who had come into the room and was lying beside me.* I had given such a great cry she had come to console me. She, too, had been weeping over the black news of yesterday. *I cried again on waking to find her beside me—It isn't true.* What? she

46

asked. But my tongue refused to budge or plead. I couldn't utter the thing aloud, the significant conversion of every dumb fact: and that in this unrestricted silent conversion lay the retrenched and elusive and invincible principle of a pure timeless kinship with. . . .

The almost unendurable unity, silence and sacrifice, departed; and I was able to voice an individual borderline existence of fear with a sense, nevertheless, of having glimpsed, however obscurely, implications of the breakdown of nightmare rule.

So it was I jumped forward into an echoing future (which is now with the dead voices of the past) and into a middle of a year—a great procession—the striking year of every man's familiar obsession (1948 or 2048?). L—— and I suddenly stumbled upon the faint but "timeless" footprints of a *self-created* self—the step-father for whom my mother wept (as if she had been weeping for *me* as well as for *him* all the time).

She had mourned long (years which wear centuries and centuries of disguise operated upon afresh by instigators of memory to probe an endless frustration and desire) hoping against hope he would still return until the news arrived that he had been drowned in the heart of the interior. I recalled him vaguely. I remembered the time he conducted me around the garden on a bicycle: I was five years old; it was all so faint and curiously disagreeable in my mind I dreamt to cut him from us altogether and to divest her of the burden of such an unreal and yet cruel dragging presence.

But in this lawful (or was it unlawful?) persuasion I failed and his life remained a millstone of responsibility: he had set foot into the past in search of proof of another's (or was it my own?) disfigured innocence. When the news came of his certain death by drowning—it was then a full month since my return home from hospital—it had seemed that *now* the obscure trial of all time was over. And yet the circumstances remained like an absurd chain drawing one up into the depths of the future and down into the image of the past.

It was this depth of recognition I feared, seeing—in this—the anti-climax of the universe continuously reflected, the law of an unlawful beginning and a lawless end, and of beginning all over again without end, a curious ill-defined substitute for someone else I had never known and whom it would have been easy to erase from consciousness were it not that one faint persistent searching memory stirs the other sleeping shape and dust: I was thinking of the tragic indistinct life of my actual parent and father—tragic I knew with the yearning bones of instinct—who died, it was reported, when I was less than a minute old. . . .

L—— was the engineer in charge of the expedition to the lost womb of a mining town, nine months journey from Water Street into the jungle of conception traversed along 'each changing river of ascent; the same scale of measurement emerged when taken from each accumulative deposit of memory in the garden East of Waterloo to the heights of Sorrow Hill.

I stood on a suspension bridge overlooking an arm of the river, conscious of Sorrow Hill at my back: a ripple, a footprint almost, appeared in the middle of the water and vanished. I stood still and waited. The sun shone with an unbending matchless stroke. Neither a feather of wind nor a fin of cloud now moved. They waited, too, for the huntsman of death to return, the hunter to become the hunted. It was a strange inviting and yet curiously un-inviting thought. Watching, listening: the body of the stream ceased to breathe, growing still as the mound of sleeping sand, the contours of which I saw, fiery and distinct, in the middle of the river; in fact the river over the sand bank was a glittering shell and enclosure, a coffin of transparency, skeleton-key deep, the colour of its shallow bed like the hot blast of snow. The dazzling sleeper of spirit, exposed within the close elements, the refraction and proximity of sun and water, awoke all too suddenly and slid, in a flash, like speechless gunfire, from crown to toe, along the slowly reddening whiteness of the sand, turning darker still like blood as it fell; and ultimately black as the river-bottom descended, vanishing into a ripple, a dying footfall again, darting across the deep roadway of water and rising once more, distinct web or trace of animation upon a flank of stone.

L— saw nothing of this and yet I could not help feeling as I turned to him that *it*, the trespass of feeling rising anew out of the stumbling labour and melting pot of history, had also touched him however indirectly or obscurely. His manner remained cool but I believed he was still deeply moved: he was pointing to the engineering merits of the bridge, the excellence and height of the site, the outcrops of rock in which the steel cable on either side was embedded. My step-father had done a remark-able job he declared. And he wondered whether he would be able to do the same. (I myself was staring into the river and I wondered if it was upon the very plank on which I stood *he* had been trapped, *stunned*). The execu-tion was perfect, L— said. The remark struck me in a flash: I gave an incredible start (as if I had been immersed very deeply, thinking, but *not* of my step-father's bridge at all) and pulled my gaze away from the water. The bridge was both a trapdoor and a poem. We had seen it from another angle yesterday, several miles away down-river and it appeared like the most fragile and beautiful web against the sky. The first enduring superstitious bastion which a spider of science had spun against the inroads of the jungle, appeared symbolically to overcome its own erosive empirical faculty and slender truth.

It was no use disclosing my thoughts to L——. His face was growing blank, devoid even of the slight hanged trace of emotion I had glimpsed. And I—as a consequence —was flooded with the kind of awe he inspired in me on certain occasions, the sheer and limitless power of re-trenchment I visualized which was capable of stirring the most profound, almost inexpressible residues of feeling.

It was on my suggestion he had sent for a woman from the ghost of the mining town some miles upriver. But when she arrived I shrank inwardly from her and could not bring myself to touch her. It was the grossness of her breasts and the enormity of her buttocks. L—— did not sense this and when I asked him how he had got on with her he looked at me with his blank look as if he had not attempted to strip her at all, had been content merely to penetrate through everything, clothing, flesh, hair and gristle, with a blind and instinctive precision, a total ac-ceptance of his responsible and her unalterable necessity, which made her naked compliance the most riddling factor of all. However ugly, however grotesque, she re-mained a fact and therefore a mystery. The thought of such unimaginable boundless freedom, such a paradox of extension born of the limitless subduction of every-thing within an essential activity, made my head spin. I clung in desperation to the rail of the bridge though it was falling into the river's snow and sun.

5

The clearing which had been made in the jungle where the suspension bridge spanned the river drew one to crane's one's neck back in order to experience a measure of blind relief—the height and depth of the sky—as if this alone, the uncovering of inner space, would overcome an approximate void in sensation one felt in spinning to a groundless fall. The *daemon* I now felt rising within such an open relationship to understanding the baselessness of sensation, was drawn to inhabit an insubstantial premise of cloud, sailing over the harbour of earth to a wider settlement and bay, trailing a rope of shadow which now gradually stretched and lengthened across the seeming gulf of incompatible reality: the flag of the sun was upheld by a broomstick of rain. Brushes of shadow were augmented by a coil of leaves rising fast to sweep the top of the forest. I had closed my eyes but I saw the muse of place descending hand over hand along the jointed rope and stick of the atmosphere.

The presence which appeared to settle within the gloom beneath me was actual I knew, but I equally knew it was folly to open my eyes and look. It might prove to be someone I loathed or despised—a base ugly trick of the matted senses: and if no one really existed I was bound to founder or wilt, of my own accord, in the self-deceptive voyage of exploratory nature.

Either way would be an absurd defeat for the true knowledge I dreamt I embraced and possessed. Scarcely moving I now felt encircled by another's rising flesh, a moving trunk, violent arms and legs, and I bowed the column of my neck at last, remaining blind nevertheless to the end, releasing myself—with the thought I had truly and deeply endured belonging to the other (as the other had truly and deeply endured belonging to me)—from the cable and rail to which both of us still clung like tendrils of flesh to a shaft of bone.

L—— was oblivious to either pillow of air or monument of fantasy. He, too, had been craning his neck backwards, nevertheless, I dreamed, pointing sightlessly to a certain tension in the nervous wires overhead and explaining to me with mute detail the distribution of load which was capable of moving upon and occupying the deck of the bridge. His voiceless witness faded from my head as if it and I had never existed. I slept and awoke and she *(the prostitute from the mining camp) was still lying beside me. It was I indeed who had penetrated her with borrowed force and intensity as she had held me and enveloped me within the rule of passion.* I could not bring myself to turn and look at her —as at the *hideousness* of all apparent charm.

But even as I turned away from her I was conscious of the jealous furious ground of instinct: I had sparked her into feeling that sheer beauty or ugliness was a fearful myth which neither L—— nor I would ever dare to face: such a gust of emotion I felt, it drew from me in turn a curious sigh, the genesis of hostility towards him. As if I could not help seeing in him my own folly laid bare at last, the emergency and divide inspired by her, his whore within the blind lust we sought, each of us, to perpetrate upon her, all alone, without conceiving of the shameful (or shameless) existence of another. It was the most difficult trial and conviction for me to begin to accept the unpalatable truth that we—who sought to make her our plaything—were her maternal joke as well (twins of buried and divided fantasy) and that a price was about to be placed upon our heads which would involve us— whether we wished it or not—in the breath of unfamiliar origins, familiar genius—in the soul of something she desired to *see*, and was prepared to nurse into existence by fair means or foul: the restoration of her spiritual bridge and sacred mining town.

L—— was protected—in the stable right of his profession—from the growing consequences of the endless goal of rehabilitation: it was never a matter of proud selfish appetite with him (whatever indifference his appearance may have reflected) or cruel self-flattery to the point of an extinction of all else. I was not however so protected (and in truth had never been) by blind innocent nature as he quite simply was. My horror of corruption and longing for vocation remained. And I began to discover a force of obsession in things I had only dimly dreamt before (it seemed to me now) to question, things and persons I had accepted too easily (it seemed now, once again) for what they were supposed to be and what they were instinctively supposed not to be. Things and persons whose life of obsession lay less within themselves and more within myself, within my lack of a universal conception, of their conception (the unborn folk). Less in the open question of their apparently submissive being and more in my ultimatum of fixed instincts, beyond which—the residual fire or magnetic field of which—I hesitated to go (even dared not go) since it would mean crossing a "dead" masked frontier as if this were a living disguise and territory in fact. . . .

This was the first obstinate difficulty we encountered in attempting to locate the ancient trails to the ghost town.

L—— decided to open a trail in the forest but the bearing he chose to follow was distorted on his compass by a magnetic instinctual load of rock in our neighbourhood. We abandoned the line, pored over the uncertain mirror of our maps, and brought the woman once more in to the picture. She was reputed to know the reflection of the country like a dog its shadow of bone. I accused her of misdirecting us and she gesticulated and pointed in all directions, needling us but apparently failing to sting us in the way she wished as if our flesh had turned to wood. *It was all our fault, our void, disorientation.* Hebra her name was, as unlikely a name as the Queen of the South (some of the dead miners of the ghost town had once so nick-named her). RAVEN'S HEAD. She spat this name at us like the dreadful severance of reflex and afterthought. Anything to make us *jump* in answer to the knife-edge of destiny. L—— was jotting each bearing down, cool as water, without the blink of a stony eyelash, anything he could glean which might prove a useful pointer later on. It was I who had urged him to accept the leadership of the engineering expedition—I wanted to claim and protest. But this seemed so pointless now (I had never been so jealous of my freedom and his authority before): how could I reasonably protest against, or on behalf of, something which was much more and so much less than any vision of responsibility I had hoped to puncture and entertain?

For centuries, everyone darkly knew, mysterious locations had been plumbed to disappear and return once more into the undisclosed astronomical wealth of the jungle. *Raven's Head*—by which name Hebra herself was sometimes known—Hebra's town—was one of these relative establishments whose life of eternity sprang from a pinpoint conception of poetic loyalty to the idea of ever-lasting justice: they (such relative establishments) belonged to those who voluntarily began to relinquish the right they deserved to a place in them—whose recovery of them lay therefore within the heart of an acceptance of great distance from them. But such a decision to relinquish what one desperately wanted to find tore at the roots of all possession and conventionality. How could I begin to endure the thought that it was I who may have instigated such an unendurable search and undemonstrable claim? No wonder my protest was stifled at the outset within the inadequacy of jealous proprietorship and conviction, the arid frame of past ruling justice or sentiment. The memory of such ruling sentiment—still undivorced from possession or place—threatened to choke me afresh, sediment rather than sentiment, the sediment of abortive constellations—the hanged man's noose over Hebra's town—within whose dry brittle air one distantly perceived the almost breathless fall of the condemned blossom of earth—the freedom of promise in dust; the very dusty insects were drawn to flight: their infinite grind and procession capable now of aerial relief. Each wall or door carved on their backs fell into the stars, disappeared in truth yet were driven to await one's logical chain of delayed recognitions of the fact. A thousand years in our sight to earn a moment in theirs. The moment of our transplantation, the conception of our roots pinpointed in their mainstream. . . .

And yet in spite of my knowledge of the truth, indeed because of this—the very apparent helplessness of dwindling truth—my rage for self-justification knew no bounds. I was forced for the first time to cry out against my own patient role of inheritance. *My father is no murderer*, I cried (no longer able to suppress the retrenched ground of emotion). *There are records in Raven's Head which will prove he was framed* and . . . I caught my breath . . . EXECUTED. Why was it—in spite of insubstantial time and eternity—the transience of everything—I still could not utter and abolish the long-standing self-injurious word of sentence? My tongue was turning to stone rather than confess to something so infamous and baffling which I had seen stitched across the years, my unlicensed censor of space. I saw the veiled silent reproof and mocking question on Hebra's black mask of a face which rose between L—— and me: she stood like a jagged daughter of cloud in the light of the moon now shining just above our shoulders; the shoulders of Sorrow Hill. All at once I dreamed that *it*—the accumulative ironies of the past, the virtuous rubbish-heap and self-parody of ancestors in death—still sought to warn me not to dig into itself so deep for the classical burden of truth (I was thinking, without clearly realizing it, of my grandfather's solid puritan instinct to dismiss the collective ghost—especially when it arrived as my outlaw and his heir, agnostic barrier and still essence of science and art and love—I was influenced as well by my mother's reflection embodied within an unreasoning tradition of fear: fear that my unwelcome (stepfather's?) attachment to her (was it true or not that he had been my own father's engineering colleague and friend?) may have compelled him—in order to win from the family of his adoption their everlasting gratitude and affection—to leave his well-ordered camp and *plunge* into the closed forbidden jurisdiction of the past in search of my open gauge and sceptical grain of fact. . . .)

It wasn't proof of a father's innocence or a stepfather's

adventure into the vanishing point of pork-knocker law and justice L—— was after. He didn't give an orphan's damn for this. He had been commissioned to re-locate Raven's Head because it was now suspected—fifteen or twenty years after its disappearance—that fantastic gold deposits lay in the river thereabouts. The difficulties were rich and enormous. A needle in the rubble of a haystack. In the first place it was uncertain whether the Raven's Head he sought lay on this river or twenty-five stitched jungled miles away on the next. (There were *two* Raven's Heads according to oral tradition.) In the second place not only did these mushroom settlements spring up overnight, they disappeared as rapidly, and often attempts at particular re-locations had to face the fact that rash new mining premises were shooting up still, here and there, each claiming to cloak an original site. This tradition and confusion of forms proved often to be the wreck of all hope for a recovery of an original nucleus of villages.

L—— knew it was imperative to do an extremely careful job in respect of Raven's Head. For his principals were contemplating an astronomical investment, labour, machinery, a new township. Once they were thoroughly satisfied they would set about establishing dredging operations in the section of the river beneath the original village and these would be accompanied by drilling work as well on both banks.

If they could not find the Raven's Head they sought they would naturally be compelled to abandon the project or to embark on expensive, possibly fruitless, prospection of the whole difficult and uncertain area.

It was no use stirring a nail to transport the parts of the dredge until they were certain they had located (and tested) their actual claim on the ground which existed on government parchment all the time. (L—— shook his head—as if he wanted to brush my cobwebs and complaints aside—when I spoke to him of probing the irresponsible legality of such licences and deceptive records.)

The war had reduced all conventional communications to paper transport services, lorry and truck—L——spoke apologetically as if by way of parable—to a standstill. And even before that there had been upheaval, feud and misery, the disruption of the self-evident normal passage of events. It was curious but he referred to the war as if it was associated with some kind of native reflex, his generation of earthquake (the implication, perhaps heretical, which arose in my mind—as he spoke—pointed to an ancient trail which was an apprehension of live response beyond the fixed limit he imposed on a residual society): an action for which no one—beyond a certain self-appointed region—stood to blame, L—— insisted—as though he read my mind and saw he could not remove the nagging seal of doubt. And if indeed any further blame was necessary, the misjudgment or misconception of reality—he agreed—then *he*—because of his insusceptibility to a continuing motion or cause outside of himself (or, in other words, because of his susceptibility to himself as his own faulty agent)—must suffer the blame, in terms of his own absolute logic of context, solely, in the numb fixture of himself. He was trapped within the riddle of his own leaden machinery—the riddle of the fixed instincts.

At such moments of absolute prejudice and resistance —within and without—immobility—L—— struck me as the advocate of the devil of humility in himself: he became the insensible nature of dreaming relationship to guilt and absurdity, the most ancient of convictions, and the most modern of sciences—empirical responsibility (and lack of responsibility) I wrestled with day and night: he fulfilled the most negative role of all—the self-imposed ratification of every closed sentence I could not truly accept and which I found myself helplessly probing in order to uncover wherein lay the movement of original compassion, the furthest point and agency of reason and the source of an active responsible *spiritual* (L—— loathed the word) tradition still.

There was one poorly constructed road running up from the coast (L—— spoke again in his unreflective way and without a germ of reproach, pointing to a map of creatures as though *it*, in truth, had no living existence) and this was in a state of almost universal neglect.

The job of moving the dismantled giant armature of the dredge, bolt by bolt, rib by rib (if the project should once be set in motion) would lie—for a time at any rate—on the slender back of what personal initiative in river transportation was available: a herculean task but not impossible. It would fall upon creatures of little weight and substance, this was true, (L—— spoke now as if he had come around, in the end, to humouring me out of some obscure necessity) legs and paddles and arms, Captain Funeral Fetish—the *one* of innumerable generations—and his fellow tenants of the bush, half-insect, half-animal, crawling in procession on the watertop and along every scant portage around the falls and rapids. In short—L—— was half-joking, half-sad, a confession amounting almost to self-defeat—there was small certainty the mission he had accepted would be successfully accomplished and *seen* to be established in his (or its?) own self-sufficient terms.

BOOK THREE

Raven's Head

Sister and wife at once; for without the use of the body
Mentally she unites, for the Spouse is God, not a man.
Out of this mother is born the Ancient as well as the
infant. . . .

PAULINUS OF NOLA

The Eyes
Closed, they are waiting. Open, they're also waiting.
They are acquainted,
but they have forgotten the name of their acquaintance.

TENNESSEE WILLIAMS

6

The horse was trotting amiably along Water Street when suddenly—without the slightest warning—it reared; neighed stridently. The respectable-looking carriage it drew lurched and appeared to be toppling on its side when it narrowly righted itself. The driver descended from his high box, held the dream-ridden horse by the reins, and began reassuring him. The horse seemed to possess a sinister memory and yet still to respond—out of a grateful and fearful desire—to the human, if not divine hand upon its neck and head. It was the custom in these parts for horses to wear shades against their eyes which allowed them to see straight ahead, up or beneath but never from side to side so whatever it was had frightened the creature may have passed right under or above its nose and then beyond the cloak of sight.

An old man and a young boy sat inside the carriage. They, too, like the supernatural driver and the supernatural horse belonged to this and every age of an insufficiency of vision. They came out into the street looking bewildered and blindfolded themselves. It was a still flowing night all around them they did not appear to see. Sightless they may have been like the bright lid of the street light overhead which had acquired a curious halo of flying insects, out of which unbroken circle every now and then a pair of wings flew straight at the vulnerable pilot of flame which revealed itself to be less vulnerable than imagined; its own alert and deadly and protective skull of a transparency like glass.

The incident occurred within a stone's throw of the ancient and modern riverwall, and the timeless river stood waiting to be discerned like a dark floating ball on which the lighted shadow of its own interior had formed itself into ships whose cargo was no less than the motion of the earth.

It was impossible to say what had startled the cryptic head of the horse. Its hide crinkled and shuddered and trembled all over and through its beaked eyes there issued a rolling and endlessly perturbed glance.

The driver endeavoured to calm its affright so that the carriage might proceed but without success. The horse stood as if riveted to the ground: with its head flung back and its presence against the river and the sky, it acquired both the illumination and the fringes of shadow inherent in Night—an extraordinary witness of Raven's Head gate or barrier. It was turning into its own forbidding gateway on the North, the Gateway of Fear.

There were, after all, four possible approaches to Raven's Head town sometimes called Hebra's Town: Raven's Head Gate on the north, Hebra's Gate on the south, the Suspension Bridge on the west and Sorrow Hill on the east. And these approaches were ceaselessly inclined to grow blurred and insensible to their origins— to be drained as it were of all consciousness of a dialogue with the emotion or genius of place and to become out-crops of common mud or stone shaped by the indifferent hand of the dead god of the seasons into an arrested weathercock.

On all sides a siege was laid to the *will*, the will to go

forward until one's resolve became—caught in its own paradox—the fortress of environment. The ancient gun which had once boomed at the gateway of the Demerara fort on the riverwall was now silent: silent as a dream of infant thunder in the heart of Sorrow Hill, a silence which was both the mature issue and the startled product of a crippled role and inborn struggle anew for comprehension within incomprehension.

Morning and night for a century or more the great gun used to shake the primitive approaches to the city and it was at such an early or late pregnant hour—though it had long ceased to fire as in the commanding years before—the horse and carriage of the Ancient of Days stopped and responded: a permanent fixture or capture this was which had nevertheless been transported into the interior, elsewhere and everywhere, appearing equally fixed—the late mental door and early battering ram of besieger and besieged.

It was—in spite of the universal predilection for waging symbolic war—a totally different ornamental approach if one sought to enter the lost town by re-discovering Hebra's Gate. It had always been, even in the best of years, a difficult problem to keep this unpredictable door and roadway open to the traffic of work-ridden and travel-ridden vehicles crawling like nightmare motorized infantry against the endless density and abstraction of space on earth. The ghosts which paraded were equally reminiscent of mechanical age and youth though it was most difficult to say who was captor and who captive. No image of respectable fantasy existed here: neither stately procession nor horse nor carriage; the landscape was genuinely wild in a manner which seemed to lay bare the true and darkest intimate recesses of the life of proliferate nature, the life of the born jungle against the life of a disintegrating tribal society.

There were even expanses along the variable road—like stitched cloth of grass within a hostile though withdrawn brooding encirclement—where the tribal shepherd appeared still intact. The grazing spirits of his cattle sometimes broke the fences and crossed the open road hereabouts, seeming still almost totally oblivious to the sudden possible acceleration of enemy traffic. In fact everything depended on the alien driver's reflex or invading clutch of instinct, the fluid brake of all vehicular times present to him, to save them (and himself from running them down) in a stationary past which was all that was present to them. The mooning cows spent an age in their slow exasperating walk from one eternal parapet to another reflecting their own archaic memory of address and landscape where the surviving march of ridge or valley was infinitely retarded, infinitely slow. The volcanic pace of everything subsided within a certain reduction of the span of lightning consciousness into an obsolescent earthborne sleep which came close to recapturing the dreamless clarity and innocence of a babe in an antique cradle. Within such a slow almost totally withdrawn figure of progress the animal of fate and patience learnt to move: its advantage over the horse, dream-ridden horsepower, gear, clutch, brake and driver, lay in its insusceptibility to the nerves of both flight and fear. It never actually ceased to move across its pedestal, however indifferently and still slowly, in response to its own scale of proportion and attunement, the universal arrested diaphragm of every glaring landslide; and with this unerring statuesque degree of just motion the animal's head lifted, swung *now, deliberately,* to address the oncoming rush and menace of an approaching machine: something which was—in the eye of the sacred cow of Raven's Head—truly lacking in all swift exposure, instant credibility, substance or dread.

But (and it was the first time the driver of the machine was deceived) a misconception arose which remained implacably framed in the mind of place—the *Inn or Resthouse of the Quartering of the Cow*—one of a number of signs pointing to the ancient mining town. *He* (the driver) was certain the animal had swung its head in order to turn and sidle to the left as well as back the way it had come. It was an elementary manœuvre, he felt, and the equilibrium and assurance of the beast made it appear obvious and inevitable. Furthermore a certain self-confidence in his own eye of judgment—room and place—had been paradoxically aroused a moment ago, when shortly before he drove out of the twilight encampment of the jungle into the shepherd's clearing he had discerned the tigercat of the bush. The tiger—known in this locality as deer-tiger—the "cat with the devil's horns"—was dressed as always in her deceptive gentle reddish brown coat. Her eyes however were naked in their own fierce right. The instant she spotted the driver upon her, there was a flash of lightning, vibration, tuning-fork, *spring*, the plucked harp of motion, *gone*. She had vanished and all that remained was the thunder of his own gasp and response. It was as if the earth had opened and swallowed her and the intervening light void of black consciousness, the open tumult of everything, nervous precipice, vicarious *impact*, death (for though she had escaped he almost dreamed he had hit her) landfall, waterfall, were all reduced to incomprehension and vast silence. Out of which emerged an

67

inflation of *his* not *her* achievement, the certainty that it was *he* who had seen *it* and skilfully avoided all.

The balloon of false reaction led straight to the roots of premature self-assurance and conviction. Far from sidling back to her side of the road, the cow, that incredibly slower beast, continued to march forward. It was too late for him to stop or for her to change her hide and escape. The mortal blow she received was like a shattering of his own barrier of stupidity and indifference and predictable image.

The closed structure of Will, the fortress of environment, had parted. The old man (clothed now in shepherd's rags) and his grandson were tending the driver of the machine. The vehicle itself was smashed: it had collided with a curious half-feminine, half-bovine obstruction. The uncertain road through the jungle was strewn with these numinous boulders.

The driver had had a miraculous escape and he was soon recovered sufficiently to accept a portion of the shepherd's evening meal. This had been prepared out of boiled plantains which were then crushed to pulp in a mortar with a pestle. The brown fatty mass which emerged was considered delicious: one could discern pale minute flecks of the original fruit or vegetable substance, which had escaped being ground, like the perfect iota of shell sprinkled here and there.

From the running ball of conversation between grandfather and grandson the driver was able—in spite of an apparently phlegmatic disposition which may have been professional and native or on the other hand the stunned immediate consequences of responsibility for his every collision—to visualize his own flight (blind passage of pitfall and footfall which lay ahead of him).

No use walking or driving or riding with one's head in the clouds. *He* (the driver) was only too well aware of this. He did not need grandfather and grandson to tell him so. But their presence had emerged upon a frontier of existence which was involved with the exploratory fact of his freedom or unfreedom, authority or lack of authority. Should self-deception (it was a thought he of all persons had never properly faced before)—in its most intimate paradox of a practical heaven of reality—fall to his lot, it was precisely because of his own acquiescence to stunned premises, the kind of engineered space in which he bargained to rule himself—and be ruled by himself—by allowing of no sensible proportion except in his own standing or stumbling experience of it. And for this reason he did not know how to begin to accept the possibility that he was being counselled or pushed, wittingly and unwittingly, fairly and unfairly, by someone and something other than himself whether apparently conservative and old or revolutionary and young.

And yet—now for the first time he was not so sure. The counsellors of past and present generations might possess—in the midst of the fruitless noises of conflict they appeared to make, the abracadabra of gesture and sound—an element of indistinct dialogue which survived within their vociferous arts of force and persuasion. Had it become vital to listen and look to them more carefully and acutely than he had ever listened and looked to anyone attending him before?

The apparent depth and horror of his position dawned on him. He felt a sharp agonized division—a sensation of being drawn convulsively *up* as well as pulled instantly *down* into the bodily (or bodiless) mystery of mysteries he dreaded: a way he had not conceived himself experiencing in a present or a future; the flock of himself—animal sub-stitute, strung-up, reflective—stood unnaturally poised within the conjunctive witness of another eye, a window within and without both shepherd and friend, ancestor and legend—the utterly retrenched and flashing instinct of the purest severance and witness of a consciousness of mute self-revolving parts in endless dialogue.

The very clearing into which he had been driven or had stumbled appeared now to have settled into an involun-tary hole in the ground. It was marked by a certain in-telligence it had taken him ages it seemed to discover, a burrowing resourceful intelligence he had been unable to stop himself from overlooking—methodical it now looked, secretive, too—layer by layer, starting with the heavy air and overgrowth of his feeling and descending into their lighter soil through different grains and lines of featureless texture and textureless feature. The iron trunk of a tree fallen from above emerged far beneath like the lantern skull of gloom. Did the shepherd's night of over-cast passage and cottage stand upon one of the lost cap-tive lighted foundations of fear of an upper world—the world to which he (the driver) apparently and solely be-longed? The driver of the broken machine laughed at himself for being an aimless fool. He was turning—or falling—into the pool or thoroughfare of someone both like and unlike himself.

He and the other—unlike and like—stood almost face to face, yet—miserable banner of all ages—masked at the same time, horse or tiger, animate cow or brute stone, sovereign or primitive device. Both were intent, beyond conventional envelope and address, on penetrating the other's vulnerable (or was it invulnerable?) carriage of secrets. Each one surmised the other's ideal stamp or picturesque emotive flag of animal landscape was clothed with danger and design, the danger of being confounded by immortal purpose and mislaid in the process by a postman or nightmare servant of design: while at the same time there stood as well the promise of a delayed telegram —movement towards the cradle of fulfilment—indistinct holes, pock-marks, monosyllabic crude lettering and utterance, canals and rivers descending into the cottage or ship of space from a projection of the moon, still rising and running forwards or backwards (no one could say which) *into* or *out of* the macroscopic script of Water Street and Ferry Road on this individual map, harbour and historical planet. (Such a tidal record of legend and impression—involving absurd codes of memory, inflation, as well as the acute thorn and nib of painted humility—witnessed to the porous skin of all oversize frontiers on earth which were drawn to gather themselves into hypothetical island or universe or pool upon the most ancient flesh of manuscript: herald and chart of precipitation, ground-plan of every modern and tribal entrepot, proud leaf of gravity adorned by names of delivery and adventure.)

Who was the engineer of such revolving barrier, despatch and arrest (birth and death) and where (or how) had it been possible to manufacture, for all eternity, in each self-important blocked device, the minuscule fleet of soul and necessary solution of origins?

It was the question one asked as though each invited the other to surrender his currency and ink of offspring, bloody password into the dark room of noble and ignoble execution, bunk of ocean, pilot and postmaster of buried access to unholy freedom, each one felt the other knew and stored for the purest selfish locked reasons.

Such a question drew one into the other's corridor of secret even treacherous mode of contemplation, the giant of place against whose enveloping, broad, plain countenance one stood so close as to lose the vision of him and indeed everything save that there existed a miniature almost forgotten universal stamp in the mind—the seal of the hanged dwarf of God. No longer were the foundations of the open city a great smashed subverted machine, destined to be anchored and helpless in time, but a rifled envelope at worst, still bearing the inner privilege of communicating with a true signature of parts. . . .

It came as a shock to the dreamer to find that the barrier which had stopped him was thin as paper, a logical stamp like a breath of air, suspended portrait, thumbprint, ghostly reflex. That it possessed such stubborn strength, such enduring power born of extension out of the catastrophic past, was the nature of the dilemma confronting the emotional dynamics of reason. It would be an admission of defeat to stop and consent to be thwarted by a bridge of obsession, the web of spirit. It was up to him, his conviction being what it was, to go forward into the future. And this was a strange uneasy way of putting the case, *his* case, after all. What conviction was it which had been propelling him and marshalling him all along in spite of everything? He resented the echo of such *naïveté*, intuition, call it what one will, and of mystical forces drawn up in retrospective battle array on a private or public ancestral front. It was all bound up with such frightful and undying exploits of spiritual conscience and absurdity. . . . He was an engineer and he practised and held himself totally responsible for an abstract form of measurement, control. It was—he paused and relented a little, standing on the verge of conceding a point to his opponent—Perhaps indeed it could be described, in all fairness, as a conviction. But the tribunal or theatre of action, courtroom, arena, living-room, bedroom, saloon, highway (the names of conviction and habit were legion) was one which it was his job solely to plan or build afresh in all emergencies in more or less precise, even though apparently mathematical, obscure, dented or insufficient material terms. It was the utilitarian spirit of improvement and responsibility which led him. But this was, once again (he knew he must watch himself) going too far. Nothing was leading him or had ever led him. Might as well say and blame inspiration for everything that happened. How could *he*—after all, be subject to such a crumbling mode of pointlessness and uncertain vagary of instinct? Could such an alien residue of motivation, outside of his proper intention, propel him beyond the ultimate marginal self-conception he held—the architect and engineer of the immediate framework of society—into discoveries of past and future associations he never dreamt of fashioning into solid residence and existence? What scale then was it he would lack either to demolish what was no longer relevant and essential or to discern and construct what was truly and clearly needed—even though no one saw it as yet?

If then the responsibility for all this still lay with him he would have to confess he had become a poor, an inefficient engineer: and he would know the necessity had now been born (the driver groaned with distaste) to feed himself and clothe himself upon eyes of mineral substitution, the artist's mask, the animal or plant of camouflage and vision. He would turn then, out of a curious despair, to someone or something he may have always unconsciously disregarded and despised, someone or something he would find himself driven now to *push* into the religious obscurity of moon or canal, the realm or depth of place he could not yet truly visualize for himself; someone who would appear surprisingly intact and whole, residual but unaffected by the landscape of fact, totally without—at that stage—the consciousness of having been actually set in motion or conscripted or wounded by another in the way the driver himself had once been free of such a dubious conviction.

And then—as if to illumine the dreamer's barricade of doubt—the dwarfed lamp of place shone like the grain of a skull: each hole of brightness which marked the ground delimited its own monstrous key of insertion and shadow like the blind solid glare of nature's fire, made tolerable to the inner camera of its reflective streaming eye within a phenomenal room of its own making, dark glasses against the sun; or like the conversion of the manufacturer's secret watermark upon an envelope held aloft against the flare of a match. So secret and inconstant the exit of image was, it concealed its dark issue in a new relationship of proportion out of disproportion.

And it was within these bars of secrecy that the framework of a parent scaffold reared its head and began to emerge again at last: the dreamer's twin obsession was clearer than ever now. And he (the driver)—stepson in vicarious stepfather, friend in vicarious brother—recoiled, on glimpsing this, as from his own growing surrender to the logic of unfamiliar truth. . . . *It* was clothing him with the necessity of acknowledging the cloak of otherness, retirement into so little and obscurity of movement into so much: the conviction drove him—and had been driving him all along though he had never seen it—into a sphere of reduction and an arm of extensive feeling; the

74

meeting ground of *two*, and he was indelibly associated with *one*.

Within it—within the globe of one and the indistinct preserves of the other—lay the key to an open consolidation the one could no longer support and carry; that one was standing ceaselessly upon the moving threshold of relinquishing it to the touch or residue of the other so that *it* (key and medium) could still exist in the grasp of one frail body of instinct as it unlocked the instant dust of another; in continual process of establishing a door for the one to issue through the other—through the logic of dreadful performance and execution into the principle of the ultimate breakdown of the wealth of injustice within the living witness of open fact.

It was both sliding rule and sliding scale of place with a reflex not merely of its own but of unpredictable room for transaction between TWO—one party to which was involved in the other's endless task of freedom (as the other was involved in the dazed circumvention of the ONE) of gauging and revising the dizzy scaffold of conceptions of the misconception—and misconceptions of the conception of revolving embrace, entrance and exit.

7

It was a strange company—TWO and IT—though who *it* was no one could say: a crumbling scarecrow perhaps, the key to. . . ? *It* possessed nevertheless a backbone and a single eye which turned and looked—without appearing to make any effort to see—both ways in the same blank crude instant: a blankness of question and expression which was as deceptive as a mirror made of headless stone or feature of glass made of heartless water. For this sculp-

75

ture of blankness—in spite of its association with a nightmare hardness or an unstable dimension—was one of the curious ways of freedom, a live negative and unsleeping signal within the field of each past footfall and of every future captive formation: it was the embodied *currency* of lifelessness to repudiate the absolute reign or stillness of death. The medium of place (the scarecrow declared) had never died as was popularly depicted in the fictions of the day. And IT was engaged—even as it supported and bore the company of TWO—in preparing a new map of the fluid role of instinct, the ancient flight and landslide of which had never ceased continuing to move and outline an inherent traverse and cradle of regeneration in answer to the arrested dialogue of legend in the model despatches of love and prisons of hate, blind of Age and fold of Youth.

Item of Reconstruction: Diary recalling Fall into Ancient Passage—20 years ago—Raven's Head. This Late Entry 30th July 1964: the Cat with Nine horned Lives painted on the Door of Present Book.

I was addressed by the walls of memory in a curious hallucinatory shorthand: STOP Equals LIGHTNING Exit. DON'T PANIC. Turn LEAVES of SUBTERRANEAN catalogue.

I framed a question in reply: was it possible to see at this stage—with emblematic eyes—or feel—with "dead" whiskers, cat—the end of the long tunnel out of blockage and catastrophe?

I can still perceive memory's chain of replies to my question like a long thundering train which still runs through this short timeless day—stranger and stranger snapshots still of those of us who recall the final—so it seemed—station of ourselves in time and space. And we (one obscure member of us, at any rate) may stumble therefore—in the end—who knows?—upon the flashing settlement and page of truth.

I confess quite openly that the picture and design of fact surrounding the crash (the crumbling reconnaissance car, plane, call it what you will, came down in the bush approximately north of Raven's Head) is—and always was from the beginning—architecturally unclear and unsound to me—unpredictable vacancy of ascent or block of descent?—and to everyone I have met to this day and hour who claim to have cleared or witnessed some such closed instantaneous event. And it is from within this stunned, breathless, post-mortem (everyone believed this to be so for a long time) vision of recollection that a conception—or misconception—of the reality of the thing emerges after centuries, ages of haphazard penetration and shifting movement it seems. To speak of it as twenty calendrical years is to frame into shorthand all eternity with two curled strokes of a pen. Truth or absurdity?

I am grateful for one childlike endless obsession I entertained for a certain length and breadth of crushed time—poetic inversion as it may seem in the light of everything—which sticks out a mile to this day. Was it he who crept and crawled that last mile to save me or I to unlock him? I still like to think it was I who saved L——'s life, and not he mine, in the nick of time. Recurring balloon of dream or gauge of reality? For on that afternoon when I (it was on the tip of my tongue to say *he*) succeeded—more dead than alive—in finding a way through the jungle, nine months after I had been left for dead, I arrived in time to prove to the authorities I was a living soul and not the dead beast they swore they had seen.

L—— was released from the prison hospital (which was all that was standing between him and execution), the conviction against him quashed. The violent quarrel we had had over the woman Hebra the day before I was killed, so it was consistently reported, had weighed heavily against me (my mind still wanders in a trap); I should have said—against him: the time of trial. Whose neck was it, after all, his or mine in our eternal triangle, parent scaffold, step-parent, jealous room for lovers? It was the old sickening arch of half-comic ancestral half-light everyone approaches by way of mortal excuse and psychological riddling instinct.

It was not only the dark brush with Hebra our self-accusers built upon. The feud and myth of Sorrow Hill went deeper still and farther back. Anything to circumscribe their own fear of explosive nature in one and to relieve (or relive) their helplessness through another.

Presumably they reckoned he had flung me out of the window, miraculously judging the space and saving himself at the same time. He was their tigercat wizard and scapegoat, after all. And I, beyond a shadow of doubt, had confirmed this by springing up, at the last minute, alive. God knows who or what I was supposed to be at this juncture save that in their minds, and mine, an equation—destined to salvage a certain area of recollection—began to form—the sweep of nothing equals everything. Or to put it in a personal nutshell—the extinction or rekindling of one confirms a witness either way which equals two.

The CRASH—which I am now aware demolished not only their conventional presence but my fixed senses as well of room and absence from them—broke through to a passage of long-lost existence wherein the total de-

privation of every clipped assumption of relative circumstance took ages to grow into the living fable of reality.
The shepherd of the prowling bush and his grandson appeared out of nowhere. (Every attempt to locate them has
been made since my recovery but the actual and original
fierce and equally mild doctors of the masked ages are
still not to be found). How did I contrive—in the void of
the mind which seems so long ago—to stitch a wild
apprehension of them together? Glaring touch of conceit:
fallacy. Needless to say it was they who obscurely
measured and needled me when they found me lying on
the ground. Rumpelstiltskin threads bristled like the
wisest whiskers. A stitch in time saves nine. Cat's eyes
fabric. Balloon skin pattern. Skyscraper tapestry. *The toy
cow jumped over the toy moon.* I felt at a growing animal loss
that they were re-fashioning me and escalating me into
the flying sequence of a dwarf and the lofty imitation of a
child.

THE FIRST BURIED IMAGES which returned to me
(long before I actually saw the face of grandfather or
grandson) were the womb and carriage of a dream I had
forgotten. I saw myself moving away from myself within
a dimension over which I appeared to have little control.
I succeeded in returning to myself and to the consciousness of where I now stood on higher ground. My recollection of rearing up over myself—if I may so put it—
actually arose in association with the feeling of a morsel
in my mouth. I tried to spit it out but the cavity of teeth
and tongue acquired an unsuspected pull and hold which
made me swallow in spite of myself. I was situated, I discerned, not beneath but above the northern gateway of
Raven's Head canal and I recalled—as I became aware of

biting into the food in my mouth—how I had walked away helplessly and fearfully from myself only a moment ago, descended into the canal, crossed an ageless pit, and recrossed back to where now once again I stood.

Whoever I was, whom I now recalled, in startled intensity, and saw as if it were actually someone else in process of being drawn helpless and obscure, appeared to have moved on the spur of one moment to gain a shelter which stood, across from him, on the opposite side of the canal. The rain had suddenly started falling (this was his apparent reason and excuse)—long sad crystal lines of water which penetrated to one's skin. He swallowed, crossed the canal, bending almost double in order to crawl into the low shelter he gained on the other bank. The rain soon stopped and like a child on a rocking-horse—half-horse, half-rider—he retraced his steps across his grave of hallucination, without actually falling as he feared.

He had no notion how food or halter came back into his mouth—as if he had never actually moved from the same spot (or as if the very ground of sustenance may have moved itself unobtrusively forwards and back): in bewilderment and frustration he wanted to spit this stubborn root of sensation out but was forced to chew and swallow as if it were a living responsible guilty thing. He knew in this instant he would have to begin from the very obscure beginnings of everything to grapple with each form of strange support and community—moving apparently at open angles in an unbridled capacity of space or time but stunned by him or stunning him all the same into a new-born sense of the active density of riding context or overlapping station. FOOD AND SHELTER. It was the quickest rationalization he (or I?) indulged in like a blurred signpost or banner, leash as well as conception of ruling spirit of place.

Slowly he was becoming aware of the presence of persons saddled by things (and things saddled by persons) in a stunned world to which he now began to perceive he belonged: so stunned everything was that each action he witnessed, the performance of hand or instrument, possessed a strange "inside-out" inevitability belonging to levels as well as agents of a certain incalculable freedom from the ancient obsessions of life. He saw each one in this new revealing light of ridiculous bondage with the eye of one freshly woken though a curious shadow of restraint still lay upon him. The unsettling conviction was dawning within that they (he and the other)—however supremely conscious now of a past relationship—doer or done, server or served, runner or run—which they had forgotten and which they now dreamt to see in all entirety—might still be involved in a blind paradox and carriage (might still be involved in a tunnel of darkness surrounding their line of sight to match, even now, the radius of presence I remembered treading in cloaked awareness of myself or itself) which distanced us still within the most intimate moments of recall—one from the other—variable degrees of magnetic obscurity or areas of illusory contact. The drama of consciousness in which we were involved, part-knowing, part-unknowing, dim and voluntary, illuminating and involuntary, was infinite and concrete, simple and complex at the same time.

He was aware all at once that his feet were standing naked on the ground. And he began descending a staircase of land. Not into the middle of an absent river this time. Down steps instead which drew him into a small

81

but unexpectedly ornate visionary room, the floor decorated with stable squares like a draughts-board. The attendant within divided his attention—polishing the floor as well as shining one shoe which he held aloft in his hand. He was a salesman of parts it appeared: SHOES FOR SALE. His reaction on seeing his customer was consistent in its divided reflection, the trespass of apparent being in all community. The fact was—he was instantly obsessed, on seeing the other, with the notion of acquiring a sturdy fellow for the reluctant shoe he had mounted on one hand. A long boot, he cried, to go with the shoe. The customer was properly taken aback but flattered all the same by the request made of him to supply—out of a forgotten store of secrets—the missing boot the salesman needed as if it was not he (the customer), after all, who wanted to clothe himself but the inverse salesman (sophisticated beggar rather than crude middleman proprietor) whose advertised wish or will he was being called upon —in a game of elaborate moves—to erect and fulfil.

As they faced each other the infant dawn of ancient recollection strengthened: he (the customer) felt he had struck a bargain with the salesman in the shape of a beggar on old Water Street. Half-bandaged feet. Decrepit suit. One trouser leg rolled up, the other dangling down. The battered serge neither wet nor dry; and the customer was drawn by the spreading gravy of fabric. Was it his own blurred spirit of seasonal image? Yellow and black and green. The worn blood of autumn, black in winter, transparent in summer.

In my Father's house are many mansions.

Blood. The customer looked startled by the canvas of *blood*. How could this be? It was yellow still and black and green.

Were these then the legend of the bargain they struck as they played for time to present the map . . . transubstantiation . . . of blood? The black and gold dress of the green beggar advertised an enigmatic fluid salesman for one project of buried innocence: the innocent unborn "soul" who was destined to be charged with an account for murder. Better not to emerge and live. What a ludicrous collective design and open self-accusation this was. Megalomania and despair or the prison of overcoming the sacrificial need in—and of—humanity? But would not someone always be found—in the midst of the "dead" seal and ransom of everything—to subscribe—without even knowing how or why—to the "living" mutilation of the scarecrow? The answer of certain death and hate was void. That of the *quick* unconscious pageant of love an appointment with the meaningful Victim of all who served to blazon and rebuke, in his own born transcendental right, the meaningless power of lust in the Victor: he might be lifeless or stunned and footsore but he still arose in the nick of time. . . . Save that it might still prove too late for all if Hebra, the vulgar muse or soul, had died —on the long buried road—of their epidemic disease, the victor's hand of strangling bodily lust, the victim's of *empty* strangled bodiless love. But how could the statuesque ghost of such painful arousal or conflict die? Hebra was equally a grotesque substitute—as repulsive as every appearance of conniving victim—for the timeless contradictory spouse they (victor and victim) both needed whether they were rich man or poor salesman, customer, artist or engineer. The art of a growing drunkard lay simply in each unthinking draught of the variegated blood of life, which made him the bloated twin of successive acts of compulsive mutilation on behalf of—was

83

it a dream from beginning to end?—the pitiful and piti-less shrunken reality of freedom.

14th–15th August 1964

Dear L——,

I am now in a position to send you this partial witness of the confession I have been promising so long to make —*The Eye of the Scarecrow*.

Thank you very much indeed for the ancient photographs, clippings, old covenant, letters etc. etc. which you despatched to me
c/o Night's Bridge Post Office.

Poor Scarecrow! it was his confession—he said he strangled her—which saved my neck. It is strange but at times I feel curiously drawn to him, then the horror of self-mutilation and self-extension—the image of con-science and consciousness—makes it seem both too evil and too good to be true. I remind myself that he may have possessed the blackest motive and to entertain a shred of affection for him—a self-confessed murderer—is the grimmest challenge to issue out of fixture and skeleton, cupboard of the past. I swear to myself—in order to re-buke every slight inclination to gratitude or love—that he did not come forward simply to stretch a helping hand to me: it was his "holy" pride which could not bear the thought of surrendering to the accursed cage of Hebra (she was the ugliest dead soul and mistress in the world one may ever hope to see); no flight was too much for him and the thought that I—project and twin in his bow of creation—should suffer punishment and death in his

84

astronomical mission and deed would have shattered all upright carriage and future hope in him. It is the contemplation of such an instrument of jealous time, *which I am at a loss to know how to bend or bear*—it is so resolute and strong—that sobers me in the end to view him once again in a new and unashamed gentle light. Yes, I confess it, after all these years, a true conception of depth and affection.

His confession it is which frees us now to make ours—if we wish. For—it is the plain arrow of truth—if he had not come forward when he did, we would have remained locked in the inertia of our time; you would have died with the uncertain conviction whether I really knew you to be innocent or guilty (in fact it would not now matter) and I in turn would have gone to my inevitable target or scaffold or end equally unknowing what you had drawn in truth out of me.

It is likely that you would have breathed not a murmur of protest and would have blamed yourself for everything. Old stoic! But I would have reacted differently. Self-mockery. Shock. How could one live to escape—as we had so often done—the string of disaster, fire and flood, to face the bar of crude unjust anti-climax? Why, our reconnaissance machine had crashed. Remember? But flung us out with a sudden snap into a jungle of miraculous survival. And still. . . .

As it was, the shock of "ultimate" liberation was the most cunning and desperate blow of all when it came. For when Scarecrow came forward—pork-knocking beggar that he was—and swore he loved the devil of a woman—I was lost in the obsession that this was our nightmare soul and trick—something you had successfully engineered (and I dreamt I performed) to give us more time to manufacture a defence and case.

And so—God forgive me—the circumstances of deception seemed so brutally open and clear—I began to identify myself with *him* and with *you* (as if there stood over me every daring midwife and extension of folly): the strongest most unbearable pregnant blinding light of misunderstanding and understanding. I began (now I see it dimly and admit it) to read the unreflecting volume which the nature of everything—both timeless and absurd—was seeking to discharge and dismantle.

And even so I am still confused by time, the truly suffering elements of pitiless direction and miraculous chance: whose and what true universal innocence—the innocence of the One we share—do these ceaselessly appoint and confirm? I do not know if Scarecrow is not still a dark invention and excuse I presented to myself and *you* were the living undistorted representative one (untimely as all time is and therefore pitiful) who paid the ugliest and dearest prospective price for me. . . .

It is this *consciousness* of the continuous erosion of self-made fortifications that is the "material" of my Confession—which you, out of some inexplicable motive and curious humour, declare yourself in need of at this time in spite of all your resources of ageless simplicity. But then you were always waiting at the door of self-exile and within the flesh of stone, without appearing to mind over much the tragic self-sufficiency and failure and meaninglessness of invented modes and self-created things. . . .

May God forgive me for what insensitive and insensible fury I believe I saw and what sensitive and sensible glory I still do not appear to make or *see*.

IDIOT NAMELESS

HIS OWN ACTION sprang out of the long unconscious habit of trying to fashion her into his own image against the fear of surprising alien beauty or ugliness in a passive state of nature. How to make her feel in the end—his hand moved from thigh to throat—what she had never suffered before—his sense of self-construction, likeness to humiliation? He had always assumed until now that it was admirable for her to be the senseless humiliated one, proper model or contemptible subject, tenant of his whim of erection, unthinking whore. This charmed circle served to give him an ascendancy over her—his principal commodity: mud and fleshpot of dreams. She was his to rule, chop, barter. To do with—on occasions—as he liked. But with each deadening stranglehold—something he had never quite bargained for in the beginning happened— the price of execution rose by leaps and bounds: the sliced features of "living" death withdrew into something as simple, direct, economic as that. It dawned on him—in a way he had never reckoned before—that she was every man's meat, the technically rich and the technically poor, and he was now being called upon to spend more and still more upon her.

IT (the transaction of indignity) had never presented itself in this harsh motive light before, the light of an incongruous initiative she possessed which was capable of overpowering him rather than being overpowered by him. It was he who was becoming the subject of her encirclement. The shock of this robbed him immediately of all feeling of arbitrary possession: and the numb consequence, wood, stone, clod of earth, grew into a new senseless demand. Like someone and something so taken by surprise in the market-place of habit, HE and IT began to dislodge themselves from an old, undeviating chain of deadly circumstance. *It* became not only a high-priced tag but a priceless jewel whose rarity bred every astonished witness of jealousy or love. And he was the most afflicted witness whose need of one model and ideal economic servant transcended the DREAMING ANCIENT link of service and demand. This magnetic dawn—age of decomposition and recomposition—drew him to make her over beyond all mere plastic lines of facile purchase or ignorant necessity into something he felt he now desired her to uphold and see. His true submissive horn of likeness. Engine of humiliation. Love.

That he had run her down and destroyed his image in the process was a possibility he never dreamt extended beyond the impotency of himself, the impotency of all men who grow from infancy into the ancient riddle of a premature acceptance of weakness, born and reborn burrowing instinct, the nebulous current of the dynamo. . . .

A transparent vehicle of age and youth he was (and she was no longer a mere crushed bone of contention), an enterprise set in incredible proportion and relation—CAPACITY and DENSITY: the capacity of unique digestion, consciousness; the density of friction between space and thing, flight and ground, making the sparks of instinct fly.

It was in this intoxicated "blind" tradition and unflinching, involuntary strength (in which he deprived her of every soft catlike option she had once been at liberty to exercise) that he killed her; and then—perceiving a glimmer of the full light of indefatigable living currency, apparent horror, integral reason and melting unreason he had unwittingly invoked—he gave himself up to be sold to the highest bidder, sensing the death of "economic" love and "ideal" opportunity but the likelihood of enduring recompense in a "soul" of liberty. And thus became truly himself a hideous engine of reality in the empirical eye of Justice, standing on the baffling scaffold of classical conversion and compassion—a new age of self-confession and self-proportion.

He had killed her in order to possess her within new limits (the ultimate cancellation of greed?)—digestion and capacity: at the jealous INN OF THE QUARTERING OF THE COW where she had taken her last promiscuous rich lover like a morsel in her own right. This was final as a blow of stone, the natural and unnatural battle-ground of the harsh senses and sexes. And yet he was still incredulous—how could he really have engineered such an impossible breathless stroke? He clung to both grain and hand of incredulity, "future" enlightenment, constitution, innocent understanding, like a Child in a womb of ancestral fantasy whose every unborn move is a refusal to bow to an inventory of mechanical fates and imprints.

Two months—even less—remained to him, and these would embrace nine in all of rude trial and conception: the Scarecrow (with which I had invested myself as if I were now intent on breaking through from within) accepted the sentence of death passed on him.

He sat in his cell like parent sculpture, pregnant witness; the feminine clay of his hands moved the pawns on a draughts-board: each piece in his fingers curiously alive, scraped clean as the dust of memory from the sole of his boot. Sometimes the game of conscience he played was blank as an empty slate, sometimes haunted by the subversive cloak of identity within, the meaning of each day's uplifted word towards the crown of silence.

For if indeed his jealous claim to the art of murder remained unflinching and still sensitive to truth, might he not have succeeded beyond his wildest dreams in supporting and re-creating the enigma of life—the twins of breath and breathlessness, animus and anima? Future instinct of the borderline. To be or not to be. In reality—how could there be in this respect any true choice since the alternatives were invested with groundless self-sufficiency? In fact they were not so invested and never had been. THE GHOST AND HAMLET. Both were the apprehensive soul or image of an unknown capacity—death the image of unreflecting life or life the soul of unreflective death: the scales of being were still melting beyond or within each other, infinitely perhaps treacherously closed or infinitely perhaps fearfully open.

The art of murder. In this lay the supreme paradox: the surprising and surprised life-blood within each invented (or inverted) pawn or thing. No man's land of living achievement. Oh to be born without the stain of death. Could it be that he was slowly going mad or inexorably and miraculously sane? He knew the child which would bear his name (most curious spirit-child of an absent parent-to-be) was expected within a couple of months. Perhaps—who could tell—within the hour of execution, *his* execution. He wanted to laugh but his lips were drawn; stiff. No wonder it became necessary, in statuesque advance, to paint, erect—invest himself with—the overriding garment of two concerted women until wife-and-mother confessed to the feature of solipsis, ageless mistress, appetite, Hebra: and Hebra herself changed and acquired the soul and expression of patented youth. Was this a self-critical and incalculable conversion . . . art . . . transubstantiation . . . of eloquent blood?

The shadow of a hidden self was his, the function of "myself" in the limbo of himself—would such an instinctive and subjective spirit-child (weaned on the disasters of the ages) consent, in turn, to be hollowed and thereby apparently inflated into an unconventional and illuminating room of endless, treacherous, growing proportions— the bed and skull and crossbones of self-discovery and self-parody, rich man, poor man, beggarman, king? He cried to me and to the skeleton proprietors of love: and with each move on his canvas and board of earth sought to lay bare each swollen, still shrunken square of flesh— an incredible design of bleeding, wounded affections which in another light appeared bloodless ingrained lines of living hardship rather than lifeless sensibility, any extension or part of which might serve—in a moment of bewildering stricken reality—to enclose or equally strip and dismantle one's preconception of guilt.

It was as if indeed I sat facing him in the dense and transparent cell of his movable, immovable, deceptive prison and person: as if I had arrived in this backward, unexpected pregnant way to the goal of my long quest. Paradoxical womb: cloak: long lost father and new-found son. Distorted mother and distorting generation. A host of terrible questions arose I needed time to ask and place in mute perspective.

I was drawn to the windows, CORPUSCLES OF SUN, glowing intermittently: the mansions of blood, illusion and reality. In one framed picture or neighbouring room the walls were almost black. The colour of smoke. A figure moved within shadow and stone: fished on his

hands and knees for a flake of soap which had slipped
from him and was skidding across the floor. He recovered
it; resumed washing his hands: basin . . . room . . . for the
grease of lust to cleanse the mud of love.

It was this shocking awareness of mutual involvement
and obsession which woke him all at once and he saw
himself within his own flowing and unwavering reflection
of shadow. For within the basin of truth he was related to
an unbending scrubbed companion, one who had never
yielded pride of place to the other until he saw himself
how black and fluid it was. And though he was looking
into what seemed the next room, under his nose, as it
were, the distance between himself and itself was enormous, light years, water years, blood years, the years of
fire and smoke; still the very enormity of intimate contact
made it impossible for him to dislodge the tie of agelessness, the sense of being tied to an age of agelessness: if one
appeared to stand nodding but still the other refracted and
moved, and when one appeared to run and sleep the
other kept a dark pace, too, and woke, moving as before
and yet still, so that the specific weight and gravity of the
distant colour of consciousness within and without one's
pool rested upon each crumb of the self-same purification
and self-recognition.

Each line, elevation, window, room—within the mansion—that he was still able to perceive from his broad
vantage point—was raised to a kind of inverse mathematical power of spirit, the indissoluble link of space,
relief from density, consciousness of unconsciousness.
As a result he was quick to jump to his own arbitrary con-
clusion: a greedy—if not bloodthirsty capacity—was on
the fringe of baring itself to him, which would support
the privilege of beholding the endless procession of the

ages, eternally and perfectly unaware of itself—within or without which—crowd scenes or bedroom scenes—he himself would therefore remain logically unremembered and unseen.

But—he caught his breath sharply—the thought had barely touched his lips like a seductive kiss, it seemed, when he felt a stifling burden and sensation of remorse, horror, stupefaction. Not that he dreaded the insubstantial jealous touch of a mere hand, heart, throat, elusive knife or blunt rope. These were, after all, transient signals, however cruel, of dimension and form leading to repose, the liberal form of death. It was the sheer limitless *contraction* he was experiencing which he now dreaded and which he had summoned all unreflecting upon himself: the heightened power of devouring hope or senseless despair to visualize a timeless ultimatum, iota of breath, infinite or infinitesimal scale: conquest of the minutest square root, *space he could not at present dream to bear.*

The fixed walls appeared to be closing in upon him inch by wall, wall by foot, and out of this arose the stifling grain of uncertainty; a trick of light falling like painted rain: rain or brush of elements sweeping over him and affecting—so it seemed—all space around him which was gradually filling and disappearing (without however emptying him, even as it threatened to obliterate him, of or from the solid dust of canvas).

It was an instinct for well-nigh unendurable contraction he had invoked and the sense of impending breathlessness began to fuse its own *breath*—mist—upon the plane surfaces of his life. In fact the image of womb as well as room was falling flat in the end as though once seen from its overwhelmed and his overwhelming angle it ceased to exist as a void. Indeed every conventional distinction between volume and surface became inextricably close and unreal.

For since a cube is subject to filling or hollowing, it subsists in potential depletion or repletion of itself (its own paradox of vain expansion): but since the thinnest film or surface into which it may ultimately resolve is susceptible to an abstract measurement in depth still, however unimaginably frail and indistinct, THIS (and no other) lives in a true body of density which demolishes at one stroke the technical, subjective hollow or void; but remains, as it were, technically full still, a dripping mist or sweat of proportion, incapable NOW of being dug into or dug out, inner space (its true unassailable possession), indestructible, faint scale or measure of One universe.

It was as if he had had his first major object lesson in spite of everything: cargo of relief: sail of consciousness. Which sought to lift from him (in a fleeting but far-reaching incalculable design) the pregnant despair of the "born" dead. Such a carriage of misconception, wheel of toppling curiosity, dread, faded into vessels it lay within him now to translate and carry like the potent irony of dust, tenants of soul whose disposition he would begin to store and build, seal of ancient hope, spiked cannon of sunrise and sunset, secret faces of sky and earth. And at the end or beginning of each light obsessed cloud, roadway of day and night, they would arise like members of his own uncertain fastness of life to shoot their instinctive ultimatum of sun at each sinister—so it seemed—barred gateway he had himself made: rainbow, condensation, constellation to enlighten him in place of the ambivalent guard or parent of old he still half-remembered he wished to question within this new almost blank goal of a past presence or present.

Was it that he had truly forgotten half of a "lived"

future, the assured dictation of the future from which he had retreated into the sentence of the womb in the way the servants and tenants of nature—mask of earth, seed, sun—were continuously striking and retiring, aiming and crumbling within the self-creation of each last burning fateful arrow?

THE DAWN OF FREEDOM. The dusty answer flashed through and through hollow artist and prisoner like grains of an unproven, even unprovable manifesto. . . .

9

MANIFESTO OF THE UNBORN STATE OF EXILE
NIGHT'S BRIDGE

Dear L——,

Language is one's medium of the vision of consciousness. There are other ways—shall I say—of arousing this vision. But language alone can express (in a way which goes beyond any physical or vocal attempt) the sheer—the ultimate "silent" and "immaterial" complexity of arousal. Whatever sympathy one may feel for a concrete poetry—where physical objects are used and adopted—the fact remains (in my estimation) that the original grain or grains of language cannot be trapped or proven. It is the sheer mystery—the impossibility of trapping its own grain—on which poetry lives and thrives. And this is the stuff of one's essential understanding of the reality of the original Word, the Well of Silence. Which is concerned with a genuine sourcelessness, a fluid logic of image. So that any genuine act of possession by one's inner eye is a subtle dispersal of illusory fact, dispossession of one's outer or physical eye.

The stillness of consciousness (which stillness is always

penetrating itself in its own activity) is not the contrived or self-created stillness of a property of the physical world. In the same way the trepass of consciousness is not the same movement one consumes with a physical immediacy, apprehension, sense. This subtle logic of image and transformation in consciousness of all one's apparent and stable and persuasive functions is the meaning of language. For language because of its untrappable source transforms—in a terrifying well-nigh unendurable perspective—every subjective block and fixture of capacity. *In my Father's house are many mansions.*

The ideal of a concrete poetry (it would be sounder I feel to say granular poetry) is an instinctive recognition of the mysterious architecture and spirit of place in the far-reaching capacity of consciousness. But to attempt to pin the grains down is to prolong the agony of misunderstanding the nature of language itself.

Of course behind this attempt—the pathetic language of "dead" things—lies a motive concealed from those who are involved in their purposeless game. It is an unconscious attempt to break down the indigestible disease of subjective fashion—to find in nature an innocent array of objects and the ground, as well, of classical unity free from a vested interest in arbitrary mood or colour. But right here a subtle misconception arises in the apparent concretization of the word "ground" which once seen in consciousness belongs to an ageless flight of "instinct".

Let this hidden motive or buried conviction appear to be *seen* (something quite different to what one sees physically on the ground) and the vision clamours for its true word of expression. So much so that it can become an appalling deaf-and-dumb show (or quest) for the wholeness of spiritual recognition and responsibility throughout every crook and cranny of things: a show which seeks unhappily to break the doom of perpetuating a "ground" of error—hereditary misconception—fixed instinct— misrepresentation starting with the very apparent birth of a "future" language of possibilities. This abortive classical grain or ground needs to suffer a truer return to the womb of subjection, subjective error and will, to see its own capacity for change which lies still and unpredictably beyond the self-evident decline of every "murdered" or "murderous" foundation. The continuous birth of poetry needs to be more (and less in its true cryptic outcry and dialectical landslide) than an imitation of a preservative fluid: it is the life-blood of *seeing* and responding without succumbing—in the very transparent mobility of consciousness—to what is apparently seen and heard.

As such it subsists on its own apparent losses as nothing else can, provided that the instincts of fluid image—inseparable from the visionary truth of nature—are indeed their own untranslatable rebuff, barrier or privilege.

Beyond this lies the original well of silence, that "silence" which language alone can evoke, a depthlessness of sound heard and digested in the blood-stream of the mind which is the closest one can come to entering the reality of the living circulation of the "dead".

I find myself laying bare what is perhaps the most secret conviction I jealously hold—I was so deeply moved by your generous acknowledgment of my Confession which you accepted, in some curious overlapping way, as if it had sprung from your own need as well. I was moved because I knew you would never have implied this if I had not—in the first place—surrendered (or tried to surrender) every obscure and thoughtless and perhaps *cun-*

97

ning gesture of will exercised by me in the past—the greedy will to action and to blanket all reaction.

In the premises of open surrender lie the equality of touch and conviction I have always inwardly desired and we both now sense and realize as never before: the true beginnings of possible dialogue, the breath of all un-obstructive physicality one receives standing upon a borderline (as silent words stand on their speaking page) between an Imagination capable of reconciling unequal forms present and past and an Imagination empty of self-determined forms to come, blank frames, indwelling non-resemblance, freedom from past, present, future form and formlessness. *It is in this unpredictable and paradoxical light one begins to forgive and be forgiven all.*

And I have much of whom and of which to ask reconciliation in the present and forgiveness in the future.

I would not have dreamt of such a possibility in the far-off days we knew without feeling either instantly ashamed of the sentiment or instantly hard-hearted: arteries of will-power: should I impose reconciliation and forgiveness on others or accept the imposition of forgiveness and reconciliation from others? Neither questionable alternative is what I now mean. . . .

The key to my present meaning lies in a crumbling of the will which may be seen in another sense as the break-down of a series of tyrannous conception or misconception—the cruel strength of individual legacy. I feel this position (from your point of view as well as mine) is clearer than ever now. For there are many approaches to this I appear to possess which seem to me indistinguish-able, in certain respects, from your own excavations or penetrations of Raven's Head. I am not suggesting that I could ever bear the continuous burden you do—unflag-

98

ging concentration and the confrontation of models of anguish. (I am thinking in particular now of the brutal snapshots of Raven's Head you sent to me which I shall soon discuss with you in my own light.) I know you will instantly turn away from the label "anguish". Why must one dwell upon or relapse into anguish of recollection you will say—except in the most relative illusory concrete terms—when confronted by an endless task which frees one from stages of subjection and subjectivity, and points towards a classical revelation of withdrawal or momentum in every part of a "living" universe?

Let it all rest in my weak part then—each confession of stifling bitterness which seems at times to settle again and lift, only with the greatest difficulty, above myself. This solitary uncreative admission remains purely individual, purely mine. As though I am capable of becoming conscious of being the rich "dead" self-sufficient, self-explanatory thing, after all, while everything else around me—despised and poor—appears to grow into a universal meaningless secret, deserving once again of contempt, because of an inward and meaningful retrenchment and participation—a brooding capacity—I fear to confess I must suffer deeply with to understand—for a new unspectacular conception of life. Which reflects something else equally subjective and paradoxical and fearful too. It was I who pushed you into your present enterprise but I am glad I do not have your classical responsibilities to bear. They frighten me to death. And for this reason I would not know how to be envious of you, whatever the ultimate "glorious" self-sacrifice and apparent reward.

Nevertheless to return to what I said a moment ago. There are certain approaches to my *crumbling of the will* which are indistinguishable—in a remote and subjective form—from your own native and professional excavations and penetrations. It is as if sometimes (I hope you will forgive me) I have an involuntary but acute awareness of changing places with you. And for a fraction of an instant I am filled with a terrible dread of place and of standing irrevocably in your shoes. I know of no more frightful tyranny of misunderstanding. Misunderstanding of what? Misunderstanding of whom? Misunderstanding of where? It is the third unknown factor and question which brings the first bewildering faint landslide of relief. *And I am able to resume, as it were, the "potential" ground of self-exile, the unborn state of the world.*

Now in connection with the latest snapshots of Raven's Head: they shook me more than I can easily say. Made me ask myself: where was it and when was it that I was invalided out of Raven's Head? I would have given much to have been able to remain with the expedition (and yet as I said before I shudder at the thought of such concentration and responsibility) and to have crossed the ancient river with you and arrived at the ruined targets your pictures disclose. I was invalided out after the CRASH. But surely you must see, my dear L——, how bewildered I still am: what was—or is—this crash one speaks of, so inconclusively, that altered nevertheless decisively our twin misconception and conception of every flamboyant possessive thing? Sexual bolt of childhood or manhood? Frantic Bull's Eye of America or Europe? Globe of fantasy—Asia or Africa? Lost chart of remembrance or new-found continent? Blindfold of Day or Night's Bridge? Way of the Ancients or Ring of the Moderns? One can go on and on firing at the shadowy long tail of memory. . . . The truth is—*I can't remember*. Evolution. Revolution. Regeneration. Collapse. All I can honestly say is that the potential fragments of recollection before and after GOD KNOWS WHAT are *alive* in a way I never suspected before.

Indeed it is here that you and I began, or still begin, to approach a meaningful conjunction and parting of the ways—essential way of "compulsive" withdrawal and incalculable way of "new" community. And yet *is it true* that I (within the person of obscurity) have really begun at last to know at the closest inviolable "negative" quarters the "flash" of explosive freedom you (within your globe or world) possess? The fear of such "exposure" arises nevertheless (even as one begins to dwell significantly in it) within premises of "privilege", bulb or state, attraction or repulsion, so that one may sometimes even discern one's individual longing and blindness in every snapshot of practical judgment (or misjudgment), absorption, calculating malice and self-indulgence: one may even discern one's fear of the capacity of another. And one may be driven as a consequence to erect one's sovereign of wish-fulfilment—as if it were the highest defence, vulgar accomplishment, presumptive darkness or light over and against the true ligament of person and thing. Which is to succumb ultimately to self-hatred or self-flattery, creed of miseducation, misrepresentation and folly. . . .

The explosive question however remains inextricably woven within each "flash", living distinctive otherness, mysterious response or lack of response. The education of freedom—(and you have been one of my unconscious tutors in whom and with whom I grew into the heart of "negative" identity, self-contradiction, even "positive" loathing of the "ground" of "spirit")—begins with a confession of the need to lose the base concretion men seek to impose when they talk of one's "native" land (or another's) as if it were fixed and anchored in place. In this age and time, one's native land (and the other's) is always *crumbling*: crumbling within a capacity of vision which rediscovers the process to be not foul and destructive but actually the constructive secret of all creation wherever one happens to be. It is in the light of wisdom or compassion—across the divide of the ages perhaps—that one looks back and accuses (as well as excuses) oneself for succumbing again and again to that individual picture of self-imposed restriction and longing which arises, and which constitutes nostalgia for what is not and the anguish of helplessness in the face of what is: the ever-recurring posture of abortive sensibility which assists one (but only at some later less self-indulgent stage—fresh insight into living detail) to sympathize with the derangement of all creatures within history and circumstance who wander the face of the earth as if they were the "living" unfulfilled part of oneself and one were the "dead" fulfilled expression of their self. . . .

Such a "graphic" inversion of privilege is the crumbling role of time in space and of one's pride and anguish. Which brings *me* face to face once again with the snapshot of your "black" cell in Raven's Head as if in one illuminating moment you and I were free of each other and yet apparently the same. And yet *you*—I cannot help feeling within the "pregnant" distance which enfolds us— must see it factually, even simply, in your explosive and elemental and indestructible right since it is I who must still confess, with a shameful start, to an ancient predisposition I have not yet shaken off, traces of lingering judgment and illness, the subjective emotion of being born into the inescapable conformity and finality of everything however liberating and far-reaching the actual kinship of event.

And indeed even now the "still" dread of change (that ancient "model" of freedom to change) still appears . . . catastrophic . . . nostalgic . . . I pored over the "black" portrait . . . forgot everything . . . remembered. . . . What? Where? Was this the room of alien judgment. . . . CONQUEST . . . into which we appeared to drop? THE ROOM OF THE FALL? Do I dream now for one choked instant as I stare into it—the figment of it—(half-comprehending, half-incomprehending nodding impractical joke) that you died there on the scaffold—distant night breathing within Raven's Head—whilst I lived and fell and gasped, hand over hand of rope, until my feet touched the floor?

The walls were black. Cloud or smoke. The Ancient of Nights. You flashed your "dead" thought like the beam of a torch towards constellation, sky or roof. Someone had died for us, you said. THE UNINITIATE. ACCEPTANCE OF BLIND MURDER. Your voice was tranquil, cold and calm. Without a trace of my fierce hunger and dread and emotion for the premature rite of ancient meaning, governing intellect and clinical understanding. Was it you who had turned the arts and tables of science and dissection on me, after all, or I on you as before? I felt my face begin to crack in the light of your clear untroubled countenance.

The meaty limbs you drew to my attention (suspended from the roof) were peeled, raw, elongated vestiges of marble. That was all. *The Inn of the Quartering of the Cow.* The name rang a bell. It was as if I stood at the door of every skeleton, lightning cupboard, curiosity shop down the secret ladder of the ages. Skyscraper dinner, menu of . . . catastrophe (or ultimate salvation and universal digestion)? Generations past and generations to come.

All reflecting the long-suffering mate or animal one saw and still slew in the mind and strove to eat or devour once and for all: the brutal art of arts—the conquest of all consuming love and jealousy which made one quick to magnify the subject of lust or anguish on every self-sufficient occasion or in every self-sufficient apparition. Until one *saw* again the sheer "negative" burden of liberation within the positive rule or maw of the senses: liberation from "divine" stomach, from premature identity of self-torture rather than self-conquest, from greed, frustration, overfed memory, vicarious desire, mechanical rape, area of preservation and prediction. On the marbles of memory (the flesh of the past) and prediction (the flesh of the future) flashed and rose the inimitable "snapshot" of spirit upon the medium of helpless and backward self-sacrificial subject. . . . And the dream of black inner space turned into new classical blood, dispossession of the strait-jacket of time. *Memory and prediction: what then could these mean?* It was as if the celebrated torch in your hand blew out and nothing remained but to grope in the uncanny realm of forgotten portrait and room.

THE BLACK ROOMS

The room of the *VISIONARY COMPANY*

One pause of sunset, in particular, I recall now, like a station of feathered branches, half-tree, half-bird, lingering a long while in the sky before a train of frozen fire part-extinguished, part-melted itself into the ground. In the fulfilled poise of this moment, like a barrier of absorption between day and night, the reluctant smoke of sky and carriage of earth were drawn into singular consciousness of each other. . . .

If I were to attempt to confine or draw an exact relationship or absolute portrait of what everything was before the stroke fell and created a void in conventional memory, I would have succumbed to the dead tide of self-indulgent realism. On the other hand, to travel with the flood of animated wreckage that followed after, is a different matter, a trusting matter in which I am involved—a confession that nothing immaterial and actual and eternal may have changed in the outlines of the past; and therefore since the nucleus of phenomenal catastrophe one envisages at any particular moment is just as likely as anything else to be an illusion, it is useless to believe one was, or is, ever possessed by articles of spirit without faith.

. . . *the starkest bier of grave memory* I knew, when as a boy on my way to school I sometimes encountered the "poor man's hearse" rolling towards me, painted black as shining coal.

. . . *fearfully and inevitably* . . . the explosive train of memory rolls along (mingling economic and political, metaphysical and dialectical physicians like an ancestral gathering of nurses. . . .) *I dreamt I was standing alone in a large room. . . .*

. . . THE STRIKING INNERMOST CHEMISTRY OF LOVE. . . .

. . . *from that moment my pagan scaffold,* my visionary

sport in nature, began crumbling secretly beyond the limits of the purity of obsession. . . . And yet little though I knew it this was to prove a lifetime's poetry of science and a stubborn terrifying task.

. . . the melted scaffolding of all the years. . . .

The Room of GENESIS

But now the very joylessness with which it had been constructed struck me like a curious revelation of mystical sorrow. I felt cold and strange, a religious stranger to all previous knowledge of emotion; and *emotion*—in such a void or context—became *new*, liberating, oblique, powerless to arouse an expenditure of energy to create the harm I saw I had already inflicted.

The sound of the clock was at first distant and somnolent but on gaining one's attentive reflection it developed into something as insistent as everything I had called upon to be made which groaned and protested. *The Night of self-initiation*, self-kinship, grew into celestial furniture, the great hearse rolled on, stitched planks held by the scissors of the universe, divisions of cloud within which glimmered the operations of space. . . .

So it was I jumped forward into an echoing future (which is now with the dead voices of the past) and into a middle of a year—a great procession—the striking year of every man's familiar obsession (1948 or 2048?) . . . the "timeless" footprints of a self-created self. . . .

. . . substitute. . . .

My dear L——,

What obsessive validity your snapshots appear to have. I have been running through them again, grain and thread from the ghost of my beginning to the spirit of my end. Two things are as obsessional as they are clear. Freak of identity or law of reality?

One—Raven's Head is constructed out of curious subjective shapes indistinguishable at times from their environment, paper, wood and stone.

Two—this subjectivity in the material is a barrier and a challenge at all times within premises of universal life whose timeless currency and continuity have nothing to do with the pseudo-objective facets and factors of subjection and stability as such which may appear (depending on one's closed standpoint) admirably "good", "successful", "pleasing" or hideously "bad", "repellent", "confusing".

The approach then to the "classical" Raven's Head— the Raven's Head into which we are still to be born like creatures who may learn to dwell in a state of penetrative relationship and self-exile—cries out for two admissions.

One—a confession or admission of humility, the limited standpoint of the active and involved human person.

Two—(in order that *One* does not become a form of nihilism, the devil's lightning and creed)—a confession or admission of the mystery of capacity, the illumination of capacity within which arises both the issue and sculpture of science, interior unpredictable dialogue, discharge of grace.

Two is of the greatest relative importance since IT confirms the "shut-in" person as both potential cornerstone and dimension (the "open" city) by confessing to a continuous and miraculous conception of "living" and "dead" nature, rehabilitation of the lost One, the unrealized One, the inarticulate One.

And this miraculous conception is timeless: since "timelessness" alone is capable of that inflation and deflation of consciousness to sift and endure every subjective "contamination" and "ground": the quest of phenomenal space rather than phenomenal time. Inevitability of direction—implicit in the iron logic of time—crumbles, the legacy of time, false or unreliable memory, false or unreliable prediction. And the "distance" between objects of assessment and reassessment—the burden of individual guilt and collective history—appears like a participation of inviolable soul or presence within and above shattering confrontation, instinctive meeting as well as conjunctive parting beyond the senseless incline or decline of chronological age, the drought of will. In the end the weakest trickle of prayer can become one's treasure of fulfilment through no virtue in the aridity of the living (such as myself) save that One (such as you) endures beyond all fluid reckoning to provide an illuminating scale and measure of self-abandonment and self-recognition. THE WELL OF SILENCE. AMEN. Amen.

IDIOT NAMELESS
25th September 1964

P9-AOF-149

FLASHMAPS!

INSTANT GUIDE TO

New York

The idea of SINGLE SUBJECT MAPS with related material was conceived for FLASHMAPS INSTANT GUIDE books in 1967. A single-subject map, color-coded and cross-indexed, has proven to be a useful tool for clearly dispensing information. FLASHMAPS INSTANT GUIDE books are used by both natives and visitors alike to save time, money and energy.

ENJOY NEW YORK!

RANDOM HOUSE

NEW YORK

EDITOR-IN-CHIEF:
  Toy Lasker
CARTOGRAPHERS:
  Timothy W. Lasker
  Sally Jarman
DIRECTOR of RESEARCH:
  Gladys F. Caterinicchio

Library of Congress Card No. 79-77622
ISBN 0-942226-35-6
Manufactured in The United States of America

CONTENTS—ALPHABETICAL

3

IMPORTANT TELEPHONE NUMBERS

Area Codes: Manhattan & Bronx (**212**) — Bklyn, Queens, S.I. (**718**)

EMERGENCIES

Police	911	**Dental Emergency**	**679-3966**
Fire	911	**Doctors on Call**	(718) **238-2100**
Ambulance	911	**Drug Abuse**	(800) **538-4840**
To report a fire	**628-2900**	**F. B. I.**	**553-2700**
Fire Headquarters	(718) **403-1403**	**Gas/Steam/Electric**	**683-8830**
Police Dept Info	**374-5000**	**Heat/Hot Water**	**960-4800**
Alcoholics Anonymous	**473-6200**	**Highway**	**566-3406**
Animal Bites	**566-7105**	**Medical Help**	(718) **326-0600**
Arson Hotline	(718) **403-1300**	**Poison Center**	**764-7667**
Battered Women	**433-7297**	**Rape Hot Line**	**777-4000**
Child Abuse	(800) **342-3720**	**Runaway Hotline**	**619-6884**
Coast Guard	**668-7936**	**Suicide Prevention**	**532-2400**
Con Edison	**683-8830**	**U.S. Secret Service**	**466-4400**
Crime Victim Hotline	**577-7777**	**Water/Sewer/Air**	**966-7500**

RECORDED INFORMATION

Lottery Winning	976-2020	Racing (OTB)	976-2121
Metropolitan Museum	535-7710	Sky Information	769-5917
MOMA Film Program	708-9490	Sports	976-1313
Parking Info	566-4121	Stock Market	976-4141
Parks Events	360-1333	Travel to/from JFK	(800) 247-7433
Passport Info	541-7700	Time of Day	976-1616
Prayer	246-4200	Weather Forecast	976-1212

SERVICES

Air Pollution	966-7500	Planned Parenthood	541-7800
Birth Control/Abortion	677-3320	Port Authority-JFK	(718) 656-4444
Boro President	669-8300	Port Auth-La Guardia	(718) 476-5000
Bus/Subway Info	(718) 330-1234	Potholes	566-2018
Chamber Commerce	561-2020	Roosevelt Island Tram	753-6626
Consumers Complaints	577-0111	Sanitation	334-8590
Convention Ctr (Javits)	216-2000	Senior Citizens	577-0800
Day Care	334-7814	Tax Info: City	(718) 935-6736
Election Board (LWV)	674-8484	State	(800) 225-5829
Family Planning	677-3040	Federal	732-0100
Foreign Exchange	883-0400	Telegrams, Cables	962-7111
Health Department	285-9503	Towaways	971-0770
Housing Authority	306-3000	Train-To-Plane	(718) 858-7272
Legal Aid Society	577-3300	Transit Authority	(718) 330-1234
Marriage Licenses	269-2900	Travelers' Aid Society	944-0013
Mayor's Office	566-5700	Unemployment Info	791-1400
Medicaid Information	594-3050	Visitors/Convention Bur	397-8200
Medicare/Soc. Security	432-3232	Welfare Assistance	344-5241

NEW YORK WEATHER

Month	Average High	Average Low	Average Temperature	Average Humidity
January	38.5	25.9	32.2	64%
April	60.7	43.5	52.1	60%
July	85.2	68.0	76.6	67%
October	66.8	50.6	58.7	67%

Average annual rainfall: **42"** — Average annual snowfall: **33.3"**
Average wind speed: summer **10** mph; winter **15** mph
Growing season: **210** days — Sunshine: **60%** of possible total
Temperature range: Extreme high **106°** F. — Extreme low **-15°** F.

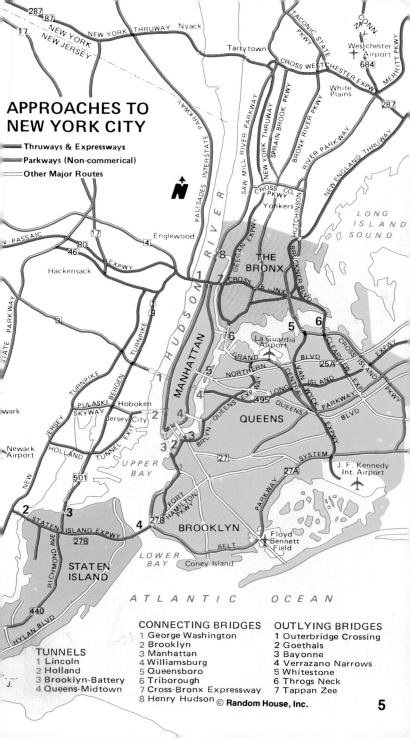

APPROACHES TO NEW YORK CITY

— Thruways & Expressways
— Parkways (Non-commerical)
— Other Major Routes

N

TUNNELS
1 Lincoln
2 Holland
3 Brooklyn-Battery
4 Queens-Midtown

CONNECTING BRIDGES
1 George Washington
2 Brooklyn
3 Manhattan
4 Williamsburg
5 Queensboro
6 Triborough
7 Cross-Bronx Expressway
8 Henry Hudson

OUTLYING BRIDGES
1 Outerbridge Crossing
2 Goethals
3 Bayonne
4 Verrazano Narrows
5 Whitestone
6 Throgs Neck
7 Tappan Zee

© **Random House, Inc.**

5

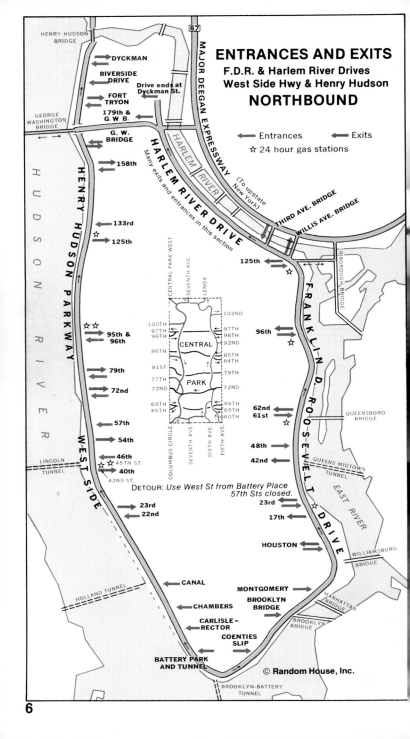

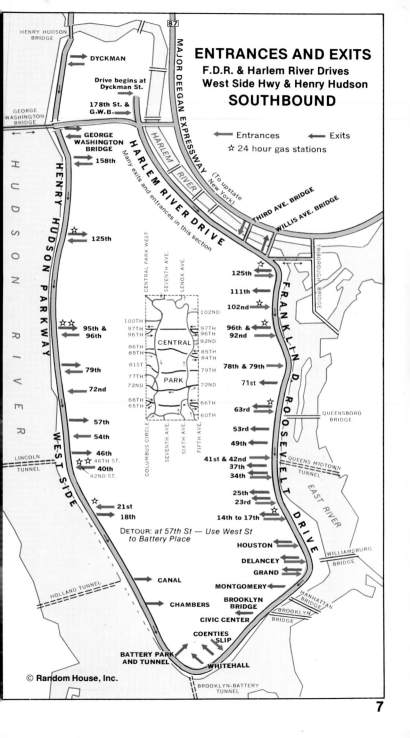

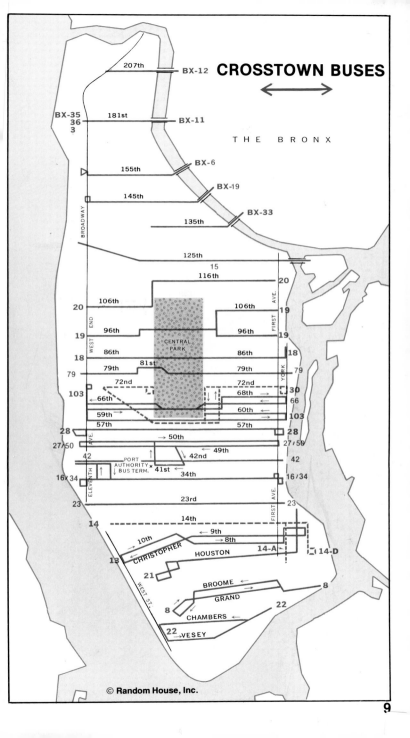

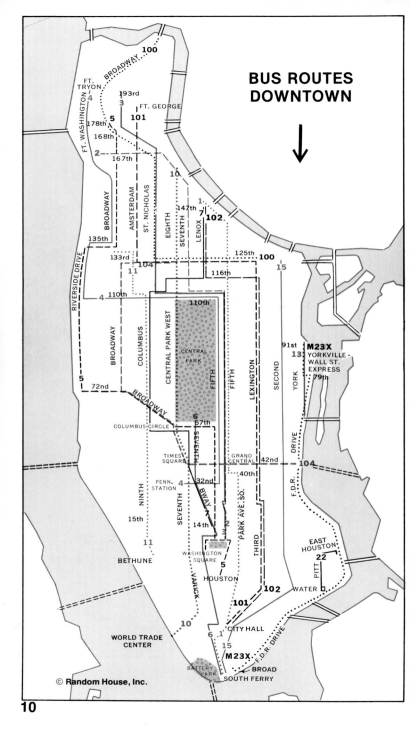

BUS ROUTES DOWNTOWN

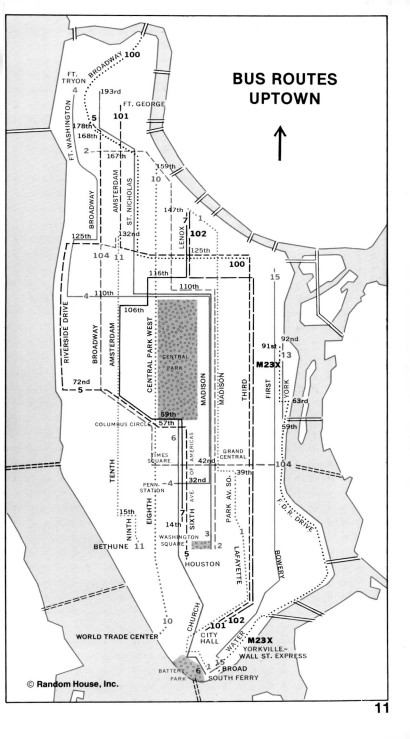

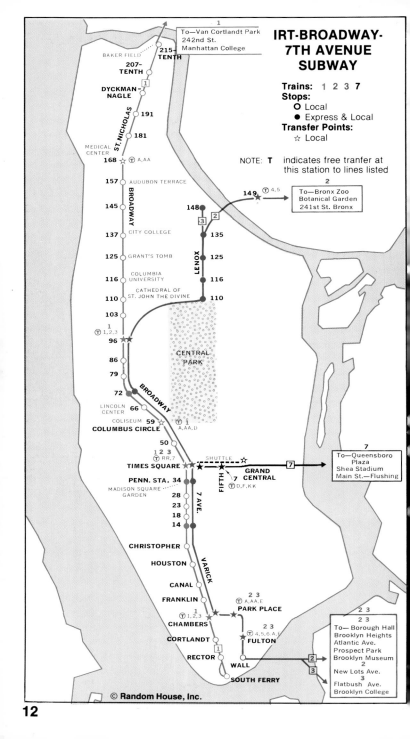

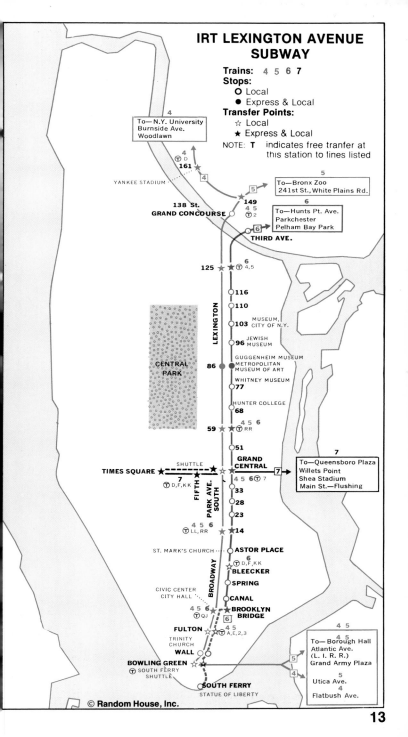

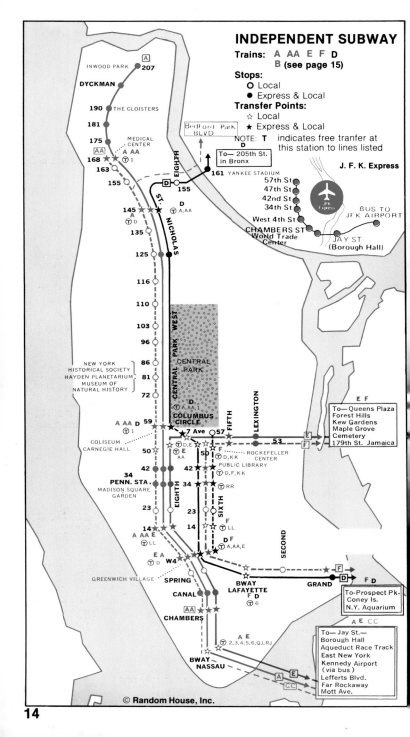

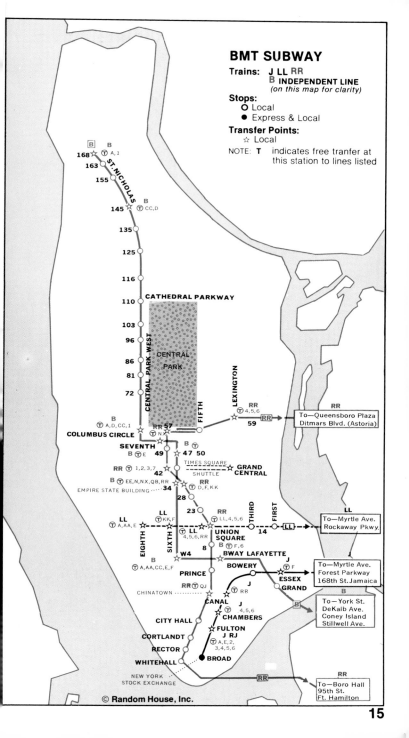

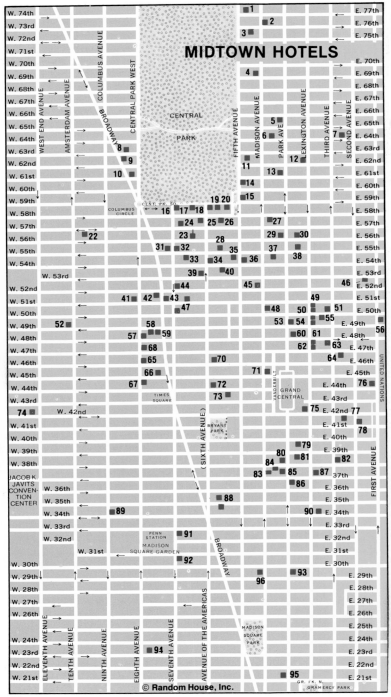

MIDTOWN HOTELS—BY MAP NUMBERS

MIDTOWN HOTELS

Hotel/Motel (Room Rate) ★	Address	Map No	Telephone	Rooms
Algonquin, The (b)	59 W 44th Street	72	840-6800	200
Barbizon, The (b)	140 E 63rd Street	12	838-5700	355
Bedford Hotel (b)	118 E 40th Street	79	697-4800	200
Beekman Tower (b)	3 Mitchell Place	56	355-7300	160
Best West Skyline (c)	Tenth Ave & 50th St	52	586-3400	240
Beverly, The (c)	125 E 50th Street	50	753-2700	300
Blackstone Hotel (c)	50 E 58th Street	27	355-4200	183
Carlton Hotel (c)	22 E 29th Street	96	532-4100	380
Carlyle, The (a)	35 E 76th Street	2	744-1600	180
Century Paramount (c) ‒	235 W 46th Street	65	764-5500	650
Chatwal Inn at UN (c-)	304 E 42nd Street	78	986-8800	500
Chatwal Inn on Park (c)	429 Park Ave South	93	532-4860	55
Collingwood Hotel (c)	45 W 35th Street	88	947-2500	200
Comfort Inn (c)	42 W 35th Street	88	947-0200	132
Consulate Hotel (c)	224 W 49th Street	58	246-5252	295
Cunard Plaza Club (a +)	The Plaza, (tel: 800 number)	20	222-0939	100
Days Inn (c)	440 W 57th Street	22	581-8100	588
Doral Court (b)	130 E 39th Street	81	685-1100	220
Doral Inn (b)	541 Lexington & 49th St	55	755-1200	700
Doral Park Avenue (b)	70 Park Avenue	80	687-7050	200

★ ROOM RATES (DOUBLE): (a) $200-270   (b) $150-200   (c) $100-150   **17**

Hotel/Motel (Room Rate) ★	Address	Map No	Telephone	Rooms
Doral Tuscany (a)	120 E 39th Street	81	686-1600	200
Dorset, The (b)	30 W 54th Street	40	247-7300	150
Drake Swissotel (a)	440 Park Ave	29	421-0900	650
Doral Park Avenue (b)	70 Park Ave	80	687-7050	200
Dumont Plaza (b)	E 34th betw 3rd & Lex	90	481-7600	257
Eastgate Towers (b)	222 E 39th Street	82	687-8000	192
Edison Hotel (c)	228 W 47th Street	68	840-5000	1000
Elysee Hotel (b)	60 E 54th Street	37	753-1066	110
Empire Hotel (c)	Broadway & 63rd Street	9	265-7400	500
Esplanade Hotel (c)	305 West End at 74th	off	874-5000	200
Essex House (a)	160 Central Park South	16	247-0300	700
Gorham Hotel (c)	136 W 55th Street	33	245-1800	170
Gramercy Park (c)	Lexington & 21st Street	95	475-4320	500
Grand Bay Hotel (a)	152 W 51st Street	47	765-1900	178
Grand Hyatt New York (a)	Lexington & 42nd St	75	883-1234	1407
Halloran House (b)	525 Lexington Avenue	54	755-4000	650
Helmsley Middletown (b)	148 E 48th Street	63	888-1624	245
Helmsley New York (a)	212 E 42nd Street	77	888-1624	800
Helmsley Palace (a+)	455 Madison Avenue	48	888-1624	1050
Helmsley Windsor (b)	100 W 58th Street	25	888-1624	300
Holiday Crown Plaza (a)	Broadway & 49th St	59	977-4000	770
Howard Johnson (c)	Eighth Ave & W 52nd	41	581-4100	300
Inter-Continental NY (a)	111 E 48th Street	60	755-5900	680
Kimberly, The (a)	145 E 50th Street	51	755-0400	160
Kitano Hotel (c)	66 Park Avenue	85	685-0022	90
Lexington Hotel (b)	Lexington & 48th St	61	755-4400	800
Loews Summit (b)	Lexington & 51st St	49	752-7000	760
Lombardy, The (b)	111 E 56th Street	30	753-8600	400
Lowell, The (a)	28 East 63rd Street	11	838-1400	60
Lyden Gardens (b)	215 E 64th Street	7	355-1230	133
Lyden House (b)	320 E 53rd Street	46	888-6070	81
Madison Towers (b)	22 E 38th Street	84	685-3700	270
Mark, The (b)	25 E 77th Street	1	744-4300	184
Marriott Marquis (a)	1535 Broadway	66	398-1900	1879
Mayfair Regent (a)	Park Ave & 65th St	5	288-0800	199
Mayflower Hotel (b)	15 Central Park West	10	265-0060	375
Milburn Hotel (c)	242 W 76th Street	off	362-1006	65
Milford Plaza (c)	270 W 45th Street	67	869-3600	1310
Morgan's (b)	237 Madison Avenue	83	686-0300	110
New York Hilton (a)	1335 Ave of Americas	39	586-7000	2131
New York Penta (b)	401 Seventh Ave & 33rd	91	736-5000	1705
Novotel (b)	226 W 52nd Street	42	315-0100	470
Omni Berkshire Place (a)	21 E 52nd Street	45	753-5800	415
Omni Park Central (b)	Seventh Ave & 55th St	31	484-3300	1450
Park Lane Helmsley (a)	36 Central Park South	19	888-1624	640
Parker Meridien (a)	118 W 55th Street	23	245-5000	700
Peninsula NY, The (a)	700 Fifth Avenue	35	247-2200	250
Pierre, The (a+)	Fifth Ave & 61st St	14	838-8000	195
Plaza Athenee (a+)	37 E 64th Street	6	734-9100	170
Plaza 50 (b)	155 E 50th Street	51	751-5710	206
Plaza, The (a+)	Fifth Ave & 59th St	20	759-3000	807
Ramada Inn (c)	Eighth Ave & 48th St	57	581-7000	363
Regency, The (a)	Park Ave & 61st St	13	759-4100	400
Ritz Carlton (a)	112 Central Park South	17	757-1900	250

18 ★ROOM RATES (DOUBLE): (a) $200-270 (b) $150-200 (c) $100-150

MIDTOWN HOTELS Continued

Hotel/Motel (Room Rate) ★	Address	Map No	Telephone	Rooms
Roger Smith Winthrop (c)	501 Lexington Avenue	62	755-1400	160
Roosevelt, The (b)	45 E 45th Street	71	661-9600	1070
Royal Concordia (a +)	151 W 51st Street	47	307-5000	500
Royalton, The (a +)	44 W 44th Street	73	869-4400	205
St. Moritz on the Park (a)	50 Central Park South	18	755-5800	772
St. Regis-Sheraton	Fifth Ave & 55th St	36	renovating	525
Salisbury Hotel (c)	123 W 57th Street	24	246-1300	320
San Carlos (c)	150 E 50th Street	55	755-1800	200
Shelburne Murray Hill (b)	303 Lexington Avenue	87	689-5200	248
Sheraton Centre (b +)	811 Seventh Ave & 52nd	44	581-1000	1850
Sheraton City Squire (b +)	Seventh Ave at 52nd St	43	581-3300	720
Sheraton Park Ave (a)	45 Park Ave at 37th	86	685-7676	160
Sheraton Towers (a)	Seventh Ave at 52nd St	44	581-1000	151
Sherry Netherland (a)	781 Fifth Avenue	15	355-2800	200
Shoreham Hotel (c)	33 W 55th Street	28	247-6700	150
Southgate Tower (b)	Seventh Ave & 31st St	92	563-1800	520
Stanhope, The (a +)	Fifth Ave & 81st St	off	288-5800	270
Surrey, The (b)	20 E 76th Street	3	288-3700	113
Travel Inn (c)	515 W 42nd Street	74	695-7171	160
UN Plaza Hotel (a)	1 United Nations Plaza	76	355-3400	288
UN Plaza Tower (a)	2 United Nations Plaza	76	355-3400	115
Viscount Manhattan (b)	127 E 55th Street	38	826-1100	102
Vista International (a)	3 World Trade Center		938-9100	825
Waldorf-Astoria, The (a)	301 Park Avenue	53	355-3000	2000
Warwick, The (b)	65 W 54th Street	34	247-2700	500
Wellington Hotel (c)	Seventh Ave & 55th St	32	247-3900	700
Wentworth Hotel (c)	59 W 46th Street	70	719-2300	250
Westbury, The (a)	Madison Ave at 69th St	4	535-2000	300
Wyndham, The (c)	42 W 58th Street	26	753-3500	200
YMCA McBurney (c-)	215 W 23rd Street	94	741-9226	279
YMCA Sloane House (c-)	356 W 34th Street	89	760-5850	1492
YMCA Vanderbilt (c-)	224 E 47th Street	64	755-2410	430
YMCA West Side (c-)	5 W 63rd Street	8	787-4400	700
Youth Hostel, Amer (c)	Amsterdam & W 103rd	off	932-2300	480

★ROOM RATES (DOUBLE): (a) $200-270   (b) $150-200   (c) $100-150

PARKING INFORMATION

Parking Area	Address	Capacity	Hourly Rate
Municipal Parking	Eighth Ave & 53rd	450	$1.20 (½ hr)
Municipal Lot	Leonard St & Lafayette	150	1.25 (1 hr)
Municipal Parking	Delancey & Essex	361	.55 (½ hr)
Municipal Parking	Park Row & Pearl	402	1.50 (½ hr)

There are about 900 private parking garages in Manhattan.
Minimum $8.50 to $11.50 (first hour); maximum $12.00 to $35.00 (12 to 24 hours).
Recorded Daily Parking Information 566-4121

PARKING VIOLATIONS

No-parking zone: Manhattan, 23rd St to 72nd St, river to river,
except where metered. (Fine for expired meter $40.00)
All parking tickets: $40.00 Double Parking: $35 to $40 Hydrants: $40
Cars towed-away: $75 plus $40 summons. Car will be found under the
West Side Hwy at 38th St (Tel: 924-6036). Storage charge per day $5.
Alternate parking: One side Mon/Wed/Fri; Other side Tues/Thur/Sat;
Sundays & Holidays: Most street parking regulations suspended.
Traffic Tickets: 770 Broadway Telephone: 477-4430.

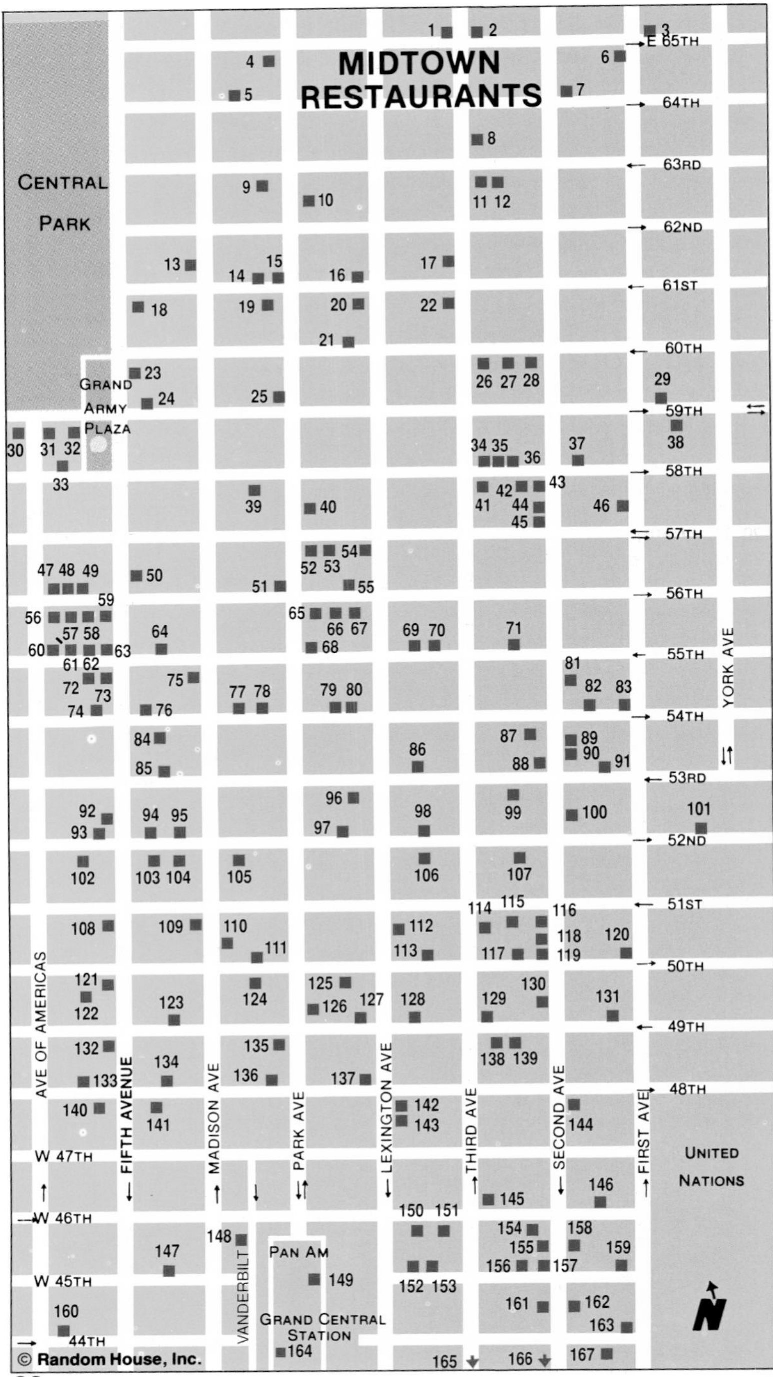
MIDTOWN RESTAURANTS
CENTRAL PARK
GRAND ARMY PLAZA
E 65TH
64TH
63RD
62ND
61ST
60TH
59TH
58TH
57TH
56TH
55TH
54TH
53RD
52ND
51ST
50TH
49TH
48TH
W 47TH
W 46TH
W 45TH
44TH
AVE OF AMERICAS
FIFTH AVENUE
MADISON AVE
VANDERBILT
PARK AVE
LEXINGTON AVE
THIRD AVE
SECOND AVE
FIRST AVE
YORK AVE
PAN AM
GRAND CENTRAL STATION
UNITED NATIONS
N
© Random House, Inc.

MIDTOWN RESTAURANTS—BY MAP NUMBERS

1 Sign of the Dove	46 Rosa Mexicano	93 Twenty-One Club
2 David K's	47 Marie-Michelle	94 La Grenouille
3 Miss Grimble	48 Il Gattopardo	95 La Galerie
4 Le Cirque	49 Abruzzi	95 Rendez-Vous
5 Le Regence	49 Aperitivo	96 Brasserie
6 Auntie Yuan	50 Terrace	97 Four Seasons
7 Primola	51 Lafayette	98 Beijing Duckhouse
8 Fiorello East	52 Mitsukoshi	99 Tang's Chariot
9 Post House	53 Bruce Ho's	100 Eamonn Doran
10 Huberts	54 Le Chantilly	101 Le Perigord
11 John Clancy's E	55 Laurent	102 San Marco
12 Bravo Gianni	56 Cafe de Nice	103 Il Menestrello
13 L'Omnibus Maxim's	57 Romeo Salta	104 Bombay Palace
13 Maxim's	58 Kurumazushi	105 Scarlatti's
14 Madame Romaine	59 Il Tinello	106 Nippon
15 Capriccio	60 Cafe Geneva	107 Maximiliano
16 Il Valletto	61 French Shack	108 Assembly
17 Alo Alo	62 L'Escargot	109 Tse Yang
18 Pierre Hotel Cafe	62 La Fondue	110 Le Trianon
19 Aureole	63 La Caravelle	111 Goucester House
20 Jacqueline's	64 La Cote Basque	112 Kenny's Steak
21 Le Veau d'Or	65 Le Manoir	114 La Table des Rois
22 Isle of Capri	66 Benihana of Tokyo	113 Nada Sushi
23 Quaglino's	67 Doriental	114 Le Bistro
24 Mondrian	68 PJ Clarke's	115 Torremolinos
25 Regine	69 Shun Lee Palace	116 Zarela
26 Contrapunto Cafe	70 Enoteca Iperbole	117 Lutece
26 Yellowfinger	71 Michael's Pub	118 La Mediterranee
27 Arizona 206	72 Aquavit	119 Leopard
28 Jane's Bar	72 Italian Pavilion	120 Wylie's Ribs
29 Brive	73 Adrienne	121 Rainbow Room
30 Cafe de la Paix	73 Le Bistro d'Adrienne	122 American Festival
30 Jockey Club	74 Raphael	122 Sea Grill
31 Nirvana	75 Quilted Giraffe	123 Sushiden
31 Park Room	76 Le Cygne	124 Giambelli
31 Mickey Mantle's	78 Lello	125 Waldorf Peacock
32 Edwardian Room	79 Cheese Cellar	126 Gin-Ray of Japan
32 Oak Room	80 Savoy Grill	127 Bull & Bear
33 Manhattan Ocean	81 Elmer's	127 Inagiku
34 Gian Marino	82 Cafe Europa	128 Christo's
34 La Camelia	83 India Pavilion	129 Smith & Wolensky
35 Le Nid	84 Prunelle	129 Tonino
36 Felidia	85 Seryna	130 San Giusto
37 Cafe Nicholson	86 Citicorp-Alfredo	131 Antolotti's
38 Sandro's	Auberge Suisse	132 La Reserve
39 Jean Lafitte	Avgerinos	133 Charley O's
40 Akbar	Charley O's	134 Hatsuhana
41 Girafe	Les Tournebroches	135 Aurora
41 Dewey Wong	Nyborg & Nelson	136 Shinbashi
41 Dawat	87 Toscana	137 Barclay's
42 Anche Vivolo	88 Il Nido	138 Chin Chin
42 Tre Scalini	89 Chez Louis	139 Box Tree
43 Bruno	90 La Mangeoire	139 Darjeeling
44 Le Steak	91 Louise Jr	140 Pearl's Chinese
45 Les Sans-Culottes	92 Top of the Sixes	141 Chalet Suisse

21

MIDTOWN RESTAURANTS—BY MAP NOS. Continued

MIDTOWN RESTAURANTS

Restaurant	Address	Map No.	Cuisine	Average Price ★	Telephone
Abruzzi	37 W 56th St	49	Italian	$20.50	489-8110
Adrienne	Peninsula Hotel	73	French	70 +	247-2200
Akbar	475 Park Ave	40	Indian	20-30	838-1717
Alfredo	Citicorp Center	86	Italian	20-30	371-3367
Algonquin · Rose Rm	59 W 44th St	160	Amer/Contl	28.00	840-6800
Ambassador Grill	UN Plaza Hotel	163	Fr/Contl	40-50	702-5014
American Festival	Rockefeller Ctr	122	American	25-35	246-6699
Anche Vivolo	222 E 58th St	42	Italian	25-30	308-0112
Antolotti's	337 E 49th St	131	N Italian	25-30	688-6767
Aperitivo	29 W 56th St	49	Italian	25-35	765-5155
Aquavit	13 W 54th St	72	Scandinavn	55.00	307-7311
Arizona 206	206 E 60th St	27	S. Western	35-45	838-0440
Assembly, The	16 W 51st St	108	Steak/Sfd	30-45	581-3580
Au Mandarin	World Financial Ctr	off	Chinese	30-35	385-0313
Auberge Suisse	Citicorp Center	86	Swiss	20-30	421-1420
Auntie Yuan	1191 A First Ave	6	Chinese	30-40	744-4040
Aureole	34 E 61st St	19	American	50.00	319-1660
Aurora	60 E 49th St	135	French	50-70	692-9292
Avgerinos	Citicorp Center	86	Greek	20-25	688-8828
Awoki	305 E 46th St	146	Japanese	50-60	759-8897
Barclay's	Intercontl Hotel	137	American	45-55	421-4389
Beijing Duckhouse	144 E 52nd St	98	Chinese	20-25	759-8260
Benihana of Tokyo	120 E 56th St	66	Japanese	25-30	593-1627
Bice	7 E 54th St	76	N Italian	50-60	688-1999
Bombay Palace	30 W 52nd St	104	Indian	18-27	541-7777
Box Tree, The	250 E 49th St	139	Continental	76.00	758-8320
Brasserie	100 E 53rd St	96	French	20-25	751-4840
Bravo Gianni	230 E 63rd St	12	Italian	40-45	752-7272
Brive	405 E 58th St	29	Fr/Contl	52-62	838-9393
Bruce Ho's Four Seas	116 E 57th St	53	Chinese	35-40	753-2610
Bruno	240 E 58th St	43	N Italian	35-40	688-4190
Bull & Bear	Lex & 49th St	127	American	25-30	872-4900
Cafe de la Paix	50 Central Pk S	30	Continental	35-45	755-5800
Cafe de Nice	56 W 56th St	56	French/Ital	15-20	586-7812
Cafe Europa	347 E 54th St	82	Modern Fr	30-35	755-0160
Cafe Geneva	69 W 55th St	60	Italian	22.95	489-7655
Cafe Nicholson	323 E 58th St	37	Continental	43.50	355-6769
Capriccio	15 E 61st St	17	N Italian	50-55	757-7795
Captain's Table	860 Second Ave	158	Seafood	45-50	697-9538
Cattleman	5 E 45th St	147	Steak/Sfd	20-30	661-1200
Chalet Suisse	6 E 48th St	141	Swiss	37.50	355-0855
Charley O's	33 W 48th St	133	American	20-25	582-7141

22

★ Prices do not include drinks or gratuities

Restaurant	Address	Map No.	Cuisine	Average Price ★	Telephone
Charley O's	Citicorp Center	86	Irish/Amer	$15-20	752-2102
Cheese Cellar	125 E 54th St	79	American	12-18	758-6565
Chef Chan	845 Second Ave	155	Chinese	15-20	687-7471
Chez Louis	1016 Second Av	89	French	35-45	752-1400
Chin Chin	216 E 49th St	138	Chinese	35-40	888-4555
Christ Cella	160 E 46th St	151	Steak/Sfd	55 +	697-2479
Christo's	143 E 49th St	128	Stk/Contl	25-35	355-2695
Contrapunto Cafe	200 E 60th St	26	Pasta	25-30	751-8616
Crystal Fountain	Grand Hyatt Hotel	165	Continental	25-35	850-5998
Darjeeling	248 E 49th	139	Indian	14.95	355-1810
David K's	1115 Third Ave	2	Chinese	30-35	371-9090
Dawat	210 E 58th St	41	Indian	30-45	355-7555
Dewey Wong	206 E 58th St	41	Chinese	25-30	758-6881
Doriental	128 E 56th St	67	Cantonese	15-25	688-8070
Eamonn Doran	998 Second Ave	100	Continental	20-25	752-8088
Edwardian Room	Plaza Hotel	32	Fr Contl	50 +	546-5310
Elmer's	1034 Second Ave	81	Steak/Sfd	35-40	751-8020
Enoteca Iperbole	137 E 55th St	70	Italian	30-40	759-9720
Felidia	243 E 58th St	36	N Italian	45-50	758-1479
Fiorello East	1081 Third Ave	8	Italian	25-30	838-7570
Flower Drum	856 Second Ave	158	Chinese	15-25	697-4280
Four Seasons	99 E 52nd St	97	Internatl	80-100	754-9494
French Shack	65 W 55th St	61	French	20-30	246-5126
Giambelli 50th St	46 E 50th St	124	N Italian	60 +	688-2760
Gian Marino	230 E 58th St	34	Italian	40-50	752-1696
Gin-Ray of Japan	148 E 50th St	126	Japanese	15-20	759-7454
Girafe	208 E 58th St	41	N Italian	45-55	752-3054
Gloucester House	37 E 50th St	111	Seafood	40-50	755-7394
Hatsuhana	17 E 48th St	134	Japanese	35-40	355-3345
Huberts	575 Park Ave	10	American	65.00	826-5911
Il Bambino d'Oro	890 Second Ave	144	Italian	25-30	308-5515
Il Gattopardo	49 W 56th St	48	N Italian	40-50	586-3978
Il Menestrello	14 E 52nd St	103	N Italian	50 +	421-7588
Il Mondo	341 E 43rd St	166	N Italian	45-75	661-5757
Il Nido	251 E 53rd St	88	N Italian	40-50	753-8450
Il Tinello	16 W 56th	59	Italian	35-40	245-4388
Il Valletto	133 E 61st St	16	N Italian	45-50	838-3939
Inagiku	111 E 49th St	127	Japanese	35-45	355-0440
India Pavilion	325 E 54th St	83	Indian	15-20	223-9740
Isle of Capri	1028 Third Ave	22	Italian	20-25	758-1828
Italian Pavilion	24 W 55th St	72	Italian	25-35	586-5950
Jacqueline's Chmpgne	132 E 61st St	20	Fr Internatl	30-45	838-4559
Jake's	801 Second Ave	166	American	30-40	687-5321
Jane's Bar & Grill	208 E 60th St	28	American	35-45	953-3353
Jean Lafitte	68 W 58th St	39	French	35-40	751-2323
Jockey Club	Ritz Carlton	30	Continental	50 +	664-7700
Joe & Rose	747 Third Ave	145	Steak/Ital	30-35	980-3985
John Barleycorn Pub	209 E 45th St	157	Irish/Amer	20-30	986-1088
J.Sung Dynasty	Lexington Htl	143	Chinese	20-30	355-1200
John Clancy's East	206 E 63rd St	11	Amer Seafd	45-50	752-6666
Kenny's Steak Pub	565 Lexington Av	112	American	20-30	355-0666
Kurumazushi	18 W 56th	58	Sushi	45-50	541-9030
L'Escargot	47 W 55th St	62	French	20-25	245-4266

★ Prices do not include drinks or gratuities

MIDTOWN RESTAURANTS Continued

Restaurant	Address	Map No.	Cuisine	Average Price ★	Telephone
L'Incontro	307 E 45th St	159	N Italian	$35-40	697-9664
L'Omnibus de Maxim	680 Madison Ave	13	Continental	50.00	980-6988
La Camelia	225 E 58th St	34	N Italian	35-45	751-5488
La Caravelle	33 W 55th St	63	French	57.00	586-4252
La Cote Basque	5 E 55th St	64	French	53.00	688-6525
La Fondue	43 W 55th St	62	Swiss Fr	12-18	581-0820
La Galerie	Omni Berkshire	95	French	30-37	753-5970
La Grenouille	3 E 52nd St	94	French	66-70	752-1495
La Mangeoire	1008 Second Ave	90	French	21-25	759-7086
La Mediterranee	947 Second Ave	118	French	20-25	755-4155
La Reserve	4 W 49th St	132	French	48.00	247-2993
La Table des Rois	135 E 50th St	113	French	30-35	223-8655
Lafayette	Drake Swissotel	51	French	65 +	832-1565
Laurent	111 E 56th St	55	French	30-45	753-2729
Le Bistro	827 Third Ave	114	French	20-25	759-5933
Le Bistro d'Adrienne	Peninsula Hotel	73	French	50-60	247-2200
Le Chantilly	106 E 57th St	54	French	42.50	751-2931
Le Cheval Blanc	145 E 45th St	153	French	21-16	599-8886
Le Cirque	58 E 65th St	4	French	55-65	794-9292
Le Cygne	55 E 54th St	77	French	58.00	759-5941
Le Manoir	120 E 56th St	65	French	15-25	753-1447
Le Nid	237 E 58th St	35	French	35-55	753-8480
Le Perigord	405 E 52nd St	101	French	45-55	755-6244
Le Regence	Plaza Athenee	5	French	59.50	734-9100
Le Steak	1089 Second Ave	44	French	35-40	421-9072
Le Trianon	Helmsley Palace	110	Continental	42-50	888-7000
Le Veau d'Or	129 E 60th St	21	French	25-30	838-8133
Lello	65 E 54th St	78	Italian	40-45	751-1555
Leopard	253 E 50th St	119	French	46.00	759-3735
Les Sans-Culottes	1085 Second Ave	45	French	15-20	838-6660
Les Tournebroches	Citicorp Center	86	French	11-22	935-6029
Louise Jr.	317 E 53rd St	91	N Italian	20-28	355-9172
Lutece	249 E 50th St	117	French	58.00	752-2225
Madame Romaine	29 E 61st St	14	French	25-30	758-2422
Manhattan Ocean	57 W 58th	33	Seafood	45-50	371-7777
Marie-Michelle	57 W 56th St	47	French	35-40	315-2444
Maximiliano	208 E 52nd St	107	Mexican	35-40	759-7373
Maxim's	680 Madison Ave	13	French	70 +	751-5111
Menage a Trois	Lexington Hotel	142	French	30-40	593-8242
Michael's Pub	211 E 55th St	71	American	25-30	758-2272
Mickey Mantle's	42 Central Pk S	31	American	20-40	688-7777
Miss Grimble	1199 First Ave	3	American	15-20	628-5800
Mitsukoshi	465 Park Ave	52	Japanese	35-50	935-6444
Mondrian	7 E 59th St	24	French	53.00	935-3434
Nada Sushi	135 E 50th St	113	Sushi	25-30	838-2537
Nanni	146 E 46th St	150	Italian	45-50	697-4161
Nippon	155 E 52nd St	106	Japanese	28-38	688-5941
Nirvana	30 Central Pk S	31	Indian	20-30	486-5700
Nyborg & Nelson	Citcorp Center	86	Scandinavian	12-18	223-0700
Oak Room	Plaza Hotel	32	American	40-45	546-5330
Oyster Bar	Grand Central	164	Seafood	20-35	490-6650
PJ Clarke's	915 Third Ave	68	American	13-18	759-1650
Palm	837 Second Ave	161	Steak	30-35	687-2953

24

★ *Prices do not include drinks or gratuities*

Restaurant	Address	Map No.	Cuisine	Average Price ★	Telephone
Palm Too	840 Second Ave	162	American	$50-55	697-5198
Park Room	Park Lane Hotel	31	Continental	45-55	371-4000
Pearl's Chinese	38 W 48th St	140	Chinese	20-35	221-6677
Pen & Pencil	205 E 45th St	156	Steak/Sfd	20-35	682-8660
Petrossian Restaurant	182 W 58th St		French	55-75	245-2214
Pierre Hotel Cafe	Fifth Ave & 61st	18	Fr Contl	45-50	838-8000
Pietro's	232 E 43rd St	165	Italian/Stk	40-45	682-9760
Polo	Westbury Hotel	off	New Amer	48.00	535-9141
Post House, The	28 E 63rd St	9	American	50-55	935-2888
Press Box	139 E 45th St	152	Ital Contl	20-25	697-4734
Primola	1226 Second Ave	7	N/S Italian	30-40	758-1775
Prunelle	18 E 54th St	84	French	45-50	759-6410
Quaglino's	783 Fifth Ave	23	N Italian	35-45	759-9047
Quilted Giraffe	Madison & 55th	75	Amer Luxury	75-100	593-1221
Rainbow Room	30 Rockefeller Plz	121	Continental	100.00	632-5100
Raphael	33 W 54th St	74	French	35-45	582-8993
Reflections	Pan Am Bldg	161	American	25-30	661-2520
Regine	502 Park Ave	25	French	57.50	826-0990
Rendez-Vous	21 E 52nd St	95	Continental	25-30	753-5970
River Cafe	1 Water St, Bklyn	off	Amer *(718)	55.00	*522-5200
Romeo Salta	30 W 56th St	57	Italian	45+	246-5772
Rosa Mexicano	1063 First Ave	46	Mexican	20-30	753-7407
San Giusto	935 Second Ave	130	N Italian	30-40	319-0900
San Marco	36 W 52nd St	102	Italian	30-35	246-5340
Sandro's	420 E 59th	38	Italian	40-50	355-5150
Savoy Grill	131 E 54th St	80	American	25-30	355-3640
Scarlatti's	34 E 52nd	105	Regional Ital	30-45	753-2444
Sea Grill	Rockfeller Center	122	Seafood	40-50	246-9201
Seryna	11 E 53rd	85	Japanese	45-50	980-9393
Shinbashi	280 Park Ave	136	Japanese	25-35	661-3915
Shun Lee Palace	155 E 55th St	69	Chinese	30-35	371-8844
Sichuan Pavilion	310 E 44th St	167	Chinese	25-30	972-7377
Sign of the Dove	1110 Third Ave	1	Continental	60+	861-8080
Smith & Wolensky	201 E 49th St	129	Steak/Sfd	45-50	753-1530
Spark's Steakhouse	210 E 46th St	154	Steak	35-45	687-4855
Sushiden	19 E 49th St	123	Japanese	25-30	758-2700
Takesushi	71 Vanderbilt	148	Japan/Sushi	20-25	867-5120
Tang's Chariot	236 E 53rd	99	Szechuan	20-30	355-5096
Terrace, The	Trump Tower	50	American	30-35	371-5030
Tonino	805 Third Ave	129	N Italian	30-35	308-2280
Top of the Sixes	666 Fifth Ave	92	Amer Contl	25-35	757-6662
Torremolinos	230 E 51st St	115	Sp Contl	25-30	755-1862
Toscana	200 E 54th St	87	N Italian	35-40	371-8144
Trattoria	Pan Am Bldg	149	Italian	15-20	661-3090
Tre Scalini	230 E 58th St	42	Italian	45-55	688-6888
Trumpet's	Grand Hyatt Hotel	165	American	40-45	850-5999
Tse Yang	34 E 51st	109	Chinese	55+	688-5447
21 Club	21 W 52nd St	93	Continental	55+	582-7200
Waldorf-Peacock Alley	301 Park Ave	125	Continental	25-35	872-4895
Water Club	East River/30th	off	Amer/Seafd	55+	683-3333
Wylie's Ribs & Co	891 First Ave	120	Texas	25-30	751-0700
Yellowfingers di Nuovo	Third Ave & 60th	26	Calif Ital	20-25	751-8615
Zarela	953 Second Ave	116	Mexican	30-35	644-6740

★ *Prices do not include drinks or gratuities*

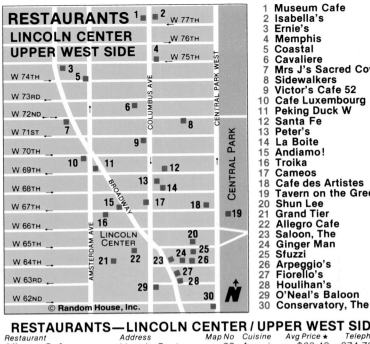

	1	Museum Cafe
	2	Isabella's
	3	Ernie's
	4	Memphis
	5	Coastal
	6	Cavaliere
	7	Mrs J's Sacred Cow
	8	Sidewalkers
	9	Victor's Cafe 52
	10	Cafe Luxembourg
	11	Peking Duck W
	12	Santa Fe
	13	Peter's
	14	La Boite
	15	Andiamo!
	16	Troika
	17	Cameos
	18	Cafe des Artistes
	19	Tavern on the Green
	20	Shun Lee
	21	Grand Tier
	22	Allegro Cafe
	23	Saloon, The
	24	Ginger Man
	25	Sfuzzi
	26	Arpeggio's
	27	Fiorello's
	28	Houlihan's
	29	O'Neal's Baloon
	30	Conservatory, The

RESTAURANTS—LINCOLN CENTER / UPPER WEST SIDE

Restaurant	Address	Map No	Cuisine	Avg Price ★	Telephone
Allegro Cafe	Lincoln Center	22	American	$30-40	874-7000
Andiamo!	1991 Broadway	15	Italian	30-35	362-3315
Arpeggio's	35 W 64th Street	26	Cont/Seafd	18-25	724-0103
Cafe Luxembourg	200 W 70th Street	10	Fr/Amer	28-35	873-7411
Cafe des Artistes	1 W 67th Street	18	Prov French	30.00	877-3500
Cameos	169 Columbus Ave	17	New Amer	35-45	874-2280
Cavaliere	108 W 73rd Street	6	N Italian	27.00	799-8282
Coastal	300 Amsterdam Ave	5	Seafood	25-30	769-3988
Conservatory, The	Mayflower Hotel	30	Continental	25-30	581-1293
Ernie's	2150 Broadway	3	Italian	15-20	496-1588
Fiorello's	1900 Broadway	27	Italian	25-30	595-5330
Ginger Man	51 W 64th Street	24	Continental	25-35	399-2358
Grand Tier	Metropolitan Opera	21	Continental	45-60	799-3400
Houlihan's	1900 Broadway	28	American	10-15	362-1340
Isabella's	359 Columbus Ave	2	Mediterr	20-25	724-2100
La Boite en Bois	75 W 68th Street	14	French	30-35	874-2705
Memphis	329 Columbus Ave	4	American	25-35	496-1840
Mrs J's Sacred Cow	228 W 72nd Street	7	American	25-35	873-4067
Museum Cafe	366 Columbus Ave	1	American	10-20	799-0150
O'Neal's Baloon	48 W 63rd Street	29	American	10-20	581-3770
Peking Duck West	Amsterdam & 69th	11	Peking	15-25	799-5457
Peter's	182 Columbus Ave	13	Contl Amer	20-25	877-4747
Saloon, The	1920 Broadway	23	Varied	15-20	874-1500
Santa Fe	72 W 69th Street	12	SW Amer	25-30	724-0822
Sfuzzi	58 W 65th Street	25	N Italian	30-40	873-3700
Shun Lee	43 W 65th Street	20	Chinese	30-40	595-8895
Sidewalkers	12 W 72nd Street	8	Seafood	15-25	799-6070
Tavern-on-the-Green	Central Pk W & 67th	19	Amer/Cont	40-45	873-3200
Troika	148 W 65th Street	16	Russian	25-35	724-0709
Victor's Cafe 71	Columbus & 71st St	9	Cuban	15-20	877-7988

26

★ Prices do not include drinks or gratuities

1 **Le Refuge**
2 **Trastevere**
3 **Primavera**
4 **Ristorante Dieci**
5 **Dining Room**
6 **Parioli Romanissimo**
7 **Gibbon**
8 **Anatolia**
9 **Sistina**
10 **Diva**
11 **Pig Heaven**
12 **Due**
13 **Il Posto**
14 **Pancho Villa's**
15 **L'Oustalet**
16 **Lusardi's**
17 **Carlyle**
18 **Csarda**
19 **Il Monello**
20 **Brighton Grill**
21 **Bravo Sergio**
22 **Vasata**
23 **Cafe San Martin**
24 **Mortimer's**
25 **Metro**
26 **Vivolo**
27 **Cafe Crocodile**
28 **Petaluma**
29 **La Signoria**
30 **La Petite Ferme**

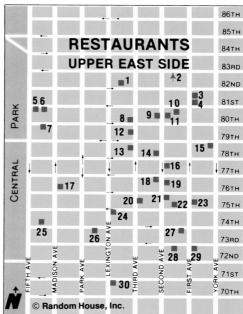

RESTAURANTS
UPPER EAST SIDE

© Random House, Inc.

RESTAURANTS—UPPER EAST SIDE

Restaurant	Address	Map No	Cuisine	Avg Price ★	Telephone
Anatolia	1422 Third Ave	8	Turkish	$35-45	517-6262
Bravo Sergio	1452 Second Ave	21	Italian	20-25	772-3629
Brighton Grill	1313 Third Ave	20	Seafood	25-35	988-6663
Cafe Crocodile	354 E 74th	27	Prov French	30-35	249-6619
Cafe San Martin	1458 First Ave	23	Spanish	25-30	288-0470
Carlyle Restaurant	983 Madison Ave	17	Fr/Contl	35-45	744-1600
Csarda	1477 2nd Ave	18	Hungarian	20-25	472-2892
Dining Room	Stanhope Hotel	5	Continental	50-55	288-5800
Diva	306 E 81st	10	N Italian	40-45	650-1928
Due	1369 Third Ave	12	Italian	25-30	772-3331
Elaine's	1703 2nd Ave	off map	Italian	25-35	534-8103
Gibbon	24 E 80th	7	Japan/Fr	35-40	861-4001
Il Monello	1460 2nd Ave	19	N Italian	25-35	535-9310
Il Posto	1378 Third Ave	13	Italian	25-30	734-0005
L'Oustalet	448 E 79th	15	French	24-28	249-4920
La Petite Ferme	973 Lexington	30	French	40-45	249-3272
La Signoria	1354 First Ave	29	N Italian	25-30	744-4400
Le Refuge	166 E 82nd St	1	French	25-35	861-4505
Lusardi's	1494 Second Ave	16	Italian	25-30	249-2020
Metro	23 E 74th St	25	Fr Amer	50-55	249-3030
Mortimer's	1057 Lexington	24	American	25-35	517-6400
Pancho Villa's	1501 2nd Ave	14	Mexican	15-20	861-5925
Parioli Romanissimo	24 E 81st St	6	N Italian	80-100	288-2391
Petaluma	1356 1st Ave	28	Italian	20-30	772-8800
Pig Heaven	1540 Second Ave	11	Chinese	25-35	744-4333
Primavera	1578 First Ave	3	N Italian	55-65	861-8608
Ristorante Dieci	1568 First Ave	4	Italian	35-40	628-6565
Sistina	1555 Second Ave	9	Italian	40-50	861-7660
Trastevere	309 E 83rd St	2	Italian	50-55	734-6343
Vasata	339 E 75th	22	Czech	20-25	650-1686
Vivolo	140 E 74th	26	Italian	20-30	737-3533

★ *Prices do not include drinks or gratuities*

27

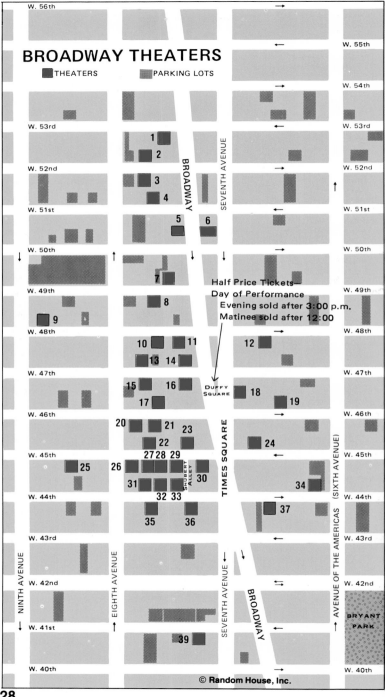

BROADWAY THEATERS

■ THEATERS　■ PARKING LOTS

W. 56th

W. 55th

W. 54th

W. 53rd

W. 53rd

1

2

BROADWAY

SEVENTH AVENUE

W. 52nd

3

W. 52nd

4

W. 51st

5

6

W. 51st

W. 50th

W. 50th

7

W. 49th

Half Price Tickets—
Day of Performance
Evening sold after 3:00 p.m.
Matinee sold after 12:00

W. 49th

8

9

W. 48th

W. 48th

10   11

12

13   14

W. 47th

W. 47th

15   16

DUFFY
SQUARE

18

17

19

W. 46th

W. 46th

20   21

TIMES SQUARE

23

22

24

W. 45th

27 28 29

W. 45th

25

26

SHUBERT ALLEY

30

31

34

32 33

W. 44th

W. 44th

35   36

37

W. 43rd

W. 43rd

NINTH AVENUE

EIGHTH AVENUE

SEVENTH AVENUE

AVENUE OF THE AMERICAS (SIXTH AVENUE)

W. 42nd

W. 42nd

BROADWAY

BRYANT PARK

W. 41st

39

W. 40th

W. 40th

© Random House, Inc.

28

BROADWAY THEATERS—BY MAP NUMBERS

1 Broadway	10 Longrace	20 Imperial	30 Minskoff
2 Virginia	11 Ritz	21 46th Street	31 Majestic
3 Neil Simon	12 Cort	22 Music Box	32 Broadhurst
4 Mark Hellinger	13 Biltmore	23 Marquis	33 Shubert
5 Circle in Sq	14 Barrymore	24 Lyceum	34 Belasco
6 Gershwin	15 Brooks Atkinson	25 Martin Beck	35 St. James
7 Winter Garden	16 Edison	26 Golden	36 Helen Hayes
8 Ambassador	17 Lunt·Fontanne	27 Royale	37 Lamb's
8 Eugene O'Neill	18 Palace	28 Plymouth	39 Nederlander
9 Jack Lawrence	19 American Place	29 Booth	

BROADWAY THEATERS

Theater	Address	Seats	Map No.	Telephones ★
Ambassador	215 W 49th	1125	7	TELE-CHARGE
American Place	111 W 46th	300	19	840-2960
Barrymore, Ethel	243 W 47th	1096	14	TELE-CHARGE
Belasco	111 W 44th	923	34	TELE-CHARGE
Biltmore	261 W 47th	949	13	NO PHONE
Booth	222 W 45th	783	29	TELE-CHARGE, TICKETRON
Broadhurst	235 W 44th	1157	32	TELE-CHARGE, TICKETRON
Broadway	1681 Broadway	1765	1	TELE-CHARGE, TICKETRON
Brooks Atkinson	256 W 47th	1090	15	719-4099
Circle in Sq Uptown	1633 Broadway	648	5	TELE-CHARGE 307-2700
Cort	138 W 48th	1089	12	TELE-CHARGE, TICKETRON
Edison	240 W 47th	505	16	TELETRON, TICK 302-2302
Eugene O'Neill	230 W 49th	1062	8	TICKETRON 246-0220
46th Street	226 W 46th	1338	21	TELETRON, TICKETRON
Gershwin	222 W 51st	1933	5	TELETRON/TICK 586-6510
Golden	252 W 45th	805	26	TELE-CHARGE
Helen Hayes	240 W 44th	499	36	TELETRON/TICK 944-9450
Imperial	249 W 45th	1452	20	TELE-CHARGE, TICKETRON
Jack Lawrence	359 W 48th	499	9	NO PHONE
Lamb's	130 W 44th	499	37	997-1780
Longacre	220 W 48th	1096	10	TELE-CHARGE
Lunt·Fontanne	205 W 46th	1478	17	TELETRON 575-9200
Lyceum	149 W 45th	928	24	TELE-CHARGE
Majestic	247 W 44th	1629	31	TELE-CHARGE, TICKETRON
Mark Hellinger	237 W 51st	1603	4	NO PHONE
Marquis	1700 Broadway	1617	23	TELE-CHARGE, TELE/TICK
Martin Beck	302 W 45th	1260	25	TELETRON 246-6363
Minskoff	B'way & 45th	1621	30	TELETRON/TICK 869-0550
Music Box	239 W 45th	1010	22	TELE-CHARGE/TICK 246-4636
Nederlander	208 W 41st	1216	39	NO PHONE
Neil Simon	250 W 52nd	1334	3	TELETRON/TICK 757-8646
Palace	B'way & 47th	1686	18	NO PHONE
Plymouth	236 W 45th	1077	28	TELE-CHARGE, TICKETRON
Ritz	219 W 48th	499	11	TELETRON/TICK 582-4022
Royale	242 W 45th	1059	27	TELE-CHARGE, TICKETRON
St. James	246 W 44th	1559	35	TELETRON/TICK 398-0280
Shubert	225 W 44th	1483	33	TELETRON, TICKETRON
Virginia	245 W 52nd	1342	2	977-9370
Winter Garden	1634 Broadway	1518	6	TELE-CHARGE, TICKETRON
Criterion Center	B'way & W 45th-Stages Right & Left			TELE-CHARGE/354-0900

LINCOLN CENTER (SEE PAGE 56)

Mitzi Newhouse & Vivian Beaumont 362-7600 **NY State Thea** 877-4700
★ **Tele·Charge** 239-6200 **Ticketmaster** 307-7171 **Ticketron** 246-0102

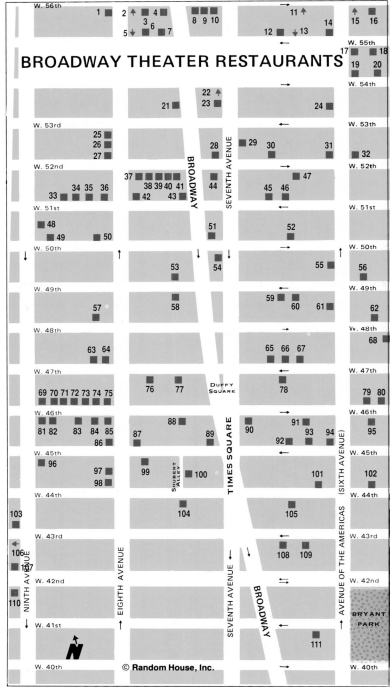

BROADWAY THEATER RESTAURANTS

BROADWAY THEATER RESTAURANTS—BY MAP NOS.

1 Coq au Vin	38 Victor's Cafe	76 Delsomma
2 Symphony Cafe	39 Gallagher's	77 Pierre au Tunnel
3 Spuntino	40 Broadway Brasserie	78 Fundador
4 El Jerez	41 Wine Bistro	79 Woo Lae Oak
5 Caramba	42 Les Pyrenees	80 Brazilian Coffee
6 Chantal Cafe	43 Beefsteak Charlie	81 Grand Sea Palace
7 Jose Sent Me	44 King of the Sea	82 Audrone's
8 India Pavilion	45 Le Bernardin	83 Le Rivage
9 Fuji	46 Palio	84 Joe Allen's
10 Patsy's	47 Sam's	85 Orso
11 Maurice	48 Sorrentinos	86 Kodama
12 Cafe Betw Breads	49 Chez Napoleon	87 Frankie & Johnnie
13 Castellano	50 Seeda Thai	88 Pergola
14 Corrado	51 Hawaii Kai	89 View, The
15 Benihana of Tokyo	52 Ho Ho	90 Celestial Empire
16 Darbar	53 Wally's & Joseph's	91 La Strada
17 Le Quercy	54 Bellini	92 Johnnie's Italian
18 La Bonne Soupe	55 Lindy's	93 Cabana Carioca II
19 Sir Walter's	56 Hurley's	94 Cabana Carioca
20 Raphael	57 Rosa's Place	95 Kitcho New York
21 Hunan Lu	58 Jackie Mason's	96 Jezebel
22 Carnegie Deli	59 La Bagh	97 Beefsteak Charlie
22 Larre II	60 Iroha	98 Charlies
23 Stage Delicatessen	61 Beanstalk	99 Mamma Leone's
24 Hurlingham's	62 Raga	100 Charlie O's
25 Bangkok Cuisine	63 Trixies	101 Cafe Un Deux Trois
26 Caffe Cielo	64 B Smith's	102 Algonquin
27 King Crab	65 Spirits	103 Le Madeleine
28 Rosie O'Grady	66 La Veranda	104 Sardi's
29 Rainier's	67 Dish of Salt	105 China Bowl
30 Pier 52	68 Pearl's Chinese	106 Manhattan Island
31 Ben Benson's	69 Crepes Suzette	107 Sukhothai West
32 China Grill	70 Lattanzi	107 West Bank Cafe
33 Cafe des Sports	71 Carolina	108 India Dining
34 Rene Pujol	72 La Vieille Auberge	109 Century Cafe
35 Cheshire Cheese	73 Barbetta	110 Cirella's
36 Tout Va Bien	74 Broadway Joe	111 Cheers
37 Russian Samovar	75 La Rivista Palatine	

BROADWAY THEATER RESTAURANTS

Restaurant	Address	Map No.	Cuisine	Avg Dinner Price ★	Telephone
Algonquin	59 W 44th	102	American	$30-40	840-6800
Audrone's	342 W 46th	82	Fr/Contl	15-25	246-1960
B Smith's	771 Eighth Ave	64	Continental	20-25	247-2222
Bangkok Cuisine	885 Eighth Ave	25	Thai	20-25	581-6370
Barbetta	321 W 46th	73	N Italian	40-45	246-9171
Beanstalk	1221 Ave of Amer	61	American	15-20	997-1005
Beefsteak Charlie	709 Eighth Ave	97	Steak	15-20	581-0500
Beefsteak Charlie	Broadway at 51st	43	Steak	15-20	757-3110
Bellini	777 Seventh Ave	54	N Italian	42-50	265-7770
Ben Benson's	123 W 52nd St	31	American	40 +	581-8888
Benihana of Tokyo	47 W 56th St	15	Japanese	20-25	581-0930
Brazilian Coffee	45 W 46th	80	Brazil/Portg	15-20	768-2766
Broadway Brasserie	226 W 52nd	40	French	20-25	315-0100
Broadway Joe	315 W 46th	74	American	25-30	246-6513

★ Prices do not include drinks or gratuities

Restaurant	Address	Map No.	Cuisine	Avg Dinner Price ★	Telephone
Cabana Carioca	123 W 45th	94	Brazil/Portg	$15-20	581-8088
Cabana Carioca II	133 W 45th	93	Brazil/Portg	15-20	730-8375
Cafe Between Breads	145 W 55th	12	American	30-40	581-1189
Cafe Un Deux Trois	123 W 44th	101	Fr/Amer	30-35	354-4148
Cafe des Sports	329 W 51st	33	French	20-30	974-9052
Caffe Cielo	881 Eighth Ave	26	N Italian	30-40	246-9555
Caramba!	918 Eighth Ave	5	Tex-Mex	20-30	245-7910
Carnegie Deli	854 Seventh Ave	22	Deli	12-15	757-2245
Carolina	355 W 46th	71	Regionl Amer	50-60	245-0058
Castellano	138 W 55th	13	N Italian	40-45	664-1975
Celestial Empire	144 W 46th	90	Mandarin	10-15	869-9183
Century Cafe	132 W 43rd	109	American	20-25	398-1988
Chantal Cafe	257 W 55th St	6	French	15-25	246-7076
Charley O's	45 Shubert Alley	100	Irish/Amer	18-23	840-2964
Charlies	705 Eighth Ave	98	Amer Contl	20-25	757-0186
Cheers	120 W 41st	111	Ital/Amer	25-30	840-8810
Cheshire Cheese	319 W 51st	35	English	30-45	765-0616
Chez Josephine	414 W 42nd	110	International	30-35	594-1925
Chez Napoleon	365 W 50th	49	French	20-30	265-6980
China Bowl	152 W 44th	105	Chinese	15-20	582-3358
China Grill	51 W 52 (CBS bldg)	32	French/Calif	35-40	333-7788
Cirella's	400 W 42nd St	110	Ital/Contl	20-30	564-0004
Coq au Vin	304 W 56th St	1	French	18.95	541-8273
Corrado	1373 Ave Amer	14	N Italian	40-50	333-3133
Crepes Suzette	363 W 46th	69	French	18-25	581-9717
Darbar	44 W 56th	16	Indian	30-35	432-7227
Delsomma	266 W 47th	76	Italian	21.50	719-4179
Devereux's	160 Central Pk S	off	American	35 +	247-0300
Dish of Salt	133 W 47th	67	Cantonese	25-30	921-4242
El Jerez	234 W 56th	4	Span/Mex	20-30	765-4535
Frankie & Johnnie	269 W 45th	87	American	30-35	997-9494
Fuji	238 W 56th	9	Japanese	15-25	245-8594
Fundador	146 W 47th	78	Spanish	15-25	819-0012
Gallagher's	228 W 52nd	39	Steak	35-40	245-5336
Grand Sea Palace	346 W 46th St	81	Thai Seafd	20-30	265-8133
Hard Rock Cafe	221 W 57th St	off	American	15-20	489-6565
Hawaii Kai	Broadway & 50th	51	Poly/Chinese	20-25	757-0900
Ho Ho	131 W 50th	52	Chinese	20-25	246-3256
Hunan Lou	1705 Broadway	21	Chinese	15-20	246-6759
Hurley's	1240 Ave of Amer	56	American	20-25	765-8981
Hurlingham's	Hilton Hotel	24	Steak/Sfd	20-35	265-1600
India Dining	102 W 43rd	108	Indian	15-18	221-6574
Indian Pavilion	240 W 56th	8	Indian	10-15	489-0035
Iroha	142 W 49th St	60	Japanese	15-20	398-9049
Jackie Mason's	224 W 49th St	58	Continental	25-32	977-9000
Jezebel	630 Ninth Ave	96	South Soul	35-40	582-1045
Joe Allen's	326 W 46th	84	American	15-25	581-6464
Johnnie's Italian	135 W 45th	92	Italian	15-25	997-9315
Jose Sent Me	253 W 55th	7	Tex Mex	18-25	246-3253
K. C. Place	807 Ninth Ave	off	Seafood	15-25	246-4258
King Crab	871 Eighth Ave	27	Seafood	15-25	765-4393
King of the Sea	808 Seventh Ave	44	Seafood	40-45	757-3522
Kitcho New York	22 W 46th	95	Japanese	20-25	575-8880
Kodama	301 W 45th	86	Japanese	15-20	582-8065

★ *Prices do not include drinks or gratuities*

Restaurant	Address	Map No.	Cuisine	Avg Dinner Price ★	Telephone
a Bagh	148 W 49th St	59	N Indian	$15-20	840-2557
a Bonne Soupe	48 W 55th	18	French	10-20	586-7650
a Rivista Palatine	313 W 46th St	75	Italian	35-40	245-1707
a Strada	134 W 46th	91	Italian	22-25	382-0060
a Veranda	163 W 47th St	66	Italian	23.00	391-0905
a Vieille Auberge	347 W 46th	72	French	20-25	247-4284
arre II	846 Seventh	22	French	20-25	586-8096
attanzi	361 W 46th	70	Italian	40-50	315-0980
e Bernardin	155 W 51st St	45	Seafood	65.00	489-1515
e Madeleine	403 W 43rd	103	French	30-35	246-2993
e Quercy	52 W 55th	17	French	20-30	265-8141
e Rivage	340 W 46th	83	French	20-25	765-7374
es Pyrenees	251 W 51st	42	French	24.00	246-0044
indy's	1256 Ave of Amer	55	Deli/Steak	10-15	586-8986
Mamma Leone's	Milford Plaza Hotel	99	Italian	20-30	869-3600
Manhattan Island	482 W 43rd St	106	Eclectic	20-25	967-0533
Maurice	Parker Meridien Htl	11	French	40.00	245-7788
Orso	322 W 46th	85	Italian	25-30	489-7212
alio	151 W 51st	46	Reginl Ital	50-60	245-4850
atsy's	236 W 56th	10	Italian	25-30	247-3491
earl's Chinese	38 W 48th	68	Chinese	25-30	221-6677
ergola	252 W 46th	88	French	15-20	840-8935
ier 52	163 W 52nd	30	Seafood	30-40	245-6652
ierre au Tunnel	250 W 47th St	77	French	20-25	575-1220
aga	57 W 48th	62	Indian	25-40	757-3450
ainier's	Sheraton Centre	29	American	31.00	581-1000
aphael	33 W 54th	20	Lt French	35-45	582-8993
ene Pujol	321 W 51st	34	French	28-32	246-3023
osa's Place	303 W 48th	57	Tex/Mex	15-25	586-4853
osie O'Grady	800 Seventh	28	Irish/Contl	20-25	582-2975
ussian Samovar	256 W 52nd	37	Russian	25-30	757-0168
ussian Tea Room	150 W 57th	off	Russian Contl	39-50	265-0947
am's	152 W 52nd St	47	American	20-30	582-8700
an Domenico	240 Central Pk S	off	Italian	60-80	265-5959
ardi's	234 W 44th	104	Continental	25-35	221-8440
eeda Thai	309 W 50th St	50	Thai	15-25	586-4040
ir Walter's	Warwick Hotel	19	Continental	25-30	247-3793
orrentino's	754 Ninth Ave	48	Italian	25-30	307-5484
pirits	165 W 47th	65	Italian	15-20	302-6186
puntino	242 W 56th	3	S Italian	12-15	247-1070
tage Delicatessen	834 Seventh Ave	23	Jewish	10-15	245-7850
ymphony Cafe	Ave of Amer	2	American	25-30	397-9595
errace - Butler Hall	Columbia Univ	off	Fr Classic	60-65	666-9490
out Va Bien	311 W 51st	36	French	20-25	265-0190
rattoria delle'Arte	900 Seventh Ave	off	Italian	15-25	245-9800
ixies	307 W 47th	63	American	20-25	840-9537
ictor's Cafe 52	236 W 52nd	38	Cuban	20-25	586-7714
ew, The	Marriott Marquis	89	Continental	50-55	704-8900
ally's & Joseph's	249 W 49th	53	Steak/Sfd	50-55	582-0460
est Bank Cafe	407 W 42nd	107	Continental	15-20	695-6909
indows on the Wrld	World Trade Ctr	off	Continental	40-45	938-1111
ine Bistro	Novotel Hotel	41	American	18.50	315-0100
oo Lae Oak	77 W 46th	79	Korean	20-30	869-9958

Prices do not include drinks or gratuities

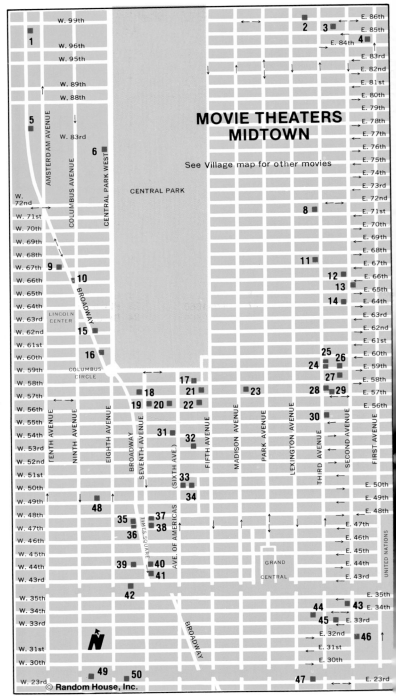

MOVIE THEATERS MIDTOWN

See Village map for other movies

CENTRAL PARK

W. 99th
W. 96th
W. 95th
W. 89th
W. 88th
W. 83rd
W. 72nd
W. 71st
W. 70th
W. 69th
W. 68th
W. 67th
W. 66th
W. 65th
W. 64th
W. 63rd
W. 62nd
W. 61st
W. 60th
W. 59th
W. 58th
W. 57th
W. 56th
W. 55th
W. 54th
W. 53rd
W. 52nd
W. 51st
W. 50th
W. 49th
W. 48th
W. 47th
W. 46th
W. 45th
W. 44th
W. 43rd
W. 35th
W. 34th
W. 33rd
W. 31st
W. 30th
W. 23rd

E. 86th
E. 85th
E. 84th
E. 83rd
E. 82nd
E. 81st
E. 80th
E. 79th
E. 78th
E. 77th
E. 76th
E. 75th
E. 74th
E. 73rd
E. 72nd
E. 71st
E. 70th
E. 69th
E. 68th
E. 67th
E. 66th
E. 65th
E. 64th
E. 63rd
E. 62nd
E. 61st
E. 60th
E. 59th
E. 58th
E. 57th
E. 56th
E. 50th
E. 49th
E. 48th
E. 47th
E. 46th
E. 45th
E. 44th
E. 43rd
E. 35th
E. 34th
E. 33rd
E. 32nd
E. 31st
E. 30th
E. 23rd

AMSTERDAM AVENUE
COLUMBUS AVENUE
CENTRAL PARK WEST
BROADWAY
LINCOLN CENTER
COLUMBUS CIRCLE
TENTH AVENUE
NINTH AVENUE
EIGHTH AVENUE
BROADWAY
SEVENTH AVENUE
(SIXTH AVE.)
AVE. OF AMERICAS
FIFTH AVENUE
MADISON AVENUE
PARK AVENUE
LEXINGTON AVENUE
THIRD AVENUE
SECOND AVENUE
FIRST AVENUE
UNITED NATIONS
TIMES SQUARE
GRAND CENTRAL
BROADWAY

© Random House, Inc.

34

MOVIES THEATERS—MIDTOWN

ALPHABETICAL

Theater	Map No	Telephone
Baronet	24	355-1663
Bay Cinema	46	679-0160
Beekman	13	737-2622
Biograph	18	582-4582
Carnegie Hall Cinema	19	265-2520
Carnegie Screening Rm	19	757-2131
Chelsea Cinema 9	50	593-5777
Cinema I, II	25	753-6022
Cinema III	17	752-5959
Cinema Studio 1, 2	10	877-4040
Cinema Third Ave	25	753-6022
Coronet	24	355-1663
Criterion Center 1-6	40	354-0900
Eastside Cinema	30	755-3020
86th St East	3	249-1144
Embassy 1 46th	37	757-2408
Embassy 2,3, 4	38	730-7262
Festival	22	307-7856
59th S East	26	759-4630
57th St Playhouse	20	581-7360
Gemini Twins	14	832-1670
Gotham	28	759-2262
Gramercy	47	475-1660
Guild	34	757-2406
Lincoln Plz Cinema 1,2,3	15	757-2280
Loews Astor Plaza	39	869-8340
Loews 34th Showplace 3	45	532-5544
Loews 84th St 1-6	5	877-3600
Loews NY Twin	12	744-7339
Loews Orpheum 1 & 2	2	289-4607
Loews Paramount	16	247-5070
Loews Tower East	8	879-1313
Manhattan I & II	27	935-6420
Metro Twins	1	222-1200
Movieland	35	757-8320
Murray Hill	44	689-6548
Museum Modern Art	32	708-9490
National Twin	41	869-0950
Naturemax-Mus Natural	6	769-5650
Paris	21	688-2013
Plaza	23	355-3320
Radio City Music Hall	33	757-3100
Regency	9	724-3700
68th St Playhouse	11	734-0302
Sutton	29	759-1411
34th St East	43	683-0255
23rd St W Triplex	49	989-0060
United Artist 85th East	4	249-5100
Warner Odeon	42	764-6760
Westside Cinema 1,2	36	398-1720
Worldwide Cinemas 1-6	48	246-1560
Ziegfeld	31	765-7600

BY MAP NUMBERS

Map No	Theater
1	Metro
2	Loews Orpheum
3	86th St East
4	U A 85th East
5	Loews 84th 1-6
6	Naturemax
8	Loews Tower East
9	Regency
10	Cinema Studio 1,2
11	68th St Playhouse
12	Loews NY Twin
13	Beekman
14	Gemini Twins
15	Lincoln Plaza
16	Loews Paramount
17	Cinema III
18	Biograph
19	Carnegie Hall
19	Carnegie Screening
20	57th St
21	Paris
22	Festival
23	Plaza
24	Baronet
24	Coronet
25	Cinema I, II
25	Cinema Third
26	59th St East
27	Manhattan I,II
28	Gotham
29	Sutton
30	Eastside
31	Ziegfeld
32	Mus Modern Art
33	Radio City
34	Guild
35	Movieland
36	Westside Cinema
37	Embassy 1
38	Embassy 2,3,4
39	Loews Astor Plaza
40	Criterion
41	National
42	Warner
43	34th St East
44	Murray Hill
45	Loews 34th St
46	Bay Cinema
47	Gramercy
48	Worldwide
49	23rd St Triplex
50	Chelsea Cinema 9

Film Forum- 57 Wall Street		431-1590
Columbia Cinema- B'way/103rd		316-6660
Harlem Movie Ctr- 235 W 125th		222-8900
Nova 1,2- B'way & W 147th St		862-5728

Little (Public)- 425 Lafayette St		598-7171
Coliseum Twin- B'way & 181st		927-7200
Olympia 1,2- B'way & 107th St		865-8128
Seaport Cinema- 210 Front St		608-7889

GREENWICH VILLAGE MOVIES PAGE 42

Streets	Central PkW	Broadway			Fifth Av	Madison
95–96	352–360	2540–2556			1140–1148	1356–13
94–95	341–351	2520–2537			1130–1136	1340–13
93–94	331–336	2501–2519			1120–1125	1316–13
92–93	322–327	2478–2500			1109–1115	1295–13
91–92	315–320	2460–2475			1100–1107	1273–12
90–91	300	2440–2459			NY Sch. Social Wk.	1254–12
89–90	293–295	2420–2439	The		1080–1089	1239–12
88–89	281–285	2400–2418			Guggenheim	1222–12
87–88	271–275	2380–2398	numbers		1060–1069	1190–12
86–87	262	2361–2379			1051–1056	1175–11
85–86	251	2341–2355	of		1040–1048	1150–11
84–85	241–249	2320–2342			1030–1035	1125–11
83–84	230–239	2300–2318	nearest		1020–1028	1109–11
82–83	225–227	2280–2299			1010–1018	1089–10
81–82	217–219	2260–2279	streets		998–1009	1072–10
80–81	Planetarium	2240–2259			990–997	1050–10
79–80	Museum of	2220–2239	will be		980–989	1033–10
78–79	Natural Hist.	2200–2219			972–973	1011–10
77–78		2180–2199	found on		960–969	998–10
76–77	170	2160–2177			950–956	974–99
75–76	151	2140–2159	the		942–947	954–97
74–75	145	2120–2139			930–936	933–95
73–74	135	2100–2114	lamp-		922–929	917–93
72–73	119	2081–2099			910–920	896–90
71–72	115	2061–2079	posts		900–907	861–87
70–71	101	2040–2062			Frick	845–87
69–70	91–99	2020–2030	in		880–885	828–85
68–69	80–88	2000–2016			870–875	813–82
67–68	75	1990–1999	Central		857–860	793–81
66–67	65–70	1960–1978			854–856	772–79
65–66	55–58	1940–1959	Park		Temple Emanu El	754–77
64–65	41–50	1920–1936			833–838	733–75
63–64	33	Lincoln C.			820–828	710–72
62–63	25	1881–1896	***Avenue***		810–817	690–70
61–62	13–20	1860–1880	***of the***		800–807	673–68
60–61	Central Pk	Coliseum	***Americas***		Central Pk.	654–66
59–60	Columbus C.	Columbus Cir.	***(Sixth Av)***		790 Hotel Pierre	635–64
	Seventh Av				Grand Army Plz	
58–59	919–933	1796–1806	1420–1439		Gen. Motors	621 Gen.
57–58	901–917	1775–1785	1400–1419		742–754	598–6
56–57	Carnegie Hall	1751–1770	Chase Man. Bk		720–730	572–5
55–56	858–880	1730–1750	1361–1377		707–718	550–5
54–55	841–855	1709–1728	1340–1357		689–703	532–5
53–54	825–838	1691–1707	1330 N.Y. Hilton	***Rockefeller Plz***	673–685	512–5
52–53	800-820 Americana	1671–1687	1301		655–671	500–5
51–52	781–799	1651–1665	1281–1297		640–653	477–4
50–51	761–780	1631–1650	1260-1277 Radio City		St. Patrick's	452–4
49–50	742–760	1612–1630	1240–1258		610-620 Saks Fifth	433–4

AVENUES FROM 14 TO 96 STREET

Park Av	Lexington Av	Third Av	Second Av	First Av	Streets
1220–1236	1476–1486	1695–1709	1840–1868	1841–1855	95–96
1199–1217	1449–1470	1678–1693	1817–1838	1817–1835	94–95
1180–1192	1424–1444	1662–1677	1800–1808	1797–1811	93–94
1160–1178	1400–1423	1644–1660	1766–1780	1756–1779	92–93
1140–1155	1380–1396	1622–1643	1748–1763	1756–1779	91–92
1120–1135	1361–1379	1601–1620	1736–1746	1740–1754	90–91
1100–1114	1342–1355	1585–1602	1716–1739	1718–1735	89–90
1080–1095	1311–1338	1568–1583	1700–1715	1701–1717	88–89
1060–1076	1300–1301	1550–1566	1682–1698	1668–1689	87–88
1040–1055	1280–1288	1529–1546	1669–1679	1653–1667	86–87
1020–1035	1263–1278	1511–1525	1640–1657	1637–1651	85–86
1000–1015	1241–1261	1480–1508	1619–1638	1618–1631	84–85
980–993	1228–1246	1470–1478	1601–1617	1602–1616	83–84
962–970	1211–1226	1453–1469	1583–1598	1577–1593	82–83
940–960	1190–1209	1430–1451	1561–1576	1569–1576	81–82
920–935	1177–1187	1410–1433	1588–1560	1533–1556	80–81
900–911	1141–1161	1390–1406	1522–1536	1514–1528	79–80
885–899	1120–1140	1367–1389	1501–1519	1495–1512	78–79
860–879	1101–1116	1356–1372	1480–1496	1479–1494	77–78
840–850	1079–1090	1329–1347	1456–1477	1462–1475	76–77
820–830	1057–1071	1311–1328	1448–1454	1444–1460	75–76
799–815	1033–1055	1291–1309	1420–1439	1429–1442	74–75
778–791	1019–1032	1271–1285	1403–1417	1370–1384	73–74
760–775	1003–1022	1251–1260	1389–1391	1352–1359	72–73
737–755	985–993	1230–1248	1339–1363	1325–1340	71–72
720–733	962–983		1341–1347	1306–1321	70–71
701–715	944–961	1187–1208	1313–1320	1286–1300	69–70
680–695	930	1175–1185	1296–1310	1265–1284	68–69
660–664	901–922	1150–1165	1283–1297	1246–1260	67–68
640–650 Armory	Armory		1260–1281	1224–1239	66–67
620–635	868–886	1110–1128	1242–1258	1205–1220	65–66
600–610	841–869	1090–1109	1226–1238	1168–1200	64–65
580–598	824–842	1066–1089	1210–1220	1152–1166	63–64
560–575	803–817	1059–1069	1177–1196	1130–1149	62–63
535–555	784–802	1030–1048	1161–1178	1113–1131	61–62
520–530	770–782	1011–1029	1140–1159	1097–1112	60–61
501–519	738–759	989–1000	Queensboro Br.	Queensboro Br.	59–60
480–500	722–741	972–989	1104–1116	1065–1082	58–59
460–475	700–721	953–968	1083–1101	1058–1063	57–58
434–446	677–698	942–948	1066–1082	1026–1044	56–57
425–430	657–665	914–933	1044–1062	1006–1021	55–56
400–417	641–652	894–908	1024–1042	984–1003	54–55
378–399	617–629	876–895	1003–1027	965–982	53–54
370–375	609–615	855–875	984–1002	945–964	52–53
341–350	575–593	845–850	964–982	930–944	51–52
320–321	557–573	824–835	943–961	891–905	50–51
300 Waldorf	538–556	797–816	923–941	883–890	49–50

37

Streets	Seventh Av	Broadway	Sixth Av	Fifth Av	Madison
48–49	721–740	1591–1611	1221–1237	595–609	412–431
47–48	701–720	1571–1590	1201–1217	579–594	400
46–47		1551–1570	1180–1197	562–578	377–385
45–46	Use	1531–1550	1160–1178	546–560	359–375
44–45	Broadway	1511–1530	1140–1156	530–545	341–356
43–44	Numbers	1499–1512	1120–1136	516–529	333–339
42–43		Times Sq	1100–1119	500–514	315–331
41–42	582–598	1451–1470	1081–1097	461–501	299–315
40–41	560–577	1440–1450	1061–1079	Public Lib.	279–298
39–40	545–558	1412–1430	1040–1056	442–462	265–280
38–39	524–530	1400–1410	1020–1036	425–439	260–261
37–38	500–515	1372–1391	1000–1017	411–420	232–245
36–37	486–499	1350–1370	980–996	392–409	218–229
35–36	462–480	1331–1350	960–977	372–390	200–215
34–35	Macy's	Macy's	Herald Sq	355–371 Altman	185–198
33–34	420–440	1282		339–353 Empire State	169–184
32–33	Penn Sta.	1260–1280	Gimbel's	320–334	152–168
	Mad. Sq. G.				
31–32	383–399	1255–1273	875–892	302–316	134–150
30–31	361–377	1220–1251	855–874	282–300	118–133
29–30	341–360	1200–1227	836–844	267–281	99–117
28–29	319–336	1178–1203	815–832	250–264	79–95
27–28	300–320	1158–1181	795–812	233–249	62–78
26–27	282–299	1140–1158	775–793	213–230	50–60
25–26	262–281	1122–1134	755–773	202–212	27–37
24–25	244–261	1101–1117	740–754	Mad. Sq	11–25
23–24	224–240	1097–1099	716–732	200	1–7
22–23	209–220	945–954	695–712	172–186	
21–22	189–208	922–939	675–692	149–170	
20–21	170–185	902–920	655–672	135–160	
19–20	153–169	889–901	635–650	119–150	
18–19	134–145	873–887	615–632	109–140	
17–18	124–133	857–872	592–612	97–128	
16–17	100–116	21–35	574–590	85–116	
15–16	78–98	13–19	552–571	79–108	
14–15	61–77	1–11	530–549	69–96	

(Union Sq W) marks Broadway 21–35, 13–19, 1–11

EVEN addresses are on the EAST side of:
Broadway, York, West End, Columbus, First, Second, Sixth, Eighth, Ninth & Tenth Avenues

ADDRESS FINDER

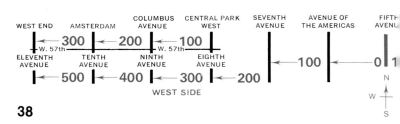

WEST END   AMSTERDAM   COLUMBUS AVENUE   CENTRAL PARK WEST   SEVENTH AVENUE   AVENUE OF THE AMERICAS   FIFTH AVENU

←300   ←200   ←100

W. 57th   W. 57th

ELEVENTH AVENUE   TENTH AVENUE   NINTH AVENUE   EIGHTH AVENUE

←100   ←0 | 1

←500   ←400   ←300   ←200

WEST SIDE

N W—E S

AVENUES FROM 14 TO 96 STS. *(Cont'd)*

	Park Av	Lexington Av	Third Av	Second Av	First Av	Streets
	280–299	518–537	776–796	902–922	861–875	48–49
	270–277	497–515	760–774	883–891	851–U.N.	47–48
	240–250	480–495	741–755	862–877	827–U.N.	46–47
Vanderbilt Av	Pan-Am	459–475	721–735	843–860	805–U.N.	45–46
	Bldg.	441–452	702–716	824–844	785–U.N.	44–45
	Grand	415–435	684–701	806–823	763–U.N.	43–44
	Central	400–416	666–679	793–801	park–U.N.	42–43
	Sta.	374–390	639–655	767–773	Tudor City	41–42
	100–103	355–373	622–633	747–765	702–720	40–41
	90–99	334–353	605–618	728–745	686–700	39–40
	67–80	314–332	579–597	707–724	666–683	38–39
	49–66	296–311	560–576	685–700	646–662	37–38
	40–45	281–288	542–558	666–673	Queens Tun.	36–37
	20–35	264–271	525–541	643–659	624–626	35–36
	5–17	239–253	507–523	623–641	599–611	34–35
	3-4 Armory	220–237	488–504	603–621	577–593	33–34
	1–2	200–218	470–487	585–601		32–33
	Park Av S				Kips Bay	
	461–470	179–196	450–467	563–581	&	31–32
	444–460	160–178	431–449	543–561	N.Y.U.	30–31
	424–431	139–159	415–430	524–541	Hospital	29–30
	403–422	119–138	394–412	500–519	479-Belle-	28–29
	386–401	99–118	375–391	484–498	463-vue	27–28
	363–381	81–98	358–365	462–479	445-Hosp.	26–27
	343–361	61–77	340–355	442–459	429–443	25–26
	323–341	40–57	321–338	420–437	411-427 Vets.	24–25
	303–322	21–39	301–318	401–416	393-409 Hosp.	23–24
	286–308	11–15	288–300	381–398	377-391 Peter	22–23
	268–285	1–8	266–281	362–380	361-375 Cooper	21–22
	251–266		244–261	345–361	345-359 Vill.	20–21
	234–250		226–243	329–343	320-343 Stuy-	19–20
	221–233		205–222	310–327	313-327 vesant	18–19
	213–220		187–203	302–308	303-311 Town	17–18
	184–201		167–177	Stuyvesant	Beth Israel H.	16–17
Union Sq E	20–34		157–165	Square	259–279	15–16
	2–18		125–133	321–240	239–257	14–15

EVEN addresses are on the WEST side of:
Amsterdam, Fifth, Third, Seventh, Madison, Park, Lexington Avenues

CROSSTOWN STREETS

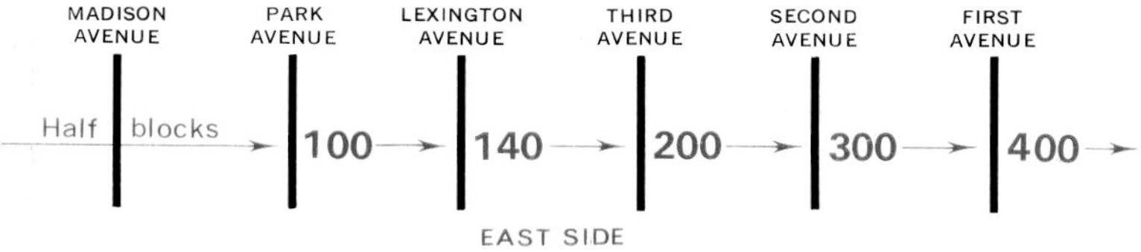

MADISON AVENUE
PARK AVENUE
LEXINGTON AVENUE
THIRD AVENUE
SECOND AVENUE
FIRST AVENUE
Half blocks
100
140
200
300
400
EAST SIDE

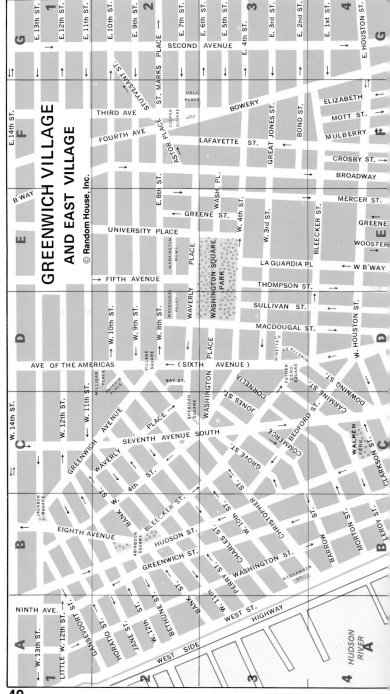

GREENWICH VILLAGE AND EAST VILLAGE STREETS

Street	Map Location	Street	Map Location	Street	Map Location
Abingdon Sq	B-2	Fourteenth St W	C-1	St Luke's Pl	C-4
Astor Place	F-2	Gansevoort St	A-1	St Mark's Pl	F-2
Ave of Americas	D-2	Gay St	D-2	Second Ave	G-2
Bank St	A-2	Great Jones St	F-3	Second St E	G-3
Barrow St	B-4	Greene St	E-2, E-4	Seventh Ave S	C-2
Bedford St	C-3	Greenwich Ave	C-1	Seventh St E	G-2
Bethune St	A-2	Greenwich St	B-2	Sheridan Sq	C-2
Bleecker St	B-2, E-4	Grove St	C-3	Sixth Ave	D-2
Bond St	F-3	Hall Pl	F-2	Sixth St E	G-3
Bowery	F-3	Horatio St	A-2	Stuyvesant St	F-2
Broadway	E-1, F-4	Houston St E	G-4	Sullivan St	D-3
Carmine St	C-4	Houston St W	D-4	Tenth St E	G-2
Charles St	B-3	Hudson St	B-2	Tenth St W	D-2, B-3
Christopher St	B-3	Jackson Sq	B-1	Third Ave	F-2
Clarkson St	C-4	Jane St	A-2	Third St E	G-3
Commerce St	C-3	Jones St	C-3	Third St W	E-3
Cooper Sq	F-2	Lafayette St	F-3	Thirteenth St E	G-1
Cornelia St	D-3	La Guardia Pl	E-3	Thirteenth St W	A-1
Crosby St	F-4	Leroy St	B-4	Thompson St	E-3
Downing St	C-4	Little W 12 St	A-1	Twelfth St E	G-1
Eighth Ave	B-2	Macdougal Alley	D-2	Twelfth St W	C-1, A-2
Eighth St E	E-2	Macdougal St	D-3	University Pl	E-2
Eighth St W	D-2	Mercer St	E-4	Village Sq	D-2
Eleventh St E	G-1	Milligan Pl	D-2	Walker, James Pk	C-4
Eleventh St W	C-1, A-3	Minetta La	D-3	Washington Mews	E-2
Elizabeth St	F-3	Minetta St	D-3	Washington Pl	C-3
Father Demo Sq	D-3	Morton St	B-4	Washington Sq	D, E-3
Fifth Ave	E-2	Mott St	F-4	Washington St	B-3
Fifth St E	G-3	Mulberry St	F-4	Waverly Pl	D, E-2, C-2
First St E	G-4	Ninth Ave	A-1	Weehawken St	B-3
Fourth Ave	F-2	Ninth St E	G-2	West Broadway	E-4
Fourth St E	G-3	Ninth St W	D-2	West Side Hwy	A-2, 3
Fourth St W	E-3, C-2	Patchin Pl	D-2	West St	A-3
Fourteenth St E	F-1	Perry St	B-3	Wooster St	E-4

GREENWICH VILLAGE LANDMARKS * National Historic Landmark

Landmark	Area	Address	Landmark	Area	Address
Bayard Building	F-4	65 Bleecker	MacDougal Alley	D-2	Wash Sq N
Cast Iron Building	F-3	67 E 11th St	New School Soc Res *	D-1	66 W 12th
Charles St House*	B-3	131 Charles	NY Public Theater*	F-3	425 Lafayette
Colonnade Row	F-3	434 Lafyette	NYU Buildings	E-3	Wash Square
Cooper Union*	F-2	7th St/4th Av	Old Merchant's Hse*	F-3	47 Fifth Ave
De Vinne Bldg	F-3	399 Lafayette	Renwick Triangle	F-2	25 Stuyvsnt
English Terrace	D-2	20 W 10th St	Scott, Gen Winfield*	D-1	24 W 12th St
Federal Office Bldg*	B-4	641 Wash St	Stuyvesant-Fish Hse*	F-2	21 Stuyvsnt
Fire House Co 33*	F-3	44 Gt Jones	St. Luke's Place	C-4	Walker Park
Grace Church*	F-2	B'way/E 10	St. Marks in Bowery*	G-2	E 10/2nd Av
Grove Court	C-3	off Grove St	St. Mark's District*	F-2	2/3 av/9-11 st
Grove St Houses	C-3	2-17 Grove	"The Row" Townhses	E-2	Wash Sq N
Isaacs-Hendrick Hse	C-3	77 Bedford	Village Comm Church	C-1	143 W 13th
Jefferson Courthse*	D-2	33 Hudson	Washington Arch	E-3	Wash Sq Pk
Judson Mem Church*	E-3	Wash Square	Washington Mews	E-2	Wash Sq/8th

Crosstown numbers increase from Fifth Ave toward both rivers.
Avenue numbers begin at 0 at Houston St and go up to 250 at 14th street.

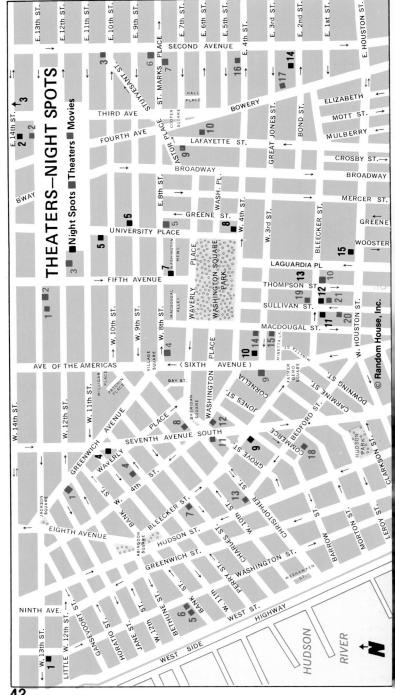

THEATERS–NIGHT SPOTS

■ Night Spots ■ Theaters ■ Movies

© Random House, Inc.

GREENWICH VILLAGE MOVIES

Theater	Address	Map No	Telephone
Art Greenwich Twin	Greenwich & 12th Street	1	929-3350
Bleecker Street 1 & 2	144 Bleecker Street	10	674-2560
Cinema Village	22 East 12th Street	3	924-3363
8th St Playhouse	52 West 8th Street	4	674-6515
Essex	Grand Street at Essex	off	982-4455
Little Theater	425 Lafayette Street	6	598-7150
Movieland 1, 2, 3	University Place & E 8th St	5	477-6600
Quad Cinema 1,2,3,4	34 West 13th Street	2	255-8800
Thalia SoHo	15 Van Dam betw 6th & 7th	off	675-0498
Theater 80 St Marks	80 St Marks Place	7	254-7400
Waverly 1 & 2	Sixth Avenue & 3rd Street	9	929-8037

GREENWICH VILLAGE NIGHT SPOTS

Night Spot	Address	Map No	Telephone
Bitter End	147 Bleecker Street	13	673-7030
Blue Note	131 W 3rd Street	10	475-8592
Bottom Line Cabaret	15 West 4th Street	8	228-6300
Bradley's	70 University Place	5	228-6440
CBGB	315 Bowery	14	473-7743
Club Mars	Tenth Ave at 13th Street	1	691-6262
Fat Tuesday's	190 Third Ave at 17th St	3	533-7902
Knickerbocker Saloon	33 University Place	6	228-8490
Knitting Factory	47 E Houston	15	869-5800
One Fifth Avenue	Fifth Avenue & 8th Street	7	260-3434
Palladium	126 East 14th Street	2	473-7171
Ritz	254 W 54th Street	off	541-8900
Sweet Basil	88 Seventh Avenue South	9	242-1785
Village Corner	142 Bleecker Street	11	473-9762
Village Gate	Bleecker & Thompson St	12	475-5120
Village Vanguard	178 Seventh Ave S at 11th	4	255-4037

OFF BROADWAY THEATERS

Theater	Address	Map No	Telephone
Actors Playhouse	100 Seventh Ave South	11	691-6226
Astor Place Playhouse	434 Lafayette Street	9	254-4370
Cherry Lane	38 Commerce Street	18	989-2020
Circle in Square D'town	159 Bleecker Street	19	254-6330
Circle Repertory Company	99 Seventh Ave South	12	924-7100
CSC Repertory	136 E 13th Street	2	677-4210
Fourth Wall Theater	79 E 4th Street	16	254-5060
Jean Cocteau Repertory	330 Bowery	17	677-0060
La Mama	74 E 4th Street	16	475-7710
Lucille Lortel	121 Christopher Street	13	924-8782
Minetta Lane	18 Minetta Lane	15	420-8000
Orpheum	126 Second Avenue	3	477-2477
Perry Street	31 Perry Street	4	255-7190
Players	115 Macdougal Street	15	254-5076
Provincetown Playhouse	133 Macdougal Street	14	477-5048
Public Theater Complex (5 theaters)	425 Lafayette	10	598-7150
Ridiculous-Charles Ludlam	1 Sheridan Square	8	691-2271
Riverwest	155 Bank Street	5	243-0359
Sullivan Street	181 Sullivan Street	20	674-3838
13th Street	50 W 13th Street	1	675-6677
Top of the Gate	160 Bleecker Street	21	475-5120
Trocadero	91 Charles Street	7	242-0636
Westbeth Theater Center	151 Bank Street	6	862-7230

BROADWAY THEATERS pg 28 — other OFF BROADWAY THEATERS pg 46 **43**

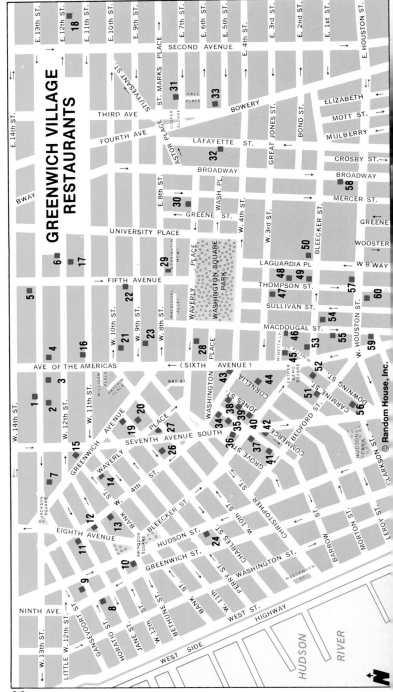

GREENWICH VILLAGE RESTAURANTS

© Random House, Inc.

GREENWICH VILLAGE RESTAURANTS — BY MAP NOS.

1 Spain	21 Texarkana	42 Manhattan Chili Co
2 Zinno	22 Mosaico	43 Tio Pepe
3 La Tulipe	23 Bondini's	44 Sabor
4 La Gauloise	24 Sazerac/Village	45 La Boheme
5 Sofi's	26 Sevilla	46 Minetta Tavern
6 Asti	27 John Clancy	47 Il Mulino
7 Cafe de Bruxelles	27 La Metaire	48 Livorno
8 El Faro	28 Coach House	49 Grand Ticino
9 Astray Cafe	29 One Fifth	49 Rincon de Espana
10 La Ripaille	30 Garvin's	50 Ennio & Michael
11 Jane St Sfd	31 McSorley's	51 Mary's
12 Beatrice Inn	32 Indochine	52 Cent'Anni
13 La Chaumiere	33 Hisae's Place	53 Da Silvano
14 Ye Waverly Inn	34 Riviera Cafe	54 Le Figaro
15 Elephant & Castle	35 One If By Land	55 Villa Mosconi
16 Gene's	36 Il Bufalo	56 Rakel/Urbino
17 Gotham Bar/Grill	37 Mitali West	57 Arturo's
18 John's	38 Bianchi & Margherita	58 Gonzalez y Gonz
19 Angelina's	40 Vanessa	59 Provence
20 El Charro	41 Melrose	60 Monsoon

GREENWICH VILLAGE RESTAURANTS

Restaurant	Address	Map No	Cuisine	Avg Price ★	Telephone
Angelina's	41 Greenwich	19	Italian	$15-20	929-1255
Arturo's	106 W Houston	57	Italian	15-20	677-3820
Asti	13 E 12th	6	Italian	25-40	255-9095
Astray Cafe	59 Horatio	9	American	20-25	741-7030
Beatrice Inn	285 W 12th	12	Italian	18-23	929-6165
Bianchi & Margherita	186 W 4th	38	Italian	20-25	242-2756
Bondini's	62 W 9th	23	N Italian	25-35	777-0670
Cafe de Bruxelles	118 Greenwich Av	7	Fr/Belgium	25-30	206-1830
Cent'Anni	50 Carmine St	52	Italian	35-40	989-9494
Coach House	110 Waverly Pl	28	American	32-38	777-0303
Da Silvano	260 Ave Americas	53	N Italian	35-40	982-2343
El Charro	4 Charles	20	Mex/Spain	15-20	242-9547
El Faro	823 Greenwich	8	Spanish	20-25	929-8210
Elephant & Castle	68 Greenwich	15	American	12-15	243-1400
Ennio & Michael	539 La Guardia Pl	50	Italian	17-30	677-8577
Garvins	19 Waverly Pl	30	Amer/Contl	25-35	473-5261
Gene's	73 W 11th	16	Ital/Contl	20-25	675-2048
Gonzalez y Gonzalez	625 Broadway	58	Spanish	15-19	473-8787
Gotham Bar & Grill	12 E 12th St	17	Amer/Fr	50-60	620-4020
Grand Ticino	228 Thompson	49	Italian	20-25	777-5922
Hisae's Place	35 Cooper Sq	33	Japanese	15-18	228-6886
Il Bufalo	87 Seventh Ave	36	Italian	30-35	243-8000
Il Mulino	86 W 3rd St	47	N Italian	75-80	673-3783
Indochine	430 Lafayette	32	Viet/Camb	25-30	505-5111
Jane St Seafood Cafe	31 Eighth Ave	11	Seafood	20-25	243-9237
John Clancy's	181 W 10th	27	Seafood	40-45	242-7350
John's	302 E 12th	18	N Italian	20-25	475-9531
La Boheme	24 Minetta Ln	45	French	25-30	473-6447
La Chaumiere	310 W 4th St	13	French	20-25	741-3374
La Gauloise	502 Ave Americas	4	French	35-40	691-1363
La Metairie	189 W 10th St	27	French	35-45	989-0343
La Ripaille	605 Hudson	10	French	25-30	255-4406
La Tulipe	104 W 13th	3	French	62.50	691-8860
Le Figaro	186 Bleecker	54	American	9-12	677-1100
Livorno	216 Thompson	48	Italian	15-20	260-1972

★ Prices do not include drinks or gratuities

GREENWICH VILLAGE RESTAURANTS Continued

Restaurant	Address	Map No	Cuisine	Avg Price ★	Telephone
Manhattan Chili Co	302 Bleecker St	42	South West	$15-20	206-7163
Mary's	42 Bedford	51	Italian	20-25	741-3387
McSorley's	15 E 7th	31	American	6-10	473-9148
Melrose	48 Barrow St	41	New Amer	40-45	691-6800
Minetta Tavern	113 Macdougal	46	Italian	20-25	475-3850
Mitali West	296 Bleecker St	37	Indian	15-20	989-1367
Monsoon	128 W Houston	60	American	8-10	674-4080
Mosaico	24 Fifth Ave	22	N Italian	25-30	529-5757
One Fifth	1 Fifth Ave	29	Steak	20-25	260-3434
One If By Land	17 Barrow	35	Amer/Contl	40-50	228-0822
Provence	38 Macdougal St	59	French	25-35	475-7500
Rakel	231 Varick St	56	French	55-65	929-1630
Rincon de Espana	226 Thompson	49	Spanish	15-20	475-9891
Riviera Cafe	225 W 4th St	34	Mex/Amer	20-25	242-8732
Sabor	20 Cornelia	44	Cuban	20-30	243-9579
Sazerac House	533 Hudson St	24	Amer Cajun	15-25	989-0313
Sevilla	62 Charles	26	Spanish	20-25	929-3189
Sofi's	102 Fifth Ave	5	American	40-50	463-8888
Spain	113 W 13th	1	Spanish	10-15	929-9580
Texarkana	64 W 10th	21	American	18-25	254-5800
Tio Pepe	168 W 4th	43	Spanish	10-20	242-9338
Urbino	78 Carmine St	56	Italian	30-35	242-2676
Vanessa	289 Bleecker	40	Continental	45-55	243-4225
Villa Mosconi	59 MacDougal St	55	N Italian	20-30	673-0390
Village Green	531 Hudson St	24	New Amer	45.00	255-1650
Ye Waverly Inn	16 Bank	14	American	20-30	243-9396
Zinno	126 W 13th	2	N Italian	35-40	924-5182

★ *Prices do not include drinks or gratuities*

OFF BROADWAY THEATERS (Not in Greenwich Village)

Theater	Address	Type	Telephone
Actors & Directors	412 W 42nd	Experimental workshops	695-5429
Apollo Theater	253 W 125th St	A theatrical landmark	749-5838
Beacon Theater	2124 Broadway	Revivals, musicals, revues	496-7070
Chelsea Playhouse	519 W 23rd	Actors' workshop	243-0397
Delacorte	Central Pk at 81	Shakespearean plays	861-7277
Douglas Fairbanks	432 W 42nd	Varied productions	239-4321
18th St Playhouse	145 W 18th	Drama comdy mime musicl	695-2884
Harold Clurman	412 W 42nd	Experimental	695-3401
Henry St Settlement	466 Grand	Dramatic workshop	598-0400
Hudson Guild	441 W 26th	Varied productions	760-9810
Improvisation	358 W 44th	Comedy sketches	765-8268
INTAR	420 W 42nd	Dramas, musicals	279-4200
John Houseman	450 W 42nd St	Drama, workshops, rep	564-8038
Joyce Theater	175 Eighth Ave	Varied productions	242-0800
Manhattan Theater Club	131 W 55th	Repertory	581-7907
Performing Garage	33 Wooster St	Experimental repertory	966-3651
Playhouse 91	316 E 91st	Light Opera of Manhattan	831-2000
Playwrights Horizons	416 W 42nd	Drama, revivals	279-4200
Promenade Theater	B'way at 76th	Drama, varied productions	580-1313
Roundabout Theatre	100 E 17th	Repertory	420-1883
SoHo Repertory	80 Varick	Revivals repertory	925-2588
Symphony Space	2537 B'way	Concerts, variety	864-5400
Theater at St Peter's	Citicorp-619 Lex	Drama, readings, music	751-9436
Theatre for New City	155 1st Ave	Varied productions	254-1109
Theater Four	424 W 55th	Negro Ensemble Co	246-8545
UBU Repertory	15 W 28th St	Readings transl Fr plays	679-7540
Westside Arts	407 W 43rd	Drama comedy	541-8394

GREENWICH VILLAGE
(See map page 40)
Random House, Inc.
SOHO · THE BOWERY · LITTLE ITALY · CHINATOWN · TRiBeCa · CIVIC CENTER

RESTAURANTS—CHINATOWN, LITTLE ITALY, SOHO

Restaurant	Address	Map No	Cuisine	Avg Price ★	Telephone
Angelo of Mulberry	146 Mulberry St	14	Italian	$25-35	966-1277
Antica Roma	40 Mulberry St	24	Italian	20-25	267-2242
Ballato's	55 E Houston	3	N. Italian	25-35	226-9683
Barocco	301 Church St	16	Italian	30-50	431-1445
Berry's	180 Spring St	7	Continental	20-30	226-4394
Bouley	165 Duane St	18	Fr Contl	45-65	608-3852
Broome St Bar	363 W Broadway	9	American	10-12	925-2086
Chanterelle	2 Harrison St	17	French	68-87	966-6960
Giambone	42 Mulberry St	23	Italian	15-20	285-1277
Great Shanghai	27 Division	29	Chinese	15-25	966-7663
Greene Street Cafe	101 Greene St	6	Fr/Amer	25-35	925-2415
Grotta Azzurra	387 Broome St	10	Italian	30-35	925-8775
Hee Seung Fung	46 Bowery	21	Chinese	16.95	374-1319
Hunan House	45 Mott St	20	Chinese	12-16	962-0010
I Tre Merli	463 W B'way	1	Italian	35-40	254-8699
Jerry's	101 Prince St	2	American	25-30	966-9494
Mandarin Inn	34 Pell St	25	Chinese	8-14	962-9061
Mezzogiorno	195 Spring St	5	N Italian	35-40	334-2112
Montrachet	239 W Broadway	15	French	25-45	219-2777
Odeon	145 W Broadway	19	Fr Amer	30-35	233-0507
Peking Duck	22 Mott St	26	Peking	15-25	962-8208
Raoul's	180 Prince St	4	French	45 +	966-3518
Ristorante SPQR	133 Mulberry	13	Italian	30-45	925-3120
Ruggero	194 Grand St	11	Italian	25-30	925-1340
Say Eng Look	5 E Broadway	28	Chinese	10-15	732-0796
Spring Street	62 Spring St	8	Natural Food	10-15	966-0290
Taormina	147 Mulberry	12	Italian	30-35	219-1007
20 Mott	20 Mott St	27	Chinese	15-25	964-0380
Villa Pensa	198 Grand St	11	Italian	25-30	966-5620

★ Prices do not include drinks or gratuities

47

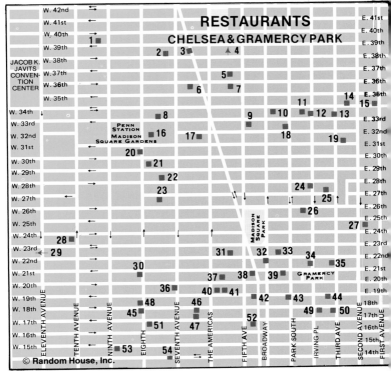

RESTAURANTS
CHELSEA & GRAMERCY PARK

RESTAURANTS—BY MAP NUMBERS

RESTAURANTS WITH A VIEW

48

RESTAURANTS— CHELSEA, GRAMERCY PK, KIPPS BAY

Restaurant	Address	Map No.	Cuisine	Average Price ★	Telephone
America	9 E 18th Street	42	American	$25-30	505-2110
American Place	2 Park Avenue	18	American	35-55	684-2122
Back Porch, The	488 Third Avenue	13	Continental	20-25	685-3828
Ballroom	253 W 28th St	22	Span/Contl	25-35	244-3005
Brandywine	274 Third Ave	35	Steak	25-40	353-8190
Cafe du Parc	106 E 19th Street	44	French	30-35	777-7840
Canastel's	229 Park Ave S	43	N Italian	35-45	677-9622
Charley O's	Madison Sq Garden	16	Irish Amer	15-20	947-0222
Chelsea Central	227 Tenth Ave	28	American	30-35	620-0301
Chelsea Trattoria Ital	108 Eighth Ave	51	Italian	30-35	924-7786
Claires	156 Seventh Ave	36	Seafood	30-35	255-1955
Club 1407	1407 Broadway	3	American	15-20	575-1407
Da Umberto	107 W 17th St	47	N Italian	25-30	989-0303
Dino Casini's	132 W 32nd Street	17	Ital Contl	15-25	695-7995
Dolphin	227 Lexington	12	Seafood	25-30	689-3010
El Parador	325 E 34th Street	15	Mexican	15-20	679-6812
Estoril Sol	382 Eighth Ave	21	Portuguese	18-22	947-1043
Giordano	409 W 39th Street	1	Italian	30-35	947-9811
Harvey's Chelsea	108 W 18th Street	46	American	20-25	243-5644
Hideaway	32 W 37th Street	5	Amer/Ital	32.50	947-8940
Hunan Fifth Ave	323 Fifth Ave	9	Chinese	15-20	686-3366
Il Galletto	120 E 34th Street	11	Italian	25-30	889-1990
Kaspar's	250 W 27th Street	23	Continental	25-30	989-3804
Keens Chop House	72 W 36th Street	7	American	55-65	947-3636
La Colombe d'Or	134 E 26th Street	26	French	35-45	689-0666
La Petite Auberge	116 Lexington	24	French	25-30	689-5003
Lavin's	23 W 39th St	4	American	45-50	921-1288
Le Parc	Gramery Pk Hotel	34	Continental	18-26	475-4320
Lino's	147 W 36th Street	6	N Italian	20-35	695-6444
Lola's	30 W 22nd St	31	Amer/Carib	30-35	675-6700
Lou G. Siegel	209 W 38th Street	2	Kosher	20-28	921-4433
Man-Ray	169 Eighth Ave	48	French	25-35	627-4220
Marchi's	251 E 31 Street	19	Italian	28.75	679-2494
Maurya Indian	129 E 27th Street	25	Indian	14-18	689-7925
Nanou	24 E 21st Street	38	Fr/Mediter	30-35	505-5252
Nicola Paone	207 E 34th Street	14	Italian	50-55	889-3239
Old Homestead	56 Ninth Avenue	53	American	16-30	242-9040
Ole	434 Second Ave	27	Spanish	15-20	725-1953
Onini	217 Eighth Avenue	30	Italian	20-25	243-6446
Periyali	35 W 20th St	37	Greek	25-35	463-7890
Pesca	23 E 22nd St	33	Seafood	30-35	533-2293
Portfolio	4 W 19th St	41	Amer Contl	25-35	691-3845
Positano	250 Park Ave S	39	N Italian	30-35	777-6211
Quatorze	240 W 14th Street	54	French	25-35	206-7006
Rascals	12 E 22nd St	32	American	15-20	420-1777
Riveranda/Empress NY	Pier 62 & Hudson	29	Continental	59-65	929-8540
Rogers & Barbero	149 Eighth Ave	45	American	20-30	243-2020
Sal Anthony's	55 Irving Place	49	Italian	20-26	982-9030
Salta in Bocca	179 Madison Ave	10	N Italian	35-45	684-1757
San Remo	393 Eighth Ave	20	N Italian	25-35	564-1819
Singalong	17 W 19th Street	40	American	15-20	206-8660
Toots Shor	233 W 33rd Street	8	American	35-40	279-8150
Tuesday's	190 Third Avenue	50	American	10-15	533-7900
Union Square Cafe	21 E 16th Street	52	Ital/French	25-30	243-4020

★ Prices do not include drinks or gratuities

49

MADISON AVENUE SHOPS

Map (Madison Avenue):

72ND

CACHE CACHE 1
LANVIN 2
3 POLO/RALPH LAUREN

71ST

PIERRE DEUX 4
MATSUDA 5
6 ST LAURENT RIVE GAUCHE

70TH

CARTIER 7
MISSONI 8
9 MADISON BOOKSHOP
10 LANVIN
11 PRATESI

69TH

KENZO 12
JAEGER 13
GIANNI VERSACE 14
15 VALENTINO
16 SIR DAVID
17 VENEZIANO
18 G. ARMANI
19 PERRIS

68TH

TAHARI 20
VERI UOMO 21
BALOGH 22
23 CERUTTI KRIZIA
24 E UNGARO
25 D.CENCI
26 PIERRE BALMAIN

67TH

S RYKIEL 27
THAXTON 28
N BEACH 29
30 CIRO
31 MONTENA-POLEONE
32 FRED LEIGHTON

66TH

AVENUE

MADISON

33 CHARLES JOURDAN
34 L.S COLLECTION

65TH

ANDREA CARRANO 35
BETSEY BUNKY NINI 36
RODIER 37
38 WALTER STEIGER
39 MANFREDI

64TH

LAURA ASHLEY 40
COACH 41
42 PILAR ROSSI
43 LA BAGAGE
44 SPREI FRER
45 BRAUN
46 DES CHAMPS
47 LOEWE

63RD

LANCEL 48
49 FURLA
50 FLORIS
51 AVENUE MONTAIGNE
52 THE LIMITED

62ND

CHRISTOFLE 53
PERRY ELLIS SHOES 54
LALIQUE 55
56 BALLY
57 JULIE
58 GEO JENSEN
59 SHERRY LEHMANN

61ST

60TH © Random House, Inc.

50

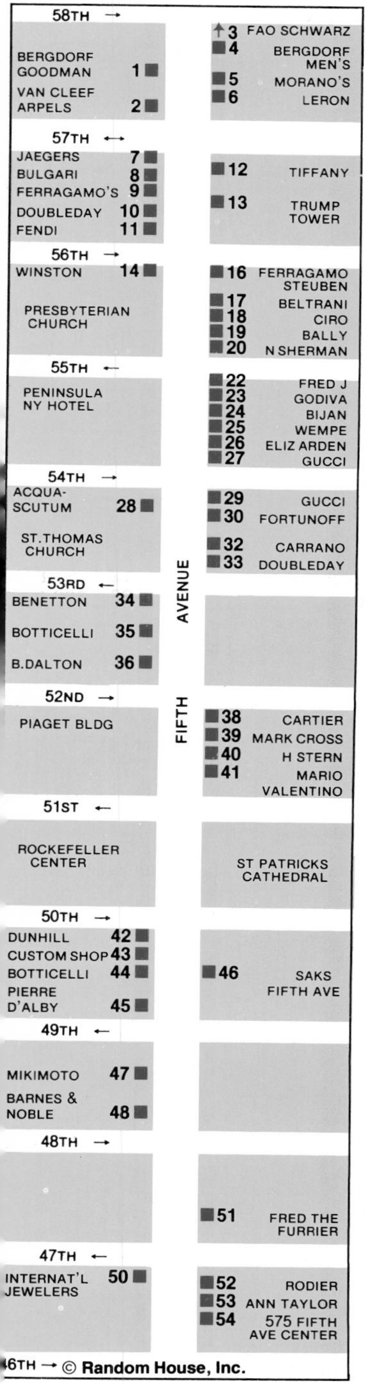
58TH →
BERGDORF GOODMAN 1
VAN CLEEF ARPELS 2
↑3 FAO SCHWARZ
4 BERGDORF MEN'S
5 MORANO'S
6 LERON
57TH ↔
JAEGERS 7
BULGARI 8
FERRAGAMO'S 9
DOUBLEDAY 10
FENDI 11
12 TIFFANY
13 TRUMP TOWER
56TH →
WINSTON 14
PRESBYTERIAN CHURCH
16 FERRAGAMO STEUBEN
17 BELTRANI
18 CIRO
19 BALLY
20 N SHERMAN
55TH ←
PENINSULA NY HOTEL
22 FRED J
23 GODIVA
24 BIJAN
25 WEMPE
26 ELIZ ARDEN
27 GUCCI
54TH →
ACQUA-SCUTUM 28
ST.THOMAS CHURCH
29 GUCCI
30 FORTUNOFF
32 CARRANO
33 DOUBLEDAY
53RD ←
BENETTON 34
BOTTICELLI 35
B.DALTON 36
FIFTH AVENUE
52ND →
PIAGET BLDG
38 CARTIER
39 MARK CROSS
40 H STERN
41 MARIO VALENTINO
51ST ←
ROCKEFELLER CENTER
ST PATRICKS CATHEDRAL
50TH →
DUNHILL 42
CUSTOM SHOP 43
BOTTICELLI 44
PIERRE D'ALBY 45
46 SAKS FIFTH AVE
49TH ←
MIKIMOTO 47
BARNES & NOBLE 48
48TH →
51 FRED THE FURRIER
47TH ←
INTERNAT'L JEWELERS 50
52 RODIER
53 ANN TAYLOR
54 575 FIFTH AVE CENTER
46TH →
© Random House, Inc.

FIFTH AVENUE SHOPS

Shop	*Map No.*	*Telephone*
Acquascutum	28	975-0250
Ann Taylor	53	972-0045
Bally	19	751-9082
Barnes & Noble	48	765-0590
Beltrani	17	838-4101
Benetton	34	399-9860
Bergdorf Goodman	1	753-7300
Bergdorf Men's Shop	4	753-7300
Bijan	24	758-7500
Botticelli	35	582-2984
Botticelli	44	582-6313
Bulgari	8	486-0086
Carrano	32	752-6111
Cartier	38	753-0111
Chandler Shoes	25	688-2140
Ciro	18	752-0441
Custom Shop	43	245-2499
Dalton Books	36	247-1740
Doubleday Books	10	397-0550
Doubleday Books	33	223-6550
Dunhill	42	489-5580
Elizabeth Arden	26	407-7900
Ferragamo's	16	759-3822
Ferragamo's	9	246-6211
575 Fifth Ave Center	54	986-4676
Fortunoff	30	758-6660
Fred Joaillier	22	832-3733
Fred the Furrier	51	765-3877
Godiva	23	593-2845
Gucci	27	826-2600
Gucci	29	826-2600
International Jewelers	50	869-1528
Jaegers	7	753-0370
Leron	6	753-6700
Mark Cross	39	421-3000
Mikimoto	47	586-7153
Morano's	5	751-7750
Nat Sherman	20	751-9100
Pierre d'Alby	45	541-7110
Rodier	52	599-2495
Saks Fifth Ave	46	753-4000
Schwarz, FAO	3	644-9410
Stern, H	40	688-0300
Steuben Glass	16	752-1441
Tiffany	12	755-8000
Valentino, Mario	41	486-0322
Van Cleef & Arpels	2	644-9500
Wempe	25	751-4884
Winston, Harry	14	245-2000
Trump Tower Shops:	13	

Abrcrmbie	832-1001	**Cartier**	308-0840
Asprey	688-1811	**Cashmere**	758-7621
Beauty Bst	888-4848	**Fred Leigh**	721-2330
Boehm	838-1562	**Gior Pap**	644-6552
Buccellati	308-5533	**Martha**	826-8855
C Jourdan	644-3830	**Pet. Etoil**	371-0388

OTHER MAJOR STORES PAGE 52

OTHER MAJOR STORES & CENTERS

Abraham & Strauss	899 Ave of the Americas	594-8500
B. Altman	Fifth Ave at 34th Street	689-7000
Barney's	106 Seventh Ave at 17th Street	929-9000
Bendel, Henri	10 W 57th Street	247-1100
Bloomingdales	1000 Third Ave at 59th Street	355-5900
Bonwit Tellers	4 E 57th Street	593-3333
Brooks Brothers	346 Madison Ave at 44th Street	682-8800
Georg Jensen	683 Madison Avenue	759-6457
Hammacher Schlemmer	147 E 57th-betw Lexington & Third Ave	421-9000
Herald Center	Broadway at 34th St-8 FLOORS	714-2530
Lord & Taylor	Fifth Ave & 38th Street	391-3344
Macy's	Broadway & 34th St-Herald Square	971-6000
Market at Citicorp Center	Lexington & 53rd Street-13 SHOPS	559-2330
Place des Antiquaires	125 E 57th Street-75 SHOPS	758-2900
South Street Seaport	Front & Water Street-110 SHOPS	732-7678
Strand Bookstore	828 Broadway at 12th Street	473-1452
World Financial Center	Hudson River betw Vesey & Liberty-25 SHOPS	945-0505
World Trade Concourse	1 World Trade Center-60 SHOPS	466-4170

GLOSSARY

	French	German	Italian	Spanish	Russian
Architecture	Architecture	Architektur	Architettura	Arquitectura	Архитектура
Art	Art	Kunst	Arte	Arte	Искусство
Buses	Autobus	Autobusse	Autobus	Autobús	Автóбусы
Churches	Églises	Kirchen	Chiese	Iglesias	Церкви
Colleges	Universités	Universitäten	Università	Universidades	Университеты
Embassies	Ambassades	Botschaften	Ambasciate	Embajadas	Посольства
Emergency Numbers	Numéros d'urgence	Notnummern	Numeri d'emergenza		Телефоны скорой
Galleries	Galléries	Gallerien	Galleria	Galería	Галлереи
History	Histoire	Geschichte	Storia	Istoria	Истóрия
Highways	Grandes Routes	Landstrassen	Autostrade	Carreteras	Дороги
Hospitals	Hopîtaux	Krankenhäuser	Ospedali	hospital	Больницы
Hotels	Hôtels	Hotels	Hotel	Hotel	Гостиницы
Libraries	Bibliotèques	Bibliotheken	Biblioteche	Bibliotecas	Биóлиотеки
Museums	Musées	Museen	Musei	Museos	Музеи
Music	Musique	Musik	Musica	Musica	Музыка
Movies	Cinémas	Filme	Cinema	Películas	Кино
Parks	Parcs	Parks	Giardini Publici	Parques	Парки
Restaurants	Restaurants	Restaurants	Ristoranti	Restaurantes	Рестораны
Science	Science	Wissenschaft	Scienza	Ciencia	Наука
Shops	Grands Magasins	Einkaufen	Negozi	Negocios	Покупки— Магазипы
Sports	Sports	Sport	Sport	Desportes	спорт
Subways	Métro	Untergrundbahnen	Metropolitana	Subterráneo	Метро
Taxi	Taxi	Taxi	Tassì	Taxi	Такси
Theaters	Théâtres	Theater	Teatri	Teatros	Театры
Zoo	Zoo	Zoo	Giardino Zoologico	Jardín Zoológico	Зоологическ

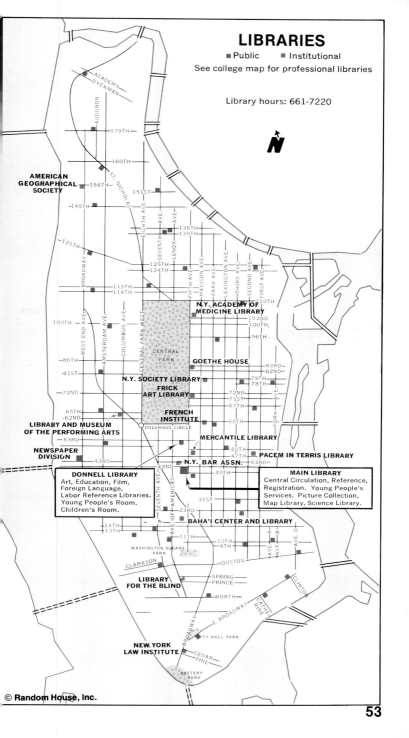

LIBRARIES

■ Public ■ Institutional

See college map for professional libraries

Library hours: 661-7220

AMERICAN GEOGRAPHICAL SOCIETY

N.Y. ACADEMY OF MEDICINE LIBRARY

GOETHE HOUSE

CENTRAL PARK

N.Y. SOCIETY LIBRARY

FRICK ART LIBRARY

FRENCH INSTITUTE

LIBRARY AND MUSEUM OF THE PERFORMING ARTS

MERCANTILE LIBRARY

NEWSPAPER DIVISION

PACEM IN TERRIS LIBRARY

N.Y. BAR ASSN.

DONNELL LIBRARY
Art, Education, Film, Foreign Language, Labor Reference Libraries. Young People's Room. Children's Room.

MAIN LIBRARY
Central Circulation, Reference, Registration. Young People's Services. Picture Collection, Map Library, Science Library.

BAHA'I CENTER AND LIBRARY

WASHINGTON SQUARE PARK

LIBRARY FOR THE BLIND

NEW YORK LAW INSTITUTE

BATTERY PARK

© Random House, Inc.

53

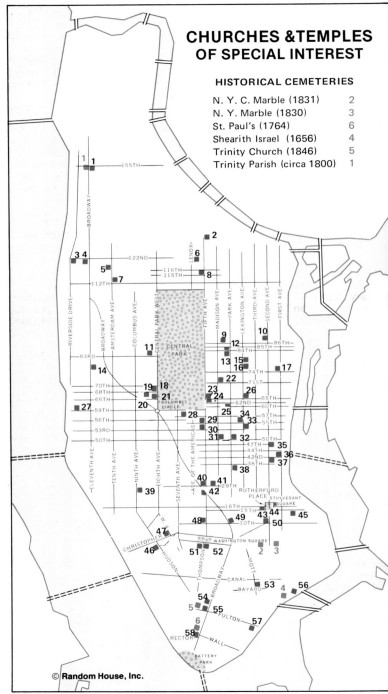

CHURCHES & TEMPLES
OF SPECIAL INTEREST

HISTORICAL CEMETERIES

N. Y. C. Marble (1831)	2
N. Y. Marble (1830)	3
St. Paul's (1764)	6
Shearith Israel (1656)	4
Trinity Church (1846)	5
Trinity Parish (circa 1800)	1

© Random House, Inc.

54

CHURCHES & TEMPLES OF SPECIAL INTEREST

(In Manhattan there are over 1200 houses of worship, representing 100 denominations)

1 Church Intercession
2 St. Andrew's
3 Riverside
4 Union Theological
5 St. Paul's Chapel
6 St. Martin's
7 St. John the Divine
8 Church of Brethren
9 Park Av Synagogue
10 Holy Trinity
11 Congr Rodeph Sholom
12 Park Ave Christian
13 St. Ignatius Loyola
14 West End Collegiate
15 All Souls Unitarian
16 St. Jean Baptiste
17 Holy Trinity Greek
18 Spanish Synagogue
19 Church of LDS

20 Stephen Wise Syn
21 Holy Trinity
22 St. James Episcopal
23 Temple Emanu-El
24 Fifth Av Synagogue
25 Christ Church
26 St. Vincent Ferrer
27 St. Paul the Apostle
28 Calvary Baptist
29 Fifth Av Presbyterian
30 St. Thomas
31 St. Patrick's
32 St. Bartholomew's
33 St. Peter's
34 Central Synagogue
35 Holy Family
36 Church of UN
37 Church of Covenant
38 Church of Our Savior

39 Church Holy Apostles
40 Marble Collegiate
41 Ltle Church Arnd Cor
42 Cathedral St. Sava
43 Friends Meeting Hse
44 St. George's
45 Immaculate Conceptn
46 St. Luke's Chapel
47 St.John's Evangelical
48 Church of Ascension
49 Grace Church
50 St. Mark's-Bouwerie
51 Judson Memorial
52 Holy Trinity Chapel
54 St. Peter's
55 St. Paul's Chapel
56 St. James R.C.
57 John St Methodist
58 Trinity Church

CHURCHES & TEMPLES

Church	Address	Map No.	Telephone
All Souls Unitarian	1157 Lexington Ave	15	535-5530
Calvary Baptist	123 W 57th Street	28	975-0170
Cathedral of St. John Divine (Episcopal) ★	Amsterdam & 112th	7	316-7400
Cathedral of St. Sava (Serbian Orthodox)	15 W 25th Street	42	242-9240
Central Synagogue (1870)	652 Lex Ave at 55th	34	838-5122
Christ Church (Methodist)	520 Park Avenue	25	838-3036
Church of Ascension (Episcopal)	Fifth Ave & 10th St	48	254-8620
Church of Brethren	27 W 115th Street	8	369-2620
Church of Latter Day Saints (Mormon)	2 Lincoln Square	19	595-1825
Church of Our Savior (Roman Catholic)	59 Park Avenue	38	679-8166
Church of the Covenant (Presbyterian)	310 E 42nd Street	37	697-3185
Church of the Intercession (Episcopal)	Broadway & 155th St	1	283-6200
Church of the UN (Non-denominational)	777 U N Plaza	36	661-1762
Congregation Rodeph Sholom	7 W 83rd Street	11	362-8800
Fifth Avenue Presbyterian	Fifth Ave & 55th St	29	247-0490
Fifth Avenue Synagogue	5 E 62nd Street	24	838-2122
Friends Meeting House (1861)	15 Rutherford Place	43	777-8866
Grace Church (Episcopal-1843)	802 Broadway	49	254-2000
Holy Apostles (Roman Catholic-1840)	296 Ninth Ave	39	807-6799
Holy Family (Roman Catholic)	315 E 47th Street	35	753-3401
Holy Trinity Cathedral (Greek Orthodox)	319 E 74th Street	17	288-3215
Holy Trinity Chapel (Roman Catholic)	Washington Square S	52	674-7236
Holy Trinity (Episcopal-1897)	316 E 88th Street	10	289-4100
Holy Trinity (Lutheran)	Central Pk W & 65th	21	877-6815
Immaculate Conception (Roman Cath.)	414 E 14th Street	45	254-0200
John Street Methodist (1841)	44 John Street	57	269-0014
Judson Memorial Baptist (1890)	55 Washington Sq S	51	477-0351
Little Church Around the Corner	1 E 29th Street	41	684-6770
Marble Collegiate (1854)	Fifth Ave & 29th St	40	686-2770
Park Avenue Christian	1010 Park Avenue	12	288-3246
Park Avenue Synagogue	50 E 87th Street	9	369-2600
Riverside (Non-denominational)	Riverside Dr & 122nd	3	222-5900
Spanish & Portuguese Synagogue	8 W 70th Street	18	873-0300
St. Andrew's (Episcopal-1889)	Fifth Ave & 127th St	2	534-0896
St. Bartholomew's (Episcopal-1917)	109 E 50th Street	32	751-1616

★ *largest Gothic cathedral in the world—10,000 worshippers*

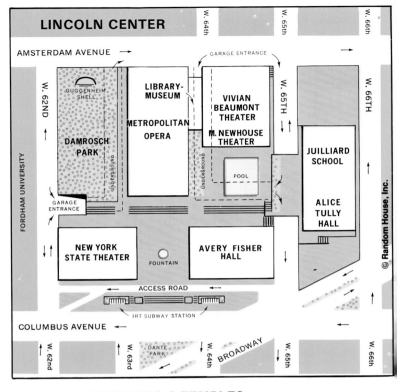

CHURCHES & TEMPLES (Continued)

Church	Address	Map No.	Telephone
St. George's (Episcopal-1846)	209 E 16th Street	44	475-0830
St. Ignatius Loyola (Roman Catholic-1895)	980 Park Avenue	13	288-3588
St. James (Episcopal)	865 Madison Ave	22	288-4100
St. James (Roman Catholic)	23 Oliver Street	56	233-0161
St. Jean Baptiste (Roman Catholic-1910)	184 E 76th Street	16	288-5082
St. John's Lutheran	81 Christopher St	47	242-5737
St. Luke's Chapel (Episcopal)	487 Hudson St	46	924-0562
St. Mark's in the Bowery (Episc-1799)	Second Ave & 10th	50	674-6377
St. Martin's Episcopal (1887)	230 Lenox Avenue	6	534-4531
St. Patrick's Cathedral (Catholic-1858)	Fifth Ave & 50th	31	753-2261
St. Paul the Apostle (Roman Catholic)	415 W 59th Street	27	265-3209
St. Paul's Chapel at Columbia (1904)	Broadway & 116th	5	854-6625
St. Paul's Chapel (Episcopal-1764) ★	Broadway & Fulton	55	602-0874
St. Peter's (Lutheran-1977)	619 Lexington Ave	33	935-2200
St. Peter's (Roman Catholic-1836)	16 Barclay Street	54	233-8355
St. Thomas (Episcopal-1909)	Fifth Ave & 53rd	30	757-7013
St. Vincent Ferrer (Roman Catholic-1918)	Lexington & 66th	26	744-2080
Stephen Wise Free Synagogue	30 W 68th Street	20	877-4050
Temple Emanu-El (1930)	1 E 65th Street	23	744-1400
Trinity Church (Episcopal-1846)	74 Trinity Place	58	602-0800
Union Theological Lampman Chapel	Broadway & 120th	4	662-7100
West End Collegiate (1892)	West End & 77th	14	787-1566

56   ★ *Site of Washington's first Inaugural address*

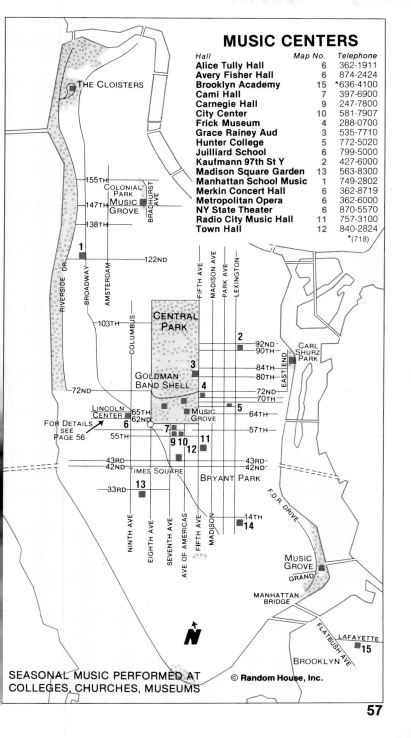

MUSIC CENTERS

Hall	Map No.	Telephone
Alice Tully Hall	6	362-1911
Avery Fisher Hall	6	874-2424
Brooklyn Academy	15	*636-4100
Cami Hall	7	397-6900
Carnegie Hall	9	247-7800
City Center	10	581-7907
Frick Museum	4	288-0700
Grace Rainey Aud	3	535-7710
Hunter College	5	772-5020
Juilliard School	6	799-5000
Kaufmann 97th St Y	2	427-6000
Madison Square Garden	13	563-8300
Manhattan School Music	1	749-2802
Merkin Concert Hall	6	362-8719
Metropolitan Opera	6	362-6000
NY State Theater	6	870-5570
Radio City Music Hall	11	757-3100
Town Hall	12	840-2824
		*(718)

THE CLOISTERS

155TH
COLONIAL
PARK
147TH MUSIC
GROVE
138TH

BRADHURST AVE

1
122ND

RIVERSIDE DR
BROADWAY
AMSTERDAM
COLUMBUS

103TH

CENTRAL PARK

FIFTH AVE
MADISON AVE
PARK AVE
LEXINGTON

2
92ND
90TH

CARL SHURZ PARK

3
84TH
80TH

GOLDMAN BAND SHELL

72ND

4
72ND
70TH

EAST END

5
MUSIC GROVE
64TH

LINCOLN CENTER
65TH
62ND

FOR DETAILS SEE PAGE 56

6

7
57TH

55TH

9 10
12
11

43RD 43RD
42ND 42ND

TIMES SQUARE

BRYANT PARK

13
33RD

F.D.R. DRIVE

NINTH AVE
EIGHTH AVE
SEVENTH AVE
AVE OF AMERICAS
FIFTH AVE
MADISON

14TH
14

MUSIC GROVE
GRAND

MANHATTAN BRIDGE

N

FLATBUSH AVE
LAFAYETTE
15
BROOKLYN

SEASONAL MUSIC PERFORMED AT COLLEGES, CHURCHES, MUSEUMS

© **Random House, Inc.**

57

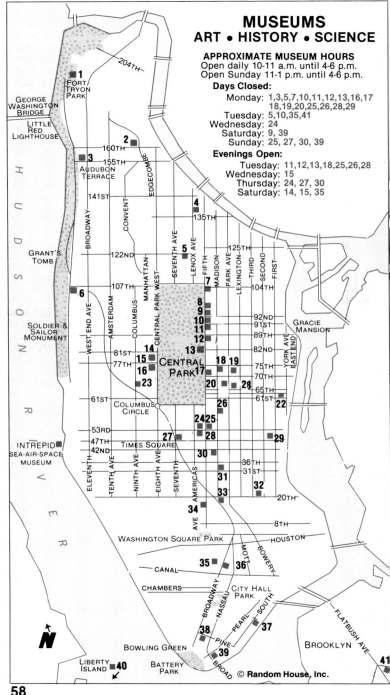

MUSEUMS
ART • HISTORY • SCIENCE

APPROXIMATE MUSEUM HOURS
Open daily 10-11 a.m. until 4-6 p.m.
Open Sunday 11-1 p.m. until 4-6 p.m.

Days Closed:
Monday: 1,3,5,7,10,11,12,13,16,17
18,19,20,25,26,28,29
Tuesday: 5,10,35,41
Wednesday: 24
Saturday: 9, 39
Sunday: 25, 27, 30, 39

Evenings Open:
Tuesday: 11,12,13,18,25,26,28
Wednesday: 15
Thursday: 24, 27, 30
Saturday: 14, 15, 35

GEORGE
WASHINGTON
BRIDGE

LITTLE
RED
LIGHTHOUSE

204TH

1 FORT
TRYON
PARK

2 160TH

3 155TH
AUDUBON
TERRACE

141ST

EDGECOMBE

CONVENT

BROADWAY

4 135TH

5 122ND

125TH

104TH

GRANT'S
TOMB

6 107TH

7

SEVENTH AVE

LENOX AVE

FIFTH

MADISON

PARK AVE

LEXINGTON

THIRD

SECOND

FIRST

MANHATTAN

COLUMBUS

AMSTERDAM

WEST END AVE

CENTRAL PARK WEST

8
9
10
11
12
13

92ND
91ST
89TH
82ND

GRACIE
MANSION

SOLDIER &
SAILOR
MONUMENT

81ST
77TH

14
15
16
23

17

CENTRAL
PARK

18 19
20 21

75TH
70TH
65TH
61ST

YORK AVE
EAST END

61ST

COLUMBUS
CIRCLE

22

26

24 25
28

53RD
47TH
42ND

27

TIMES SQUARE

29

INTREPID
SEA-AIR-SPACE
MUSEUM

ELEVENTH AVE

TENTH AVE

NINTH AVE

EIGHTH AVE

SEVENTH

AVE AMERICAS

30

31

33

32

36TH
31ST

20TH

34

8TH

WASHINGTON SQUARE PARK

HOUSTON

35

36

MOTT

BOWERY

CANAL

CHAMBERS

CITY HALL
PARK

BROADWAY

NASSAU

PEARL

SOUTH

38

37

FLATBUSH AVE

BOWLING GREEN

PINE

39

BROAD

BROOKLYN

N

LIBERTY
ISLAND

40

BATTERY
PARK

41

© Random House, Inc.

HUDSON RIVER

58

MUSEUMS — BY MAP NUMBERS

1 Cloisters, The	10 Cooper Hewitt	20 Americas Soc	31 Morgan Lib
2 Morris-Jumel	11 Natl Ac Design	21 China Institute	32 Police Acad
3 Amer Aca Arts	12 Guggenheim	22 A Adam Smith	33 Theo Roosevlt
3 Amer Indian	13 Metropolitan	23 Mus Amer Folk	34 Forbes Gallery
3 Hispan/Numis	14 Hayden Planet	24 Mus Mod Art	35 New Mus Contp
4 Schomburg	15 Am Natural His	25 Mus Broadcst	36 Hispanic Cont
5 Studio Mus	16 NY Historical	26 AT &T	37 So St Seaport
6 Nichls Roerich	17 Frick	27 Whitney Equit	38 NY Stock Exch
7 Mus City NY	18 Whitney Amer	28 Amer Craft	39 Fraunces Tvrn
8 Intern'l Photo	19 Asia House	29 Afric-Amer/Japn	40 Amer Immigrtn
9 Jewish Mus	20 African Art	30 Whitney PM	41 Brooklyn Mus

MUSEUMS

Museum	Address	Map No	*(Area 718) Telephone
Abigail Adams Smith House	421 E 61st Street	22	838-6878
African American Institute	833 UN Plaza	29	949-5666
African Art Center	54 E 68th Street	20	861-1200
American Academy of Arts & Letters	633 W 155th Street	3	368-5900
American Craft Museum	40 W 53rd Street	28	956-6047
American Indian Heye Foundation	Broadway & 155th St	3	283-2497
American Museum of Immigration	Statue of Liberty	40	363-3267
American Museum of Natural History	Central Pk W & 79th	15	769-5100
Americas Society	680 Park Avenue	20	249-8950
Asia Society Gallery	Park Ave at 70th St	19	288-6400
AT & T Infoquest	550 Madison Avenue	26	605-5555
Brooklyn Museum	200 Eastern Pkwy	41	*638-5000
China House	125 E 65th Street	21	744-8181
Cloisters, The	Fort Tryon Park	1	923-3700
Cooper Hewitt/The Smithsonian	2 E 91st Street	10	860-6898
Forbes Magazine Galleries	60 Fifth Avenue	34	206-5548
Fraunces Tavern Museum	54 Pearl Street	39	425-1778
Frick Collection	Fifth Ave & 70th St	17	288-0700
Guggenheim Museum	Fifth Ave & 89th St	12	360-3500
Hayden Planetarium/Laserium	Central Pk W & 80th	14	769-5920
Hispanic Contemporary	584 Broadway	36	966-6699
Hispanic Society of America	Broadway & 155th St	3	690-0743
Internt'l Center of Photography	1130 Fifth Avenue	8	860-1777
Japan Society	333 E 47th Street	29	832-1155
Jewish Museum	1109 Fifth Ave at 92nd	9	860-1888
Metropolitan Museum of Art	Fifth Ave & 82nd St	13	535-7710
Morgan, Pierpont Library	29 E 36th Street	31	685-0610
Morris-Jumel Mansion	Edgecombe & W 160th	2	923-8008
Museum of American Folk Art	2 Lincoln Square	23	595-9533
Museum of Broadcasting	1 E 53rd Street	25	752-7684
Museum of the City of New York	Fifth Ave & 103rd St	7	534-1672
Museum of Modern Art (MOMA)	11 W 53rd Street	24	708-9480
National Academy of Design	1083 Fifth Avenue	11	369-4880
New Museum of Contemporary Art	583 Broadway	35	219-1222
New York Historical Society	170 Central Pk W	16	873-3400
New York Stock Exchange	20 Broadway	38	656-5168
Nicholas Roerich Museum	319 W 107th Street	6	864-7752
Numismatic Society America	Broadway & 156th St	3	234-3130
Police Academy Museum	235 E 20th Street	32	477-9753
Schomburg Black Culture Collection	515 Lenox Avenue	4	862-4000
South Street Seaport Museum	Fulton & South Street	37	669-9424
Studio Museum in Harlem	144 W 125th Street	5	864-4500
Theodore Roosevelt House	28 E 20th Street	33	260-1616
Whitney Museum American Art	Madison Ave& 75th St	18	570-3676
Whitney Museum-Equitable Ctr	787 Seventh Avenue	27	554-1000
Whitney Museum-Philip Morris	120 Park Avenue	30	878-2550

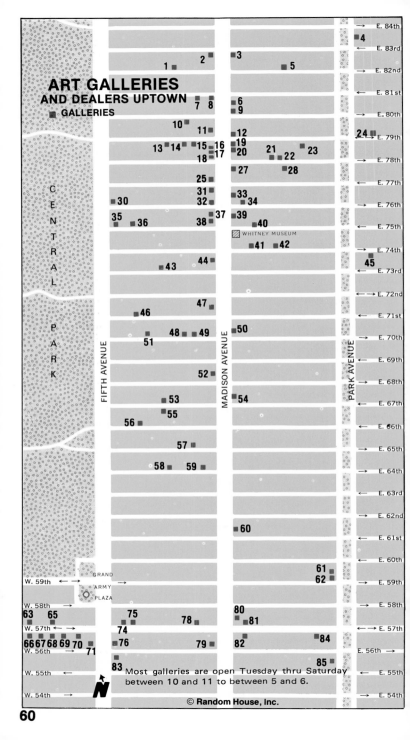

ART GALLERIES
AND DEALERS UPTOWN
■ GALLERIES

Most galleries are open Tuesday thru Saturday between 10 and 11 to between 5 and 6.

© Random House, Inc.

60

ART GALLERIES UPTOWN—BY MAP NUMBERS

ART GALLERIES UPTOWN

★ off map

61

Gallery	Address	Map No
Elkon, Robt	18 E 81st	7
Emmerich, A	41 E 57th	81
Feigen, Richard	113 E 79th	24
Findlay, David	984 Madison	31
Findlay, David Jr	41 E 57th	81
Findlay, Peter	1001 Madison	27
Fischbach	24 W 57th	69
Fitch-Febvrel	5 E 57th	74
Forum	1018 Madison	16
Frumkin, Allan	50 W 57th	66
Gagosian	980 Madison	32
Galerie Le Long	10 W 57th	70
Galerie Rienzo	922 Madison	44
Galer. St Etienne	24 W 57th	69
Galer. Schreiner	1046 Madison	8
Gallery 84	30 W 57th	68
Gallery Urban	500 Park Ave	62
Gimpel & W	724 Fifth Ave	71
Godel & Co	969 Madison	34
Goodman, Jas	41 E 57th	81
Goodman, M	24 W 57th	69
Graham	1014 Madison	18
Grand Central	24 W 57th	69
Green, Richard	24 W 57th	69
Haime, Nohra	41 E 57th	81
Hamilton, M	19 E 71st	46
Hammer	33 W 57th	65
Heidenberg, L	50 W 57th	66
Herstand & Co	24 W 57th	69
Hilde Gerst	685 Madison	60
Hirschl/Adler	21 E 70th	49
Hirschl/Adlr Mod	851 Madison	50
Hutton, Leonard	33 E 74th	42
IBM Gallery	Madison at 56	79
Isman, Neil	1100 Madison	2
Isselbacher	41 E 78th	21
Janis, Sidney	110 W 57th	★
Johnson, Jay	1044 Madison	11
Jordan/Volpe	958 Madison	38
Kennedy	40 W 57th	67
Kenneth Lux	1021 Madison	19
Kent Fine Arts	41 E 57th	81
Kerr, Coe	49 E 82nd	5
Knoedler, M	19 E 70th	48
Kouros Gallery	23 E 73rd	43
Kovesdy, P	19 E 71st	46
Kraushaar	724 Fifth Ave	71
Krugier, Jan	41 E 57th	81
La Boetie/Serger	9 E 82nd	1
La Magna, Carlo	50 W 57th	66
Lafayette Parke	58 E 79th	23
Leloup	1044 Madison	11
Lefebre	411 West End	★
Luhring, Aug	41 E 57th	81
Madison Ave	985 Madison	33
Manhattan Art	1050 Second Av	★
Marlborough	40 W 57th	67
Mathes, Barbara	851 Madison	50
Matisse, Pierre	41 E 57th	81
Mazoh, Stephen	43 E 75th	40
McCoy, Jason	19 E 71st	46
McKee, David	41 E 57th	81
Merrin Gallery	724 Fifth Ave	71
Midtown	11 E 57th	75
Miller, Robt	41 E 57th	81
Multiples	24 W 57th	69
Newhouse	19 E 66th	56
Orrefors	58 E 57th	84
Pace Edition/Gal	32 E 57th	82
Perls	1016 Madison	17
Portraits Inc	985 Park Ave	4
Ralph, Anthony	43 E 78th	22
Raydon	1091 Madison	3
Reece Galleries	24 W 57th	69
River Run	135 Central Pk W	★
Ronin	605 Madison	80
Rosenberg, Alex	20 W 57th	70
Rosenberg, Paul	20 E 79th	15
Rosenberg/Stieb	32 E 57th	82
Safani	960 Madison	37
Saidenberg	1018 Madison	16
Salander-O'Reilly	22 E 80th	10
Schaeffer	983 Park Ave	12
Schlesinger Ltd	822 Madison	52
Schoelkopf, Robt	50 W 57th	66
Schweitzer	1015 Madison	20
Sculpture Center	167 E 69th	★
Shea & Beker	20 W 57th	70
Shippee	41 E 57th	63
Siegel, Ruth	24 W 57th	69
Simpson Gallery	1063 Madison	6
Sindin	1035 Madison	12
Smith Gallery	1045 Madison	9
Solomon, Holly	724 Fifth Ave	71
Sotheby's	1334 York Ave	★
Spanierman, Ira	50 E 78th	28
Sportsman's Edge	136 E 74th	45
Steuben	715 Fifth Ave	83
Studio 53	424 Park Ave	85
Sumers, Martin	50 W 57th	66
Tatistcheff	50 W 57th	66
Uptown	1194 Madison	★
Urban Center The	457 Madison	★
Urdang, Bertha	23 E 74th	41
Vercel, Felix	17 E 64th	58
Viridian	52 W 57th	66
Wally Findlay	17 E 57th	78
Ward, Michael	9 E 93rd	★
Washburn	41 E 57th St	81
Weintraub	988 Madison	25
Wildenstein	19 E 64th St	59
Wittenborn	1018 Madison	16
York, Richard	21 E 65th	57
Zabriskie	724 Fifth Ave	71

★ off map

SOHO ART GALLERIES—BY MAP NUMBER

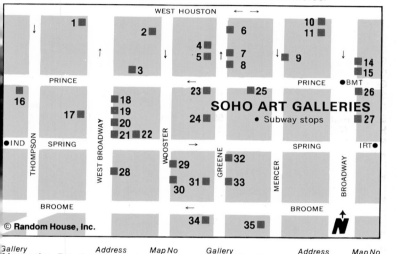

© Random House, Inc.

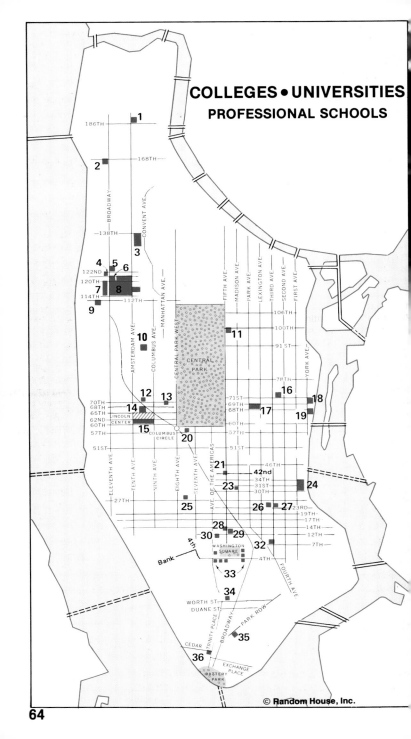

COLLEGES • UNIVERSITIES
PROFESSIONAL SCHOOLS

© Random House, Inc.

COLLEGES & UNIVERSITIES — BY MAP NUMBERS

1 Yeshiva University	12 NY Institute of Tech	25 Fashion Institute
2 Columbia Physicians	14 Juilliard School Music	26 Baruch College
3 City College	14 School Amer Ballet	27 School Visual Arts
4 Manhattan Music	15 Fordham Ed/Law/SS	28 Parsons
5 Jewish Theological	15 John Jay	29 Yeshiva Law
6 Union Theological	16 Marymount/Manhattan	30 New School
7 Barnard College	17 Hunter College	32 Cooper Union
8 Columbia University	18 Cornell Medical	33 Hebrew Union
8 Columbia Social Work	19 Rockefeller University	33 New York Univ
8 Teachers College	20 Art Students League	33 NYU Law
9 Bank Street	21 City Univ Graduate	34 New York Law
10 Mannes College	23 Amer Academy Drama	35 Pace
11 Mt Sinai Medical	24 NYU Medical	36 NYU Business

COLLEGES & UNIVERSITIES

College	Address	Map No	Telephone
American Academy Dramatic Arts	120 Madison Avenue	23	686-9244
Art Students League	215 W 57th Street	20	247-4510
Bank Street College of Education	610 W 112th Street	9	222-6700
Barnard College	3009 B'way at 120th St	7	854-5262
Baruch College	155 E 24th Street	26	725-3000
Cardozo Law (Yeshiva Univ)	55 Fifth Avenue	29	790-0200
City College of New York	Convent & 138th Street	3	690-6977
City University Graduate	33 W 42nd Street	21	642-1600
Columbia Physicians/Surgeons	630 W 168th Street	2	305-3596
Columbia School Social Work	622 W 113th Street	8	854-4088
Columbia University	Broadway & 116th St	8	854-1754
Cooper Union	41 Cooper Sq at 7thSt	32	254-6300
Cornell University Medical	1300 York Avenue	18	746-5454
Fashion Institute Technology	227 W 27th Street	25	760-7700
Fordham Law	140 W 62nd Street	15	841-5190
Fordham Education/SS	Columbus Ave & 60th St	15	841-5430
Hebrew Union School Ed/Religion	1 W 4th Street	33	674-5300
Hunter College	695 Park Avenue	17	772-4000
Jewish Theological Seminary	Broadway & 122nd St	5	678-8000
John Jay College	445 W 59th Street	15	237-8000
Juilliard School of Music	Lincoln Center Plz at 66th	14	799-5000
Manhattan School of Music	120 Claremont	4	749-2802
Mannes College of Music	150 W 85th Street	10	580-0210
Marymount Manhattan	221 E 71st Street	16	517-0555
Mount Sinai School of Medicine	Fifth Ave & 100th Street	11	241-6696
New School Social Research	66 W 12th Street	30	741-5600
NY Institute of Technology	1855 Broadway	12	399-8300
New York Law	57 Worth Street	34	431-2100
New York University	Washington Square	33	998-1212
NYU Business/Public Admin.	100 Trinity Place	36	285-6000
NYU Law	40 Washington Sq South	33	998-6060
NYU Medical	550 First Avenue	24	340-5290
Pace University	1 Pace Plaza	35	488-1200
Parsons School of Design	66 Fifth Avenue	28	741-8900
Rockefeller University	York Ave & 66th Street	19	570-8000
School of American Ballet	144 W 66th Street	14	877-0600
School of Visual Arts	209 E 23rd Street	27	679-7350
Teachers College Columbia	525 W 120th Street	8	678-3000
Union Theological Seminary	Broadway & 120th St	6	662-7100
Yeshiva University	Amsterdam Ave & 185th	1	960-5400

CONSULATES

CENTRAL PARK

© Random House, Inc

CONSULATES

Consulate-Address	Map No.	Telephone	Consulate-Address	Map No.	Telephone
Argentina 12 W 56th	15	603-0400	Japan 299 Park Av	27	371-8222
Australia 636 5th Av	45	245-4000	Kenya 424 Madison Av	25	486-1300
Austria 31 E 69th	6	737-6400	Korea 460 Park Av	14	752-1700
Bahamas 767 3rd Av	31	421-6420	Kuwait 321 E 44th	38	973-4318
Bangladesh 821 UN Plz	37	867-3434	Lebanon 9 E 76th	3	744-7905
Barbados 800 2nd Av	42	867-8435	Liberia 820 2nd Av	41	687-1033
Belgium 50 Rckfellr Plz	44	586-5110	Lithuania 41 W 82nd	★	877-4552
Bolivia 211 E 43rd	39	687-0530	Luxembourg 801 2nd Av	40	370-9870
Brazil 630 5th Av	46	757-3085	Madagascar 801 2nd Av	40	986-9491
Burma 10 E 77th	2	535-1310	Malaysia 140 E 45th	36	490-2722
Canada 1251 Av Amer	24	586-2400	Malta 249 E 35th	59	725-2345
Chile 866 Un Plz	29	980-3366	Mexico 8 E 41st	50	689-0456
China,P. R. 520 12th Av	★	868-7752	Monaco 845 3rd Av	21	759-5227
Colombia 10 E 46th	35	949-9898	Morocco 437 5th Av	55	758-2625
Costa Rica 80 Wall St	★	425-2620	Nepal 820 2nd Av	41	370-4188
Cyprus 13 E 40th	52	686-6016	Netherlands 1 Rckf Plz	47	246-1429
Denmark 825 Third Av	22	223-4545	New Zealand 630 5th Av	46	698-4650
Dominican 17 W 60th St	8	265-0630	Nigeria 575 Lexington	20	715-7200
Ecuador 18 E 41	51	683-7555	Norway 825 3rd Av	22	421-7333
Egypt 1110 2nd Av	12	759-7120	Pakistan 12 E 65th	9	879-5800
El Salvador 46 Park Av	57	889-3608	Panama 1270 Av Amer	38	246-3771
Estonia 9 Rockfeller Plz	48	247-1450	Paraguay 1 World Trade	★	432-0733
Finland 540 Madison	16	832-6550	Peru 805 3rd Av	22	644-2850
France 934 5th Av	4	606-3688	Philippines 556 5th Av	34	764-1330
Germany 460 Park Av	14	308-8700	Poland 233 Madison	56	889-8360
Ghana 19 E 47th	26	832-1300	Portugal 630 5th Av	46	246-4580
Great Britain 845 3rd Av	21	752-8400	San Marino 350 5th Av	60	736-3911
Greece 69 E 79th	1	988-5500	Saudi Arabia 866 Un Plz	29	752-2740
Grenada 820 2nd Av	41	599-0301	South Africa 326 E 48th	30	371-7997
Guatemala 57 Park Ave	58	686-3837	Spain 150 E 58th	13	355-4080
Guyana 866 UN Plz	29	527-3215	Sri Lanka 630 3rd Av	54	986-7040
Haiti 60 E 42nd	49	697-9767	St Vincent 801 2nd Av	40	687-4490
Honduras 80 Wall St	★	269-3611	Sudan 210 E 49th	28	421-2680
Hungary 8 E 75th	5	879-4127	Sweden 825 3rd Av	22	751-5900
Iceland 370 Lexington	53	686-4100	Switzerland 665 Fifth Av	18	758-2560
India 3 E 64th	10	879-7800	Thailand 53 Park Pl	★	732-8166
Indonesia 5 E 68th	7	879-0600	Trinidad Tobago -420 Lex	39	682-7272
Ireland 515 Mad Av	17	319-2555	Turkey 821 UN Plz	37	949-0160
Israel 800 2nd Av	42	351-5200	Uruguay 747 3rd	32	753-8193
Italy 390 Park Av	23	737-9100	Venezuela 7 E 51st	19	826-1660
Jamaica 866 2nd Av	33	935-9000	Yugoslavia 767 Third Av	31	838-2300

UNITED NATIONS MISSIONS - without New York Consulates

Afghanistan	866 UN Plz	754-1191	Mauritius	221 E 43rd	949-0190
Bahrain	2 UN Plaza	223-6200	Mongolia	6 E 77th	861-9460
Botswana	103 E 37th St	889-2277	Nicaragua	820 2nd Av	490-7997
Byelorussian	136 E 67th	535-3420	Niger	417 E 50th	421-3260
Cameroon	22 E 73rd	794-2295	Oman	866 UN Plz	355-3505
Centrl Africa	386 Pk Av S	689-6195	P.L.O.	115 E 65th	288-8500
Ceylon	630 Third Ave	986-7040	Qatar	747 3rd Av	486-9335
Congo	14 E 65th	744-7840	St Lucia	820 2nd Av	697-9360
Cuba	315 Lex	689-7215	St Vincent	801 2nd Av	687-4490
Ethiopia	866 UN Plz	421-1830	Senegal	238 E 68th	517-9030
Gabon	820 2nd Av	686-9720	Sierra Leone	57 E 64th	570-0030
Gambia	820 2nd Av	949-6640	Somalia	425 E 61st	688-9410
Germany Dem	58 Park Av	686-2596	Surinam	1 UN Plz	826-0660
Guinea	820 2nd Av	486-9170	Syrian Arab	820 2nd Av	661-1313
Guinea-Bissau	211 E 43rd	661-3977	Tanzania	205 E 42nd	972-9160
Iran	622 3rd Av	687-2020	Tunisia	405 Lex Av	557-3344
Iraq	14 E 79th	737-4433	Ukraine	136 E 67th	535-3418
Ivory Coast	117 E 55th	988-3930	Un.Arab Emir.	747 3rd Av	371-0480
Jordan	866 UN Plz	752-0135	U.S.A.	799 UN Plz	415-4000
Laos	321 E 45th	986-0227	U.S.S.R.	136 E 67th	861-4900
Lesotho	866 UN Plz	421-7543	Yemen	866 UN Plz	355-1730
Mauritania	9 E 77th	737-7780	Zambia	237 E 52nd	758-1110

★ off map

67

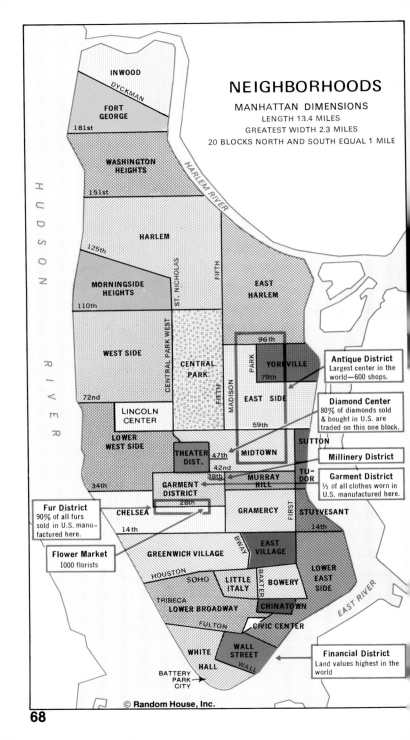

NEIGHBORHOODS

MANHATTAN DIMENSIONS
LENGTH 13.4 MILES
GREATEST WIDTH 2.3 MILES
20 BLOCKS NORTH AND SOUTH EQUAL 1 MILE

INWOOD
DYCKMAN
FORT GEORGE
181st
WASHINGTON HEIGHTS
151st
HARLEM
125th
MORNINGSIDE HEIGHTS
110th
WEST SIDE
72nd
CENTRAL PARK WEST
CENTRAL PARK
ST. NICHOLAS
FIFTH
EAST HARLEM
PARK
96th
YORKVILLE
79th
MADISON
FIFTH
EAST SIDE
59th
LINCOLN CENTER
LOWER WEST SIDE
THEATER DIST.
47th
MIDTOWN
42nd
SUTTON
34th
GARMENT DISTRICT
28th
MURRAY HILL
38th
TU-DOR
CHELSEA
14th
GRAMERCY
FIRST
STUYVESANT
14th
GREENWICH VILLAGE
BWAY
EAST VILLAGE
HOUSTON
SOHO
LITTLE ITALY
BAXTER
BOWERY
LOWER EAST SIDE
TRIBECA
LOWER BROADWAY
CHINATOWN
FULTON
CIVIC CENTER
WHITE HALL
WALL STREET
WALL
BATTERY PARK CITY

HUDSON RIVER

HARLEM RIVER

EAST RIVER

Antique District
Largest center in the world—600 shops.

Diamond Center
80% of diamonds sold & bought in U.S. are traded on this one block.

Millinery District

Garment District
⅓ of all clothes worn in U.S. manufactured here.

Fur District
90% of all furs sold in U.S. manufactured here.

Flower Market
1000 florists

Financial District
Land values highest in the world

© Random House, Inc.

68

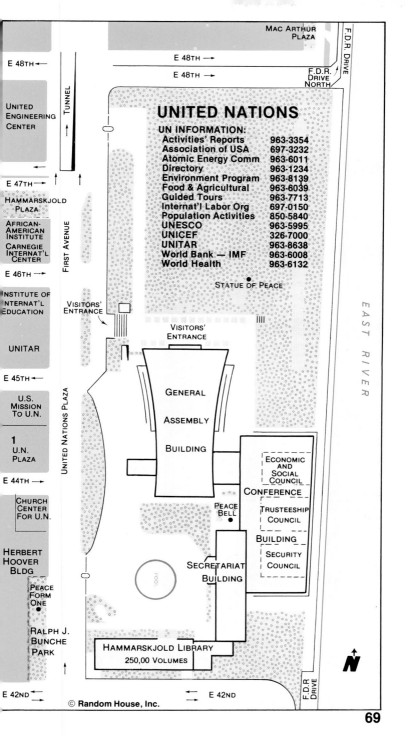

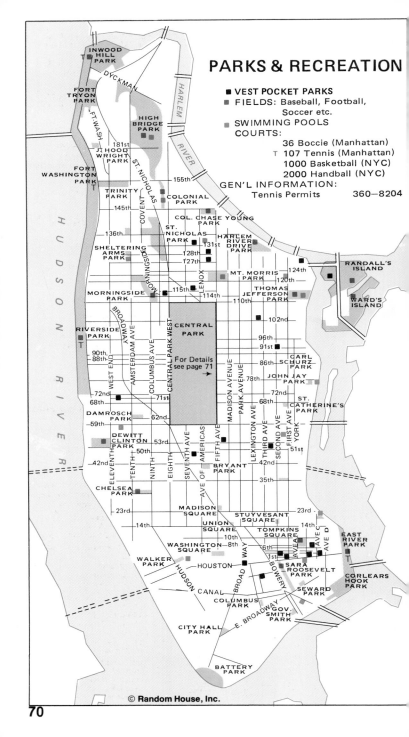

PARKS & RECREATION

- ■ VEST POCKET PARKS
- ■ FIELDS: Baseball, Football, Soccer etc.
- ■ SWIMMING POOLS
  COURTS:
  - 36 Boccie (Manhattan)
  - T 107 Tennis (Manhattan)
  - 1000 Basketball (NYC)
  - 2000 Handball (NYC)

GEN'L INFORMATION:
Tennis Permits   360—8204

© Random House, Inc.

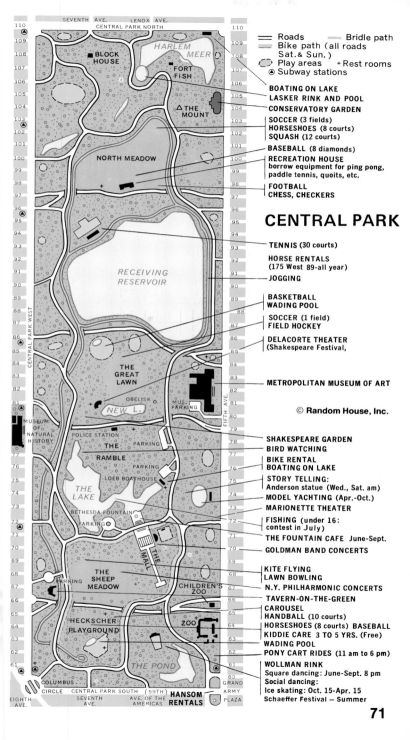

CENTRAL PARK

Roads — Bridle path
Bike path (all roads
Sat. & Sun.)
Play areas + Rest rooms
Subway stations

BOATING ON LAKE
LASKER RINK AND POOL
CONSERVATORY GARDEN
SOCCER (3 fields)
HORSESHOES (8 courts)
SQUASH (12 courts)
BASEBALL (8 diamonds)
RECREATION HOUSE
borrow equipment for ping pong,
paddle tennis, quoits, etc.
FOOTBALL
CHESS, CHECKERS

TENNIS (30 courts)
HORSE RENTALS
(175 West 89-all year)
JOGGING

BASKETBALL
WADING POOL
SOCCER (1 field)
FIELD HOCKEY
DELACORTE THEATER
(Shakespeare Festival,

METROPOLITAN MUSEUM OF ART

© Random House, Inc.

SHAKESPEARE GARDEN
BIRD WATCHING
BIKE RENTAL
BOATING ON LAKE
STORY TELLING:
Anderson statue (Wed., Sat. am)
MODEL YACHTING (Apr.-Oct.)
MARIONETTE THEATER
FISHING (under 16:
contest in July)
THE FOUNTAIN CAFE June-Sept.
GOLDMAN BAND CONCERTS

KITE FLYING
LAWN BOWLING
N.Y. PHILHARMONIC CONCERTS
TAVERN-ON-THE-GREEN
CAROUSEL
HANDBALL (10 courts)
HORSESHOES (8 courts) BASEBALL
KIDDIE CARE 3 TO 5 YRS. (Free)
WADING POOL
PONY CART RIDES (11 am to 6 pm)
WOLLMAN RINK
Square dancing: June-Sept. 8 pm
Social dancing:
Ice skating: Oct. 15-Apr. 15
Schaeffer Festival – Summer

71

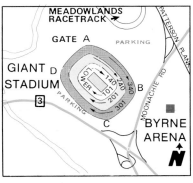

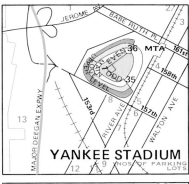

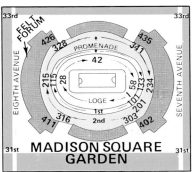

SPECTATOR SPORTS

	Playing Field	Address	Telephone
BASEBALL:			
NY Mets	**Shea Stadium**	Flushing, NY	(718) 507-8499
NY Yankees	**Yankee Stadium**	Bronx, NY	(212) 293-6000
BASKETBALL:			
NY Knicks	**Madison Sq Garden**	Seventh Ave & 32nd	(212) 563-8000
NJ Nets	**Brendan Byrne Arena**	Meadowlands, NJ	(201) 935-3900
FOOTBALL:			
NY Giants	**Giant Stadium**	Meadowlands, NJ	(201) 935-8222
NY Jets	**Giant Stadium**	Meadowlands, NJ	(212) 421-6600
HOCKEY:			
NJ Devils	**Brendan Byrne Arena**	Meadowlands, NJ	(201) 935-6050
NY Islanders	**Nassau Coliseum**	Uniondale, LI	(516) 794-4100
NY Rangers	**Madison Sq Garden**	Seventh Ave & 32nd	(212) 563-8300
HORSE RACING:			
Aqueduct Race Track		Rockaway Blvd, Ozone Park	(718) 641-4700
Belmont Raceway		Hempstead Tpke, Belmont, LI	(718) 641-4700
Meadowlands Race Track		Meadowlands, New Jersey	(201) 935-8500
Roosevelt Raceway		Westbury, Long Island	(516) 222-2000
Yonkers Raceway		Yonkers Ave, Yonkers, NY	(914) 968-4200

ANNUAL SPORTING EVENTS   **MADISON SQUARE GARDEN   563-8300**

Colgate Grand Prix Tennis (Jan)   Millrose Wanamaker Track (Jan-Feb)
Golden Gloves Boxing (Jan-Feb)   Nat'l Invitation Tournament (Mar)
International Horse Show (Nov)   Westminster Kennel Show (Feb)

NY Marathon · 26½ miles thru 5 boroughs · last Sun of Oct   (212) 860-4455
US Open Tennis · Flushing Meadows, N. Y. (Sept)   (718) 271-5100
Sports Complex Info · Meadowlands, N. J.   (201) 935-3900

SKYSCRAPERS AND BEST VIEWS

★ Best panoramic views

MIDTOWN MANHATTAN

LOWER MANHATTAN

SKYSCRAPERS

Building · No. stories	Height in ft.	Map No.
World Trade · 110	1,350	35
Empire State · 102	1,250	30
Chrysler · 77	1,046	26
American Interntl · 66	950	41
40 Wall Tower · 71	927	40
Citicorp Center · 54	914	8
RCA Rockefeller · 70	850	15
Chase Manhattan · 60	813	39
Pan Am · 59	808	23
Woolworth · 58	792	34
1 Penn Plaza · 57	764	31
1 Liberty Place · 52	743	36
Citibank · 56	741	7
20 Exchange Pl · 47	741	43
Exxon · 54	735	14
1 Astor Place · 54	730	22
9 W 57th · 52	725	3
Union Carbide · 52	707	18
General Motors · 50	705	2
Metropolitan Life · 50	700	33
500 Fifth · 60	697	25
Chem-NY Trust · 50	687	19
55 Water · 53	686	44
Chanin · 56	680	28
Gulf & Western · 44	679	1
Marine Midland · 52	677	38
McGraw Hill · 51	674	17
Lincoln · 54	673	27
1633 Broadway · 48	670	12
Trump Tower · 68	664	5
Museum Towers · 54	650	9
American Brands · 47	648	21
AT & T · 37	647	4
Irving Trust · 52	640	42
345 Park Ave · 44	634	11
Grace · 50	636	24
1 N.Y. Plaza · 50	630	45
Home Insurance · 44	630	37
1 Hammarskjold · 50	628	20
Burlington House · 50	625	6
Waldorf Astoria · 47	625	16
Olympic Towers · 51	620	10
10 E 40th · 48	620	29
General Electric · 51	616	13
N.Y. Life · 36	615	32
J.C. Penney · 46	609	9
I.B.M. · 41	607	5

© Random House, Inc.

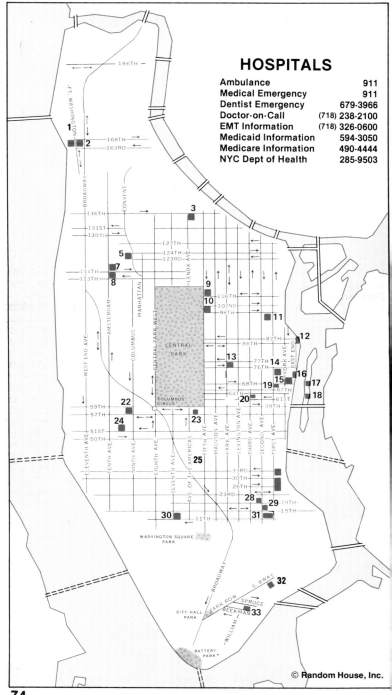

HOSPITALS

Ambulance	911
Medical Emergency	911
Dentist Emergency	679-3966
Doctor-on-Call	(718) 238-2100
EMT Information	(718) 326-0600
Medicaid Information	594-3050
Medicare Information	490-4444
NYC Dept of Health	285-9503

HOSPITALS — BY MAP NUMBERS

1 Columbia Presbyterian
2 Babies Hospital
2 Harkness Eye Institute
2 New York Orthopedic
2 Sloane Hospital for Women
3 Harlem Hospital
5 Sydenham Family Care
7 Women's · Roosevelt
8 St. Luke's · Roosevelt
9 Cardinal Cooke Health Center
10 Mount Sinai
11 Metropolitan Hospital
12 Doctors Hospital
13 Lenox Hill
14 Gracie Square
15 New York Hospital · Cornell
15 Payne Whitney Pavilion
16 Hospital Special Surgery

17 Coler Memorial
18 Goldwater Memorial
19 Memorial · Sloan-Kettering
20 Manhattan Eye & Ear
22 Roosevelt-St. Luke's
23 Medical Arts
24 St. Clare's
25 Strang Clinic
26 New York University
27 Bellevue/VA Hospital
28 Cabrini-Columbus
29 Beth Israel
29 Hospital Joint Diseases
30 St. Vincent's
31 New York Eye & Ear
32 Gouverneurs
33 Beekman Downtown
33 New York Infirmary

HOSPITALS

Hospital	Address	Map No	Telephone
Babies Hospital-Presby	Broadway & 166th Street	2	305-2500
Beekman Downtown	170 William Street	33	312-5000
Bellevue Medical Center	First Ave & 27th Street	27	561-4141
Beth Israel	First Ave & 16th Street	29	420-2000
Cabrini-Columbus	227 E 19th Street	28	995-6000
Cardinal Cooke Health Center	Fifth Ave & 106th Street	9	360-1000
Coler Memorial	Roosevelt Island	17	848-6000
Columbia-Presbyterian Med Ctr	Broadway & 168th Street	1	305-2500
Harkness Eye Institute	635 W 165th Street	2	305-2500
New York Orthopedic	622 W 168th Street	2	305-2500
Doctors Hospital	East End Ave & 87th	12	870-9000
Goldwater Memorial	Roosevelt Island	18	750-6800
Gouverneurs Hospital	227 Madison Street	32	238-7000
Gracie Square	420 E 76th Street	14	988-4400
Harlem Hospital	Lenox Ave & 135th Street	3	491-1234
Hospital for Joint Diseases	301 E 17th Street	29	598-6000
Hospital for Special Surgery	535 E 70th Street	16	606-1000
Lenox Hill Hospital	Park Ave & 77th Street	13	439-2345
Manhattan Eye & Ear	210 E 64th Street	20	838-9200
Medical Arts Center	57 W 57th Street	23	755-0200
Memorial-Sloan-Kettering	York Ave & 68th Street	19	639-2000
Metropolitan Hospital	First Ave & 98th Street	11	230-6262
Mount Sinai	Fifth Ave & 100th Street	10	241-6500
New York Hospital-Cornell	525 E 68th Street	15	746-5454
New York Eye & Ear	310 E 14th Street	31	598-1313
New York Infirmary	170 William Street	33	312-5000
New York University Medical Ctr	550 First Ave	26	340-7300
Payne Whitney Pavilion	525 E 68th Street	15	746-3800
Roosevelt-St. Luke's	Ninth Ave & 59th Street	22	523-4000
St. Clare's	426 W 52nd Street	24	586-1500
St. Luke's - Roosevelt Hospital	Amsterdam & 114th Street	8	523-4000
St. Vincent's	Seventh Ave & 11th Street	30	790-7000
Sloane Hospital for Women	Broadway & 166th Street	2	305-2500
Strang Clinic	55 E 34th Street	25	684-6969
Sydenham Family Care	215 W 125th St	5	932-6500
Veterans Administration	First Ave & 24th Street	27	686-7500
Women's-Roosevelt Hospital	Amsterdam Ave & 114th St	7	523-4151

LOWER MANHATTAN

GREENWICH VILLAGE
(See map page 40)

THE BOWERY

LITTLE ITALY

EAST VILLAGE

EAST HOUSTON

WEST HOUSTON

LOWER BROADWAY

LOWER CANAL

LOWER EAST SIDE

CHINATOWN

CRIMINAL COURTS BUILDING

FOLEY SQUARE

N.Y. COUNTY COURTHOUSE

U.S. COURTHOUSE

HALL OF RECORDS

CIVIC CENTER

CITY HALL

CITY HALL PARK

MUNICIPAL BUILDING

POLICE HEADQUARTERS

WORLD TRADE CENTER

CHASE MANHATTAN PLAZA

SOUTH ST. MUSEUM

TRINITY CHURCH

N.Y. STOCK EXCHANGE

WALL STREET

Financial District

EXCHANGE PLACE

CUSTOM HOUSE

FRAUNCES TAVERN

BOWLING GREEN

DOWNTOWN HELIPORT

WHITEHALL

BATTERY PARK

NEW YORK PLAZA

HUDSON RIVER

EAST RIVER

BROOKLYN BRIDGE

HOLLAND TUNNEL

HOLLAND TUNNEL ENTRANCE

HOLLAND TUNNEL EXIT

WEST SIDE HIGHWAY

ELEVATED HIGHWAY

BMT BATTERY TUNNEL

FERRY TO STATUE OF LIBERTY

FERRY TO STATEN ISLAND

© Random House, Inc.

LOWER MANHATTAN STREETS

AREAS AND CENTERS

J. F. KENNEDY INTERNATIONAL AIRPORT

SOUTHERN PKWY
ROCKAWAY
VAN WYCK
150 ST

United **A**
American **B**

Cargo Center Road
Animal Shelter
Medical Building
Post Office

POLICE/GENERAL HEADQUARTER

British Airways **A**

PARKING LOT 3
PARKING LOT 5

TWA **F**

EASTERN **A**

PARKING LOT 1
PARKING LOT 2
PARKING LOT 4

B

TWA **B**

B

C PAN AM
A **B**
INTERNATIONAL ARRIVALS

N

© Random House, Inc.

Parking Rates:
Lots 1-5 $4.00 an hr - $24.00 24 hrs
Long Term (8-9) $5.00 for 24 hrs

Fare between Terminals:
Interline Buses: Free
Taxis $4.00 to $6.00

Rates to/from Manhattan:
JFK Express $6.50 (See Pg 14)
Carey Trans $8.00 — Taxis $30-35.00

AIRLINES

Airline	Map Area	★800 ☆718 Telephone
Aer Lingus	B	557-1110
Aero Argentinas	B	★333-0276
Aero Mexico	B	★237-6639
Aeroflot	C	397-1660
Air Afrique	A	247-0100
Air France	A	247-0100
Air India	A	751-6200
Air Jamaica	B	★523-5585
Alitalia	A	☆656-2828
Allegheny	A	736-3200
ALM-Antillean	B	★327-7230
American	B	619-6991
American Eagle	B	619-6991
Avianca	C	★327-1330
British Airways	A	★247-9297
BWIA	B	581-3200
CAAC	C	☆656-4722
China Air	B	399-7877
Czechoslovak	B	682-5833
Delta	B	239-0700
Dominicana	A	★635-3560
Eastern	A	986-5000
Ecuatoriana	B	★327-1348
Egyptair	B	☆997-7700
El Al	A	486-2600
Finnair	A	656-7477
Guyana	B	☆693-8000
Iberia	B	★772-4642
Icelandair	B	967-8888
Japan	B	838-4400

Airline	Map Area	★800 ☆718 Telephone
KLM	B	759-3600
Korean	B	371-4820
Kuwait	B	308-5454
Lan Chile	B	★735-5526
Lot Polish	B	869-1074
Lufthansa	B	☆895-1277
MGM Grand	B	★422-1101
Mexicana	B	★531-7921
NY Helicopter	B	★645-3494
Nigeria	A	935-2700
Northwest	A	★225-2525
Olympic	A	838-3600
Pakistan	A	☆656-4027
Pan Am	C	687-2600
Piedmont	B	★251-5720
Qantas	B	★227-4500
Royal Air Maroc	B	750-6071
Royal Jordanian	A	949-0050
Sabena	B	★521-0135
SAS	A	☆657-7700
Saudi Arabian	B	758-4727
Swissair	A	☆995-8400
TAP Air Portugal	B	944-2100
TWA	B	290-2121
Tarom	B	687-6013
United	A	☆803-2200
US Air	A	736-3200
Varig	B	682-3100
Viasa	A	★327-5454
Yugoslav	C	246-6401

Transportation Info to/from JFK: ★247-7433

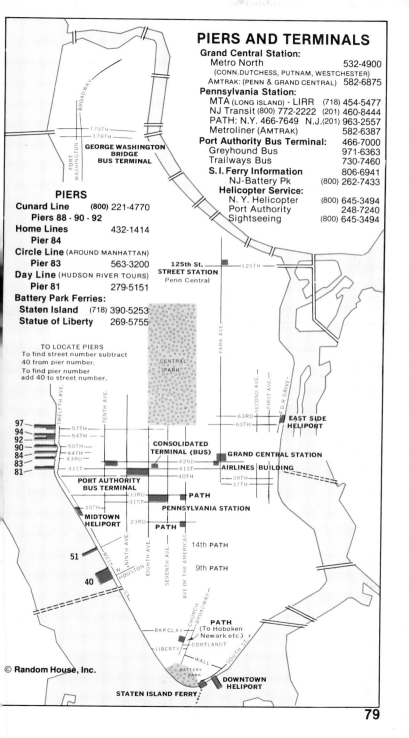

PIERS AND TERMINALS

Grand Central Station:
Metro North   532-4900
(CONN. DUTCHESS, PUTNAM, WESTCHESTER)
AMTRAK: (PENN & GRAND CENTRAL)   582-6875

Pennsylvania Station:
MTA (LONG ISLAND) - LIRR   (718) 454-5477
NJ Transit (800) 772-2222   (201) 460-8444
PATH: N.Y. 466-7649   N.J.(201) 963-2557
Metroliner (AMTRAK)   582-6387

Port Authority Bus Terminal: 466-7000
Greyhound Bus   971-6363
Trailways Bus   730-7460

S. I. Ferry Information   806-6941
NJ-Battery Pk   (800) 262-7433

Helicopter Service:
N. Y. Helicopter   (800) 645-3494
Port Authority   248-7240
Sightseeing   (800) 645-3494

PIERS
Cunard Line   (800) 221-4770
   Piers 88 · 90 · 92
Home Lines   432-1414
   Pier 84
Circle Line (AROUND MANHATTAN)
   Pier 83   563-3200
Day Line (HUDSON RIVER TOURS)
   Pier 81   279-5151
Battery Park Ferries:
   Staten Island   (718) 390-5253
   Statue of Liberty   269-5755

TO LOCATE PIERS
To find street number subtract
40 from pier number.
To find pier number
add 40 to street number.

© Random House, Inc.

79

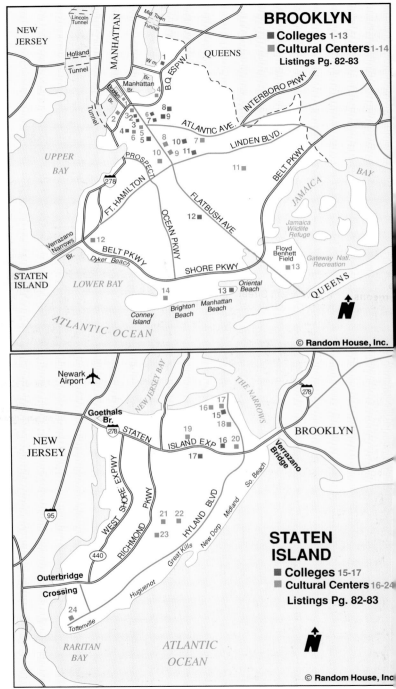

BROOKLYN

■ Colleges 1-13
■ Cultural Centers 1-14

Listings Pg. 82-83

NEW JERSEY

MANHATTAN

QUEENS

Lincoln Tunnel

Holland Tunnel

Mid Town Tunnel

W m.

B.Q. ESPW

Br. Manhattan Br.

INTERBORO PKWY

Tunnel

ATLANTIC AVE.

LINDEN BLVD.

UPPER BAY

PROSPECT

BELT PKWY

JAMAICA BAY

Jamaica Wildlife Refuge

FT. HAMILTON

OCEAN PKWY

FLATBUSH AVE.

Verazano Narrows Br.

BELT PKWY

Floyd Bennett Field

Gateway Natl. Recreation

Dyker Beach

SHORE PKWY

QUEENS

STATEN ISLAND

LOWER BAY

Conney Island

Brighton Beach

Manhattan Beach

Oriental Beach

ATLANTIC OCEAN

N

© Random House, Inc.

Newark Airport

NEW JERSEY BAY

THE NARROWS

278

Goethals Br.

278

STATEN

ISLAND EXP

BROOKLYN

Verrazano Bridge

95

WEST SHORE EXPWY

RICHMOND PKWY

440

HYLAND BLVD

Midland

So. Beach

New Dorp

Great Kills

Huguenot

STATEN ISLAND

■ Colleges 15-17
■ Cultural Centers 16-24

Listings Pg. 82-83

Outerbridge Crossing

Tottenville

RARITAN BAY

ATLANTIC OCEAN

N

© Random House, Inc

80

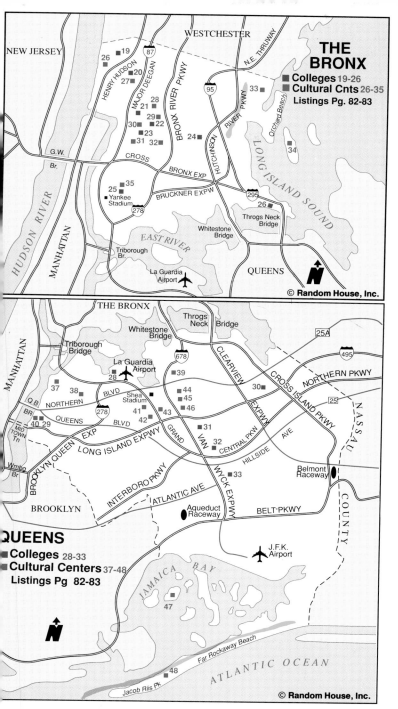

THE BRONX

■ **Colleges** 19-26
■ **Cultural Cnts** 26-35
Listings Pg. 82-83

WESTCHESTER

NEW JERSEY

HENRY HUDSON

MAJOR DEEGAN

BRONX RIVER PKWY

N.E. THRUWAY

RIVER PKWY

Orchard Beach

LONG ISLAND SOUND

G.W. Br.

CROSS

BRONX EXP

Hutchinson

BRUCKNER EXPW

Yankee Stadium

Triborough Br.

EAST RIVER

Whitestone Bridge

Throgs Neck Bridge

La Guardia Airport

QUEENS

© **Random House, Inc.**

THE BRONX

Throgs Neck Bridge

Whitestone Bridge

Triborough Bridge

25A

495

La Guardia Airport

CLEARVIEW EXPWY

CROSS ISLAND PKWY

NORTHERN PKWY

MANHATTAN

Q B

NORTHERN BLVD

Shea Stadium

QUEENS BLVD

GRAND

VAN

CENTRAL PKWY

HILLSIDE

AVE

25

NASSAU COUNTY

BR

MID TOWN Tn

BROOKLYN QUEEN EXP

LONG ISLAND EXPWY

INTERBORO PKWY

Wmbg Br

ATLANTIC AVE

WYCK EXPWY

Belmont Raceway

BROOKLYN

Aqueduct Raceway

BELT·PKWY

J.F.K. Airport

QUEENS

■ **Colleges** 28-33
■ **Cultural Centers** 37-48
Listings Pg 82-83

JAMAICA BAY

Far Rockaway Beach

Jacob Riis Pk.

ATLANTIC OCEAN

© **Random House, Inc.**

81

BRONX·BROOKLYN·QUEENS·STATEN ISLAND
CULTURAL CENTERS·HISTORIC SITES·MUSEUMS — By Map Nos

CULTURAL CENTERS·HISTORIC SITES·MUSEUMS

(Area 718)

Name	Address	Map No	Telephone
Bartow-Pell Mansion-1836*	Shore Rd & Pelham Bay Pkwy, Bx	33	*885-1461
Billopp Conference Hse-1680*	7455 Hyland Blvd, S.I.	24	984-2086
Bowne House-1661*	37-01 Bowne, Flushing, Q	44	359-0528
Bronx Historic·Valentine Varian	3266 Bainbridge Avenue, Bx	28	*881-8900
Bronx Museum of the Arts	1040 Grand Concourse, Bx	35	*681-6000
Bronx Zoo	Bronx Rvr Pkwy·Fordham Rd	32	*367-1010
Brooklyn Botanic Gardens	1000 Washington Ave, Bklyn	9	622-4433
Brooklyn Children's Museum	145 Brooklyn Avenue, Bklyn	7	735-4432
Brooklyn Historical Society	128 Pierpont St, Bklyn	5	624-0890
Brooklyn Hgts/Esplanade*	Atlantic/Fulton/Court/Montague	2	no phone
Brooklyn Museum	Eastern Pkwy/Wash Ave, Bklyn	8	638-5000
Brooklyn Navy Yard	Navy Yard, Bklyn	4	no phone
Empire Fulton Ferry Park	New Dock/Cadman Plz W, Bklyn	1	858-4708
Fort Hamilton Museum	Fort Hamilton 101st St, Bklyn	12	630-4349
Fort Tilden·Gateway	Ft Tilden, Breezy Point, Q	48	474-4600
Friends' Meeting Hse-1694*	137-16 Northern Blvd, Q	39	358-9636
Garibaldi·Meucci Museum	420 Tompkins Avenue, S.I.	20	442-1608
Gateway National Rec Ctrs	Hdq Floyd Bennet Field, Bklyn	13	338-3338
High Rock Conservation Ctr*	200 Nevada Avenue, S.I.	22	987-6233
Hall of Fame Great Americans	University at W 181st St, Bx	31	*220-6366
Hunter's Point Hist Dist-1870*	45th Ave betw 21-23rd Sts Q	40	no phone
Jamaica Bay Wildlife Refuge	Broad Channel & 1st Road, Q	47	474-0613
Museum of Moving Image	35th Ave at 36th St, Astoria, Q	38	784-0077
Mus Tibetan Art·Marchais Ctr	338 Lighthouse Avenue, S.I.	21	987-3478
New York Aquarium	Boardwalk/W 8th, Bklyn	14	265-3474
New York Botanical Gardens*	200th St, Southern Blvd, Bx	29	*220-8777
New York Hall of Science	Flushing Meadow Park, Q	41	699-0675
New York Transit Museum	Boerum & Schermerhorn St, Bkly	6	330-3060
Newhouse Contemporary Art Ctr	1000 Richmond Terrace, S.I.	16	448-2500
Noguchi Garden Museum	32-37 Vernon Blvd, L.I.C. Q	37	204-7088
North Wind Undersea Mus	610 City Island Avenue, Bx	34	*885-0701
Plymouth Church Pilgrim-1849*	Orange & Hick Street, Bklyn	3	624-4743
Poe Cottage-1812	Grand Concrse/Kingsbrdg, Bx	30	*881-8900
Prospect Pk Zoo/Lefferts Hs	Prospect Park, Bklyn	10	965-6560
Queens Botanical Gardens	43-50 Main St, Flushing, Q	46	886-3800
Queens Hist Soc Kingslnd-1774*	143-35 37th Ave, Flushing Q	45	939-0647
Queens Museum	Flushing Meadow Park, Q	43	592-5555

82 *National Historic Landmark   *(Area 212)*

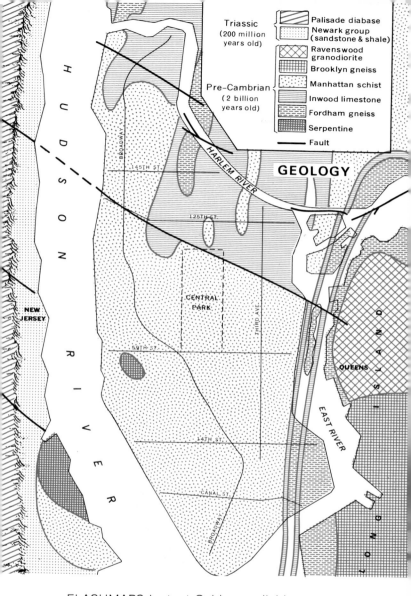

GEOLOGY

Triassic
(200 million
years old)

Pre-Cambrian
(2 billion
years old)

Palisade diabase

Newark group
(sandstone & shale)

Ravenswood
granodiorite

Brooklyn gneiss

Manhattan schist

Inwood limestone

Fordham gneiss

Serpentine

Fault

HUDSON RIVER

NEW JERSEY

HARLEM RIVER

EAST RIVER

LONG ISLAND

QUEENS

BROADWAY

145TH ST.

125TH ST.

CENTRAL PARK

THIRD AVE.

59TH ST.

14TH ST.

CANAL ST.

BROADWAY

FLASHMAPS

50 MAPS
3,000 LISTINGS

TABLE OF CONTENTS

ISBN 0-942-22635-6

50595

9 780942 226355

>>$5.95

CULTURAL CENTERS·HISTORIC SITES·MUSEUMS Continued

Queens Zoo Children's Farm	Flushing Meadow, Q (reopens 1990)	42	699-7239
Richmondtown Restoration	441 Clarke Avenue, S.I.	23	351-1611
Snug Harbor Center/Gardens	1000 Richmond Terrace, S.I.	16	448-2500
S.I. Children's Museum	Snug Hrbr Rd/Rchmnd Ter, S.I.	18	273-2060
S.I. Museum	75 Stuyvesant Place, S.I.	17	727-1135
S.I. Zoo	614 Broadway, S.I.	19	442-3100
Van Cortlandt Mansion -1748*	B'way at W 246th St, Bx	27	*543-3344
Voorlezer's House -1695*	Arthur Kill & Center, S.I.	23	351-1611
Wave Hill -c 1844*	675 W 252nd Street, Bx	26	*549-2055
Wyckoff Pieter Claesen Hs -1652*	5816 Clarendon Road, Bklyn	11	629-5400

COLLEGES & UNIVERSITIES — By Map Numbers

1	Boricua	8	Pratt Inst	17	College S.I.	26	NY Maritime
2	Polytech Inst	9	St. Joseph's	19	Coll Mt St Vinc	28	Acad Aeronau
2	NY Tech	10	Medgar Evers	20	Manhattan	29	La Guardia
3	St. Francis	11	Downstate	21	Herb Lehman	30	Queensboro
4	Bklyn Law	12	Bklyn College	22	Fordham Univ	31	Law School
5	Bklyn Conserv	13	Kingsborough	23	Bx Communty	31	Queens Collg
6	Long Island U	15	College S.I.	24	Einstein Med	32	St. John's U
7	Bklyn Acad	16	Wagner	25	Hostos Comm	33	York College

COLLEGES & UNIVERSITIES*

College	Address	Map No	(Area 718) Telephone
Academy of Aeronautics	86-01 23 rd Ave, Elmhurst, Q	28	429-6600
Boricua College	186 N 6th Street, Bklyn	1	782-2200
Brooklyn Academy of Music	30 Lafayette Ave, Bklyn	7	636-4100
Brooklyn College CUNY	Bedford Av & Av H, Bklyn	12	780-5485
Brooklyn Conservatory Music	58 7th Ave/Lincoln Pl, Bklyn	5	622-3300
Brooklyn Law School	250 Joralemon, Bklyn	4	625-2200
CUNY Community Colleges			
Bronx Community	University Av & 181st St, Bx	23	*220-6450
Hostos Community	475 Grand Concourse, Bx	25	*960-1200
Kingsborough Community	2001 Oriental Blvd, Bklyn	13	934-5000
La Guardia Community	31-10 Thomson Avenue, Q	29	482-7200
Medgar Evers Community	1150 Carroll Street, Bklyn	10	735-1750
Queensborough Community	56th Av/Springfield, Q	30	631-6262
College Mount St Vincent	Riverdale & W 263rd St, Bx	19	*549-8000
College S.I. St George CUNY	130 Stuyvesant Place, S.I.	17	390-7951
College S.I. Sunnyside CUNY	715 Ocean Terrace, S.I.	15	390-7733
Downstate Medical SUNY	450 Clarkson Ave, Bklyn	11	270-1000
Einstein Med Coll (Yeshiva U)	1300 Morris Pk Avenue, Bx	24	*430-2000
Fordham University	E Fordham & 3rd Ave, Bx	22	*579-2000
Herbert Lehman College CUNY	Bedford Pk Blvd W, Bx	21	*960-8000
Law School Queens College	65-21 Main Street, Q	31	575-4200
Long Island University	University Plaza, Bklyn	6	834-6000
Manhattan College	Parkway & W 242nd St, Bx	20	*920-0100
NY Maritime College SUNY	Fort Schuyler, Bronx	26	*409-7200
NYC Technical College CUNY	300 Jay Street, Bklyn	2	643-4900
Polytechnic Institute NY	333 Jay Street, Bklyn	2	260-3600
Pratt Institute	200 Willoughby Ave, Bklyn	8	636-3600
Queens College CUNY	65-30 Kissena, Flushing, Q	31	520-7000
St. Francis College	180 Remsen Street, Bklyn	3	522-2300
St. John's University	Grand Centrl/Utopia Pkwy, Q	32	990-6161
St. Joseph's College	245 Clinton Avenue, Bklyn	9	636-6800
Wagner College	631 Howard Avenue, S.I.	16	390-3100
York College CUNY	94-20 Guy Brewer Blvd, Q	33	262-2000

*MANHATTAN COLLEGES PAGE 64

*(Area 212)   **83**

ART TREASURES—OUTDOORS

Museum of Modern Art Garden—designed by Philip Johnson

Sculptures by: Alexander Calder · Gaston Lachaise · Jacques Lipchitz ·
Henri Matisse · Henry Moore · Eli Nadelman · Pablo Picasso · David Smith ·
Pierre Auguste Renoir · Auguste Rodin

★ Labeled on ma

ARCHITECTURAL LANDMARKS—ALPHABETICAL

uilding	Architect	Date	Map Page	Map No.
mer Mus Natural History	John Russell Pope	1936	58	14
mer Tel & Telegraph	Welles Bosworth	1917	76	E-2
ssociation of the Bar	Cyrus L. W. Eidlitz	1895	42 W	44
udubon Terrace	Charles P. Huntington	1908	58	★
very Fisher Hall	Max Abramowitz	1962	56	★
ayard-Condict	Louis H. Sullivan	1898	40	D-2
owery Savings	York & Sawyer	1923	110 E	42
rooklyn Bridge	John A. Roebling	1883	76	E-4
arnegie Hall	Tuthill, Adler & Hunt	1891	57	9
ath St. John the Divine	Heins & La Farge	1892+	54	7
hanin	Sloan & Robertson	1929	73	28
hase Manhattan Plaza	Skidmore Owings & Merrill	1960	76	E-2
hrysler	William Van Alen	1929	73	26
iticorp Center	H. Stubbins & E. Roth	1977	73	8
ity Hall	Mangin McComb	1811	76	D-2
olonnade Row	Alexander Jackson Davis	1838	40	F-3
ooper Union Hall	Frederick A. Peterson	1859	40	F-2
akota Apartments	Henry J. Hardenbergh	1884	1 W	72nd
mpire State	Shreve Lamb Harmon	1931	73	30
ederal Reserve Bank	York & Sawyer	1924	76	E-2
latiron	Daniel H. Burnham	1902	B'way & 23	
ord Foundation	Roche & Dinkeloo	1967	320 E 43	
eneral Motors	Edward Stone & E. Roth	1968	73	2
eo Washington Bridge	Cass Gilbert & O.H. Ammann	1931	8	★
race Church	James Renwick, Jr	1843	54	49
rand Central Terminal	Warren Wetmore Reed Stem	1920	79	★
uggenheim Museum	Frank Lloyd Wright	1959	58	11
aughwout	John P. Gaynor	1856	76	B-3
untington Hartford	Edward Durell Stone	1964	200 W 58	
iilliard School Music	Pietro Belluschi	1968	56	★
ever House	Skidmore Owings & Merrill	1952	390 Park	
ow Memorial Library	McKim Mead & White	1897	64	8
letropolitan Museum Art	Richard Morris Hunt	1890	58	12
letropolitan Opera House	Wallace K. Harrison	1966	56	★
organ Library	McKim Mead & White	1901	58	26
.Y. Historical Society	York & Sawyer	1908	58	15
.Y. Public Library	Carrere & Hustings	1911	53	★
.Y. State Theater	Philip C. Johnson	1964	56	★
.Y. Stock Exchange	George B. Post	1903	76	F-2
.Y. Telephone Hdqtrs	Ralph T. Walker	1917	76	E-2
ld Merchant's House	Minard Lafeber	1800	29 E 4th	
an Am	Walter Gropius	1963	73	23
. C. A.	Raymond Hood	1933	73	15
iverside Church	Ralph Cram & Chas Collens	1930	54	3
t. Patrick's Cathedral	James Renwick, Jr.	1879	54	31
t. Paul's Church	Thomas McBean	1766	54	27
eagram	Mies van der Rohe	1958	Park & 52	
emple Emanu-el	Clarence S. Stein	1929	54	23
rinity Church	Richard Upjohn	1846	76	F-2
nited Nations	Wallace K. Harrison	1952	69	★
.S. Customs House	Cass Gilbert	1907	76	F-2
illard Houses	McKim Mead & White	1886	Mad & 50	
ivian Beaumont Theater	Eero Saarinen	1965	56	★
Vhitney Museum of Art	M. Breuer & H. Smith	1966	58	16
Voolworth	Cass Gilbert	1913	73	34
Vorld Trade Center	Yamasaki & Roth	1974	73	35

★ *Labelled on Map*

NEW YORK TREASURES

Museums and Institutions are located by Map No. and Page

	Map No	Map Page
ANCIENT CULTURES		
Asia · Rockefeller collection; Pan-Asian from earliest to 19th century	19	5
Egyptian · 40,000 artifacts · largest collection outside Cairo	12	5
Egyptian & Classical Art · sculpture, friezes textiles from 5 millenia	8	8
Indians · No./Cent./So. Amer. · Aborigine cultures, pre-historic to date	3	5
Primitive Art · Rockefeller's: 15,000 items fr Africa, Americas, Pacific	12	5
BOOKS & MANUSCRIPTS		
Art Books · over 80,000 books and periodicals	22	5
Black Culture · 75,000 vols, 50,000 photos, music, Afro-Amer artifacts	4	5
Guttenberg Bibles · & Medieval, Renaissance illuminated manuscripts	26	5
Hispanic · 102,000 volumes, also paintings, murals, artifacts	3	5
Judaica · most extensive collection of artifacts in the world	8	5
Presidential Papers · 2,500 historical documents and memorabilia	29	5
Rare Books · 91,000 volumes including Guttenberg Bible, first folio Shakespeare, Bay Psalm bk 1640, Christopher Columbus' letter 1493	MAIN LIB	5
FURNITURE & DECORATIVE ARTS		
American · period rooms, paintings · Colonial thru the 20th century	12	5
Designs · over 30,000: theater, furniture, textile, ceramic, ornaments...	9	5
Faberge · 200 *objets de luxe* including 10 Russian Easter Eggs	29	5
Tiffany Collection · over 200 items · lamps, windows, *objets d'art*	15	5
NATURAL SCIENCES		
Bronx Zoo · 262 acres, 3,600 animals, 700 species, World of Darkness · day/nite reversal; World of Birds · Jungle World, reptiles	32	8
Gems · 21,000 carat topaz, 563 carat sapphire, 100 carat star ruby...	14	5
Gardens · 50 acres, 13,000 species of plants, 13 specialized gardens	9	8
Haupt Conservatory · Victorian glass palace with 11 environments	29	8
Marine Life · 20,000 specimens of over 225 species; 4 Beluga whales	14	8
25 Million Artifacts · dinosaurs, primates, whales, mammals, birds	14	5
PAINTINGS & SCULPTURE		
American Contemporary · complete collection also Calder's "Circus"	16	5
Audubon · 433 original watercolors depicting birds of North America	15	5
Drawings · Renaissance · 19th century, Michaelangelo, Rembrandt...	26	5
European · 14th to 18th century Masters, world renowned collection	12	5
European · paintings, furniture, tapestries in 14th-19th century setting	17	5
Impressionist · largest collection outside of France	12	5
Medieval · 8th to 16th cen Gothic & Romanesque art and architecture; part of 4 cloisters; a chapel, 12th cen apse, unicorn tapestries	1	5
Modern · 100,000 paintings, sculpture, drawings · 1880 to present	22	5
Non Objective Art · International collection including Brancusi's "Muse"; viewed from Frank Lloyd Wright's spiraling ramp	11	5
MISCELLANEOUS		
Costumes · worldwide collection 17th cen to present couturier fashions	12	5
Film Collection · 8,000 films and over 3 million stills, also screenings	22	5
Maps · over 370,000 maps of the world from the beginning of time	LABEL	5
Miniature Models · 12,000 toy soldiers in 'action' · 500 crafts & ships	29	5
New York Panorama · 9,000 sq ft model, 855,000 bldgs (1" equals 100')	43	82
Richmondtown Restoration · 96 acres, 30 historic bldgs, 17-19th cen	23	8
Statue of Liberty · 1886 gift of France, restored by 2.5 million donations	36	5

See pages 84-85 for Architectural Landmarks and Outdoor Statuary

SUBURBS & METROPOLITAN AREA COMMUNITIES

Community	1980 census	Approx *miles	Community	1980 census	Approx *miles
WESTCHESTER COUNTY — NEW YORK					
Bedford	15,137	40	New Rochelle	70,794	18
Briarcliff	7,115	30	Ossining	20,196	35
Bronxville	6,267	17	Rye	15,083	26
Chappaqua	15,425	35	Scarsdale	17,650	21
Harrison	23,046	26	Tarrytown	10,648	18
Mamaroneck	17,616	20	White Plains	46,999	25
Mt. Kisco	8,025	39	Yonkers	195,351	14
Mt. Vernon	66,713	16	Yorktown	31,988	40
NASSAU · SUFFOLK COUNTIES — NEW YORK					
Amityville	9,076	39	Levittown	57,045	27
Babylon	12,388	45	Lindenhurst	26,919	41
Bay Shore	10,784	50	Long Beach	34,073	27
Bethpage	16,840	33	Lynbrook	20,424	22
Commack	34,719	44	Manhasset	8,485	18
Copiague	20,132	40	Massapequa	19,779	36
East Meadow	39,317	26	Merrick	24,478	29
Farmingdale	7,946	60	Mineola	20,757	26
Floral Park	16,805	20	New Hyde Pk	9,801	24
Freeport	38,272	28	Oyster Bay	6,497	35
Garden City	22,927	23	Port Washington	14,521	23
Glen Cove	24,618	25	Rockville Centre	25,412	24
Great Neck	9,168	20	Roslyn Heights	6,546	23
Hempstead	40,404	22	Syosset	9,818	32
Hicksville	43,245	31	Valley Stream	35,769	22
Huntington	21,727	37	Wantagh	19,817	32
Islip	13,438	52	Westbury	13,871	26
FAIRFIELD COUNTY — CONNECTICUT					
Bridgeport	142,546	61	New Canaan	17,931	44
Darien	18,892	39	Norwalk	77,767	43
Fairfield	54,849	56	Stamford	102,453	35
Greenwich	59,578	31	Westport	25,290	46
BERGEN COUNTY — NEW JERSEY					
Bergenfield	25,568	14	Lodi	23,956	14
Cliffside Park	21,464	6	Palisades Pk	13,732	11
Dumont	18,334	15	Paramus	26,474	16
Englewood	23,701	9	Ridgefield (area)	23,032	12
Fair Lawn	32,229	20	Rutherford	19,608	9
Fort Lee	32,449	7	Teaneck	39,007	11
Hackensack	36,039	14	Tenafly	13,552	14
HUDSON · ESSEX · MORRIS COUNTIES — NEW JERSEY					
Bayonne	64,047	10	Lyndhurst	20,326	10
Bloomfield	47,792	13	Madison	15,357	29
Clifton	74,388	13	Maplewood	22,950	18
E. Orange	77,690	17	Montclair	38,321	15
Hoboken	42,460	4	Morristown	16,614	33
Irvington	61,493	16	Newark	329,248	12
Jersey City	223,532	5	No. Bergen	47,019	5
Kearny	35,735	15	Union City	50,184	4
UNION · MIDDLESEX COUNTIES — NEW JERSEY					
Elizabeth	106,201	17	Springfield	13,955	22
Linden	37,836	21	Summit	21,071	26
Rahway	26,723	24	Westfield	30,447	26
Roselle	20,641	22	Woodbridge	90,074	27

*To midtown NYC-(Because of the many routes into the city, mileages may vary.)

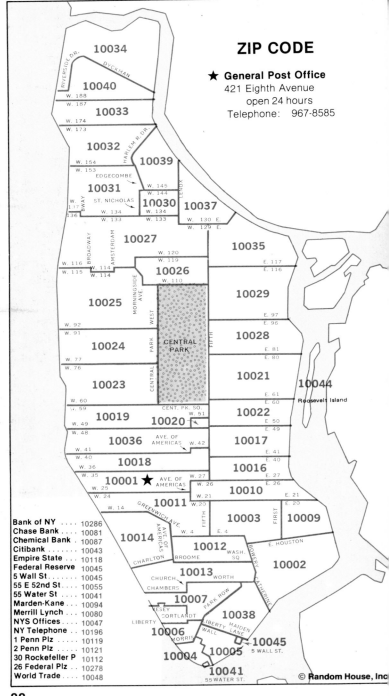

ZIP CODE

★ **General Post Office**
421 Eighth Avenue
open 24 hours
Telephone: 967-8585

Bank of NY 10286
Chase Bank 10081
Chemical Bank . 10087
Citibank 10043
Empire State ... 10118
Federal Reserve 10045
5 Wall St....... 10045
55 E 52nd St.... 10055
55 Water St 10041
Marden-Kane ... 10094
Merrill Lynch ... 10080
NYS Offices 10047
NY Telephone .. 10196
1 Penn Plz 10119
2 Penn Plz 10121
30 Rockefeller P 10112
26 Federal Plz .. 10278
World Trade 10048

© **Random House, Inc**